# Corrupting Chastity

### A Reverse
### Harem Romance

## Krista Wolf

## KRISTA'S VIP EMAIL LIST:

Join to get free book offers, and learn release dates for the hottest new titles!

Tap here to sign up: http://eepurl.com/dkWHab

# ~ Other Books by Krista Wolf ~

Corrupting Chastity - Krista Wolf

<u>Three Christmas Wishes</u>
<u>Trading with the Boys</u>

# <u>Chronicles of the Hallowed Order</u>

Book one: <u>Ghosts of Averoigne</u>
Book two: <u>Beyond the Gates of Evermoore</u>
Book three: <u>Claimed by the Pack</u>

Corrupting Chastity - Krista Wolf

# One

## CHASTITY

"Thank *GOD.*"

I breathed the words in tandem with the slamming of the door behind me, followed immediately by the ceremonial dropping of my keys on the kitchen counter. Two twists of the lock later, and that was it. Silence descended over my little apartment.

I was finally *home*.

"Another one bites the dust."

Stepping out of my shoes was a religious experience. My feet felt so good, it was almost orgasmic.

Just one more random engagement party in the books.

At least this time it was Lexi, so I really didn't mind. Alexa was one of my closest friends; a freshman year roommate who'd gone on to meet a truly amazing guy. They'd been dating just long enough that his proposal — hiding the ring-box in a snowman during their getaway trip to Vermont — had been perfect and adorable.

5

The whole thing was so sweet I didn't know whether to cry tears of joy for her or throw up.

I spun through the kitchen, grabbing two Advils and pouring myself a glass of water. The nagging sensation of having to do something else lingered at the back of my mind, until finally it manifested itself:

*Feed the cat.*

For a half-second I actually turned in the direction of the little green feeding bowl, purely out of habit. Then my shoulder slumped, and the usual sadness washed over me.

The feeding bowl wasn't there. It was tucked away — out of sight, out of mind — deep in the pantry. And that's because Athena was gone.

I sighed heavily. "I miss you, you little punk."

She'd passed away... what? Six months ago now? The little calico was my childhood pet. A cat who'd lived long enough to survive my teenage and college years, then come along to live with me afterward. My parent's last parting gift before shipping off to Florida.

I downed my Advil and half my water, shaking off the sadness a little slower than usual. My dress danced around my calves as I fled to the bedroom. I began shrugging it off along the way, eager to get into something comfy.

*Lexi. Engaged.*

Holy fucking shit.

It was one thing to be twenty-five and single, without a prospect in sight. To watch your closest friends all fall in love and get married. To attend their weddings one by one,  and listen to them talk about starting families.

But it was quite another to do it all as a virgin.

*And... there it is.*

I did have several other things though. Two failed relationships. A miserably failed business startup. Borderline personality disorder coupled with a history of pushing men away — all based on some vague fear of intimacy I'd picked up from God-knows-where.

At least my brains had gotten me far: a double major in computer science and information technology, followed by a masters of science in software engineering. I'd sacrificed my social life for academia. I'd dedicated still more years to a risky venture, one that would've set me up for life if only it had paid off.

Instead it had set me back down right where I'd started: lonely and alone, in a bleak field of nothingness. Watching. Enduring.

Seeing my friends and colleagues get happily hitched.

*Oh come on now!* I chastised myself. *It's not all bad.*

I flopped back on the bed, enjoying the feel of my back against the cool mattress. At least I was free. Free to do what I wanted, to come and go whenever I pleased. Take tonight for instance. The party had been a good one, the food outstanding. The drinks had flowed — probably a little too much — and everyone involved had a fantastic time.

Especially when it came to Sierra and Eric.

The thought of what I'd seen sent a flash of heat rushing through me.

It was sometime toward the end of the night when I'd stumbled upon Lexi's maid of honor and one of Donovan's groomsmen, going at each other hot and heavy in the unisex bathroom. Until tonight the two members of the bridal party were complete strangers who'd never met. Right now Sierra and Eric were most likely hooking up at one or the other's apartment, where they'd fuck like rabbits until morning. Hell, maybe they already were.

I stretched further into my bed, curling my wrists and ankles. They'd hook up at the wedding too, most likely. Maybe they'd be dating by then. Perhaps they'd even get engaged, and I'd end up being invited to *that* wedding, and the whole crazy cycle would begin anew.

*And there you'll be, frozen in time. In exactly the same place.*

I sat up in frustration and took a deep breath, staring at myself in the dresser-mounted mirror. I was twenty-five. *Twenty five!* And still a virgin!

*Fuck.*

I might as well wait the extra five years, and become a sorceress. That was the old wives' tale anyway. That if you made it to thirty without having sex, you somehow became a wizard. The whole thing would be funny if it weren't so sad.

*At least if I became a wizard I'd have cool spells.*

Lexi and Donovan. Sierra and Eric. Me and... well...

Rolling over I slipped quickly into a pair of sweats and a T-shirt. I'd shower come morning. For now though...

For now I opened my laptop and clicked on the link I had bookmarked for over a month.

The images loaded quickly, having already been cached dozens of times before.  Broad, massive shoulders.  A gorgeous, immaculately-sculpted chest and arms, all covered in black-and-grey tattoos.

*Mmmmmm....*

And then that mouth, framed by a dark, sexy beard. Full, beautiful lips, set grimly above a strong, chiseled jawline.

The mouth I'd so often dreamt of kissing.

"Senan."

I said the name aloud, tasting it for what it was. Strong.  Sensual.  Unique.

And of course, totally and completely made up.

"Whatever."

The man on the screen could be mine, if I really wanted him.  His contact info was right there.  His email address, his Instagram handle.  I'd gone down that rabbit hole before too, sifting through another three or four dozen photos of his hard, muscular body.

Yes, Senan could be all mine if I so desired.  And that's because I was on a greyhat site, and Senan was an escort.

A beautiful, flawless escort.

Already I could feel the heat rising in my belly. Clicking away reluctantly, I switched to the neighboring photo — another escort, also in my area.

Ander was every bit as hard as Senan, only a little leaner.  He had lighter hair.  A smile that could — and often did — melt the panties right down my thighs, to where I was kicking them off and letting them land on my bedroom floor.

What I did after that, well... that was all between me and them.

For a while I was opening my laptop two or three times a week to visit my fantasy boyfriends. Lately though, it was more. I'd scrolled through their photos almost every night this week. I'd read their little bios, parsing through their likes and dislikes, their rates and requirements.

I'd even come close to opening my own email program... and finally contacting them.

*Imagine that?*

Actually I could. I had the money, I had the time. And either of these men had exactly what *I* needed, whether I wanted to admit to it or not.

*Losing my cherry to a male escort?*

It had seemed laughable at first, but over the weeks the idea became more and more reasonable. I didn't know these men, and they didn't know me. That eliminated the social awkwardness. It took the edge off the fear of intimacy.

Even better there would be no embarrassing morning after. No nervousness that I might run into them, or work alongside them, or ever have to see them again. It would be a simple transaction: money for sex. Each party getting exactly what they wanted from the deal. Nothing more. Nothing less.

I swallowed hard, looking back at the screen. What the hell was stopping me? It wasn't like I was 'saving myself.' I'd done just about everything else with a guy *but* have sex. When you looked at it that way, that one final step was little more than an annoying formality.

*Senan...*

I stared down at the screen again. The heat was all-consuming now, worse than ever.

*Or Ander?*

Images of Sierra and Eric flashed through my mind, their bodies twisting each other in the shadows of the bathroom. They'd been so *into* it. Even for the brief two seconds I'd witnessed before apologetically closing the door, it all seemed so unspeakably hot.

*Pick one already.*

Something inside me snapped loose. I recognized it instantly as the last ounce of my resolve, finally breaking away.

"Screw it."

Reaching out, I grabbed a coin from the jar of loose change on my nighttable. Tossing it so high it almost scraped the ceiling, I let it land on my comforter and stared down at the result.

My stomach erupted in butterflies as I clicked on the contact email for Senan.

"Sorry Ander."

# Two

## CHASTITY

I moved past Webster Hall, crossing Wentworth street and stepping into The Green. It was chilly but not cold. Last week's snow was still frozen into crust-covered mounds, pushed to the sides of the criss-crossing paths in patterns that were both geometric and beautiful.

In reality, all of Dartmouth's campus was breathtakingly gorgeous. Especially in winter.

The library had always been a source of reflection for me, and as a postgraduate it was no different. I went there to do research, and to read up on things. To open my laptop in the beautiful, book-bound silence and sharpen whatever skills I needed on that particular day.

Today though, I couldn't think about anything but tonight.

And Senan.

*Holy fucking shit.*

I still couldn't believe I'd actually done it.  Last night I'd sent a simple email, from a brand new throwaway email address.  It had taken no more than a minute.  Ten seconds to hammer out the words, and another fifty seconds to read them over and over again before hitting the send button:

# I'd like to see you tomorrow evening, if you're available.  — Chastity

That's it.  It was that quick and easy.  A simple sentence that would change my life, or at least my sex life, and hopefully for the better.

*Definitely couldn't be for the worse.*

I crossed through the center of The Green, nodding politely to a pretty young woman clutching a stack of books against her chest.  My feet crunched noisily against the salted path.  It was getting dark fast, maybe faster than usual.

*Two hours.*

I gulped my way past the little lump in my throat. That's how long I had left.  That's how much longer I'd technically be a maiden, give or take however many minutes it took to hop into bed with the gorgeous, muscle-bound model I'd been drooling over for so many days and weeks.

*Escort, not model.  There's a difference.*

The voice in my head was annoying, even if it was correct. Honestly I didn't care.  I was still viewing the whole thing as a business transaction, and getting my virginity out of the way would open the door — so to speak — for future relationships.

*How's that for a metaphor?*

I had to get home. Primp and preen a bit. Get myself all ready... to go out and meet up.

And yes, go out. I'd made myself familiar with some of the terms of the escort service industry, including incall and outcall. Senan didn't offer an incall service, not that it mattered. I wasn't brave or foolhardy enough to go to a complete stranger's house or apartment.

Yet at the same time, I wasn't willing to have him over to my place either. I didn't know this man, except for his photos. I had no feel for who he was. What he might be like...

For that reason I decided upon a neutral location. Somewhere public, somewhere we could sit down and discuss what would happen. It was the curse of being organized; I liked to plan ahead. I needed to know when, where, what, and why. All of those variables had to be decided before I would finally go through with the whole crazy idea.

*And... you're over-thinking things again.*

"Professor!"

I glanced up, looking in about five different directions before I saw the source of the call. A young man was waving to me from the other end of the path. He came hurrying over, sprinting the last thirty yards or so as I stood there waiting for him.

"Professor, I'm sorry, I just..."

Already he was out of breath. Kids these days.

"It's okay," I smiled. "Relax. Take your time."

I recognized him as someone from my Software Design and Implementation class, last semester. He sat in the back. He always carried a giant backpack too, although right now he was empty-handed.

"I wanted to know if you'd look at something for me," he breathed, and his breath left little puffs of white steam in the crisp winter air. "It's not from your course though," he added apologetically. "It's from my Algorithms class. Professor Hennessey. But I know you're very familiar with—"

"Of course I'll look at it," I said right away.

"Cool," the young man smiled. "Thanks!" Before I could say anything else he stood up a little straighter, then pointed back toward the library. "Now?"

I stiffened instantly. "Um, no. I can't do it right *now...*"

"Sorry," he apologized. "It's just that—"

"I— I have an appointment," I stammered.

*Yes. You sure as hell do.*

"Tomorrow though?"

The young man smiled and nodded. "Whatever time's good for—"

"Two O'clock," I told him. "Meet me in the Baker library."

"Got it." He grinned and tipped an imaginary hat. "Thanks so much, professor."

"No problem."

15

He ran off across The Green, and I watched him go. For some reason I felt needlessly guilty. Like I was letting him down, for the sake of my own needs and perversions.

*Really? Needs and perversions?*

I took a deep breath as the sky darkened further. No, I wasn't letting anyone down, I decided. If anything I was putting myself first for once, and that made me happy. For far too long I'd been trading pieces of my life away to make everyone else's life easier.

And for tonight at least, that was going to change.

# Three

## CHASTITY

He entered the room right on time, walking with confidence rather than swagger. Tight black shirt. Tighter jeans. He looked even taller than in the photos, more handsome, more masculine. And his eyes...

His eyes were a beautiful hazel color, set beneath thick dark brows. I hadn't seen those eyes before, in any of his photos. Like most escorts protecting their identities, he'd only taken pictures from the nose down.

*My God, he's perfect.*

It had been my first worry — that Senan would show up and somehow he wouldn't be the man in the photos. Or the photos would've been old. Or any number of things that could've screwed this up for me.

Instead though, he was absolutely gorgeous.

*And shouldn't he be? It's his job to look like this.*

It took him a moment to find me based on my outfit:

17

a blue and white checkered sweater with my most hip-hugging black skirt. Matching black boots. Black-rimmed glasses and a nervous smile.

"Ah, there you are."

I stood as he approached, winding his way through the coffee nook in the back of the bookstore. The place had been open forever, but by now the ratio of coffee shop to books was almost fifty-fifty. It didn't bode well for the book side of things.

"Chastity, right?"

He extended his hand, which was as smooth and handsome as he was. I took it mechanically, marveling at the size. Wondering if it meant what I thought it could mean.

"Hi."

We sat down across from each other at the little round table, like two opponents squaring off. In fact there was a game board painted in the middle, for chess or checkers. You could get the pieces for either from the barista, if you went up and asked.

"Can I get you anything?"

His voice was smooth and velvety, his smile warm and charming as hell. I could tell it was probably his opening line. I wondered how many times he'd uttered it.

"Coffee?" he asked, looking back over his shoulder at what was available. "A pastry? Or—"

"No, thank you," I cleared my throat. "Actually I don't drink coffee."

Senan seemed immediately taken aback, but also a little

amused. "Well I don't know if I trust you then."

"Why?" I asked. "Because I don't drink coffee?"

"Well you *did* ask me to a coffee shop."

"Technically I asked you to a bookstore with a coffee shop in it," I replied. "Although I don't know how much longer they're going to be selling books here."

His smile widened as he glanced around. "Me neither."

"I guess it was more so we could meet in public than anything else," I admitted. "I'm wary, obviously. And not that good with strangers."

My guest leaned forward in the little seat that was way too small for him, and folded his arms on the table. His tattoos danced as the barista approached and he waved her away.

"You're doing great so far," he said nonchalantly.

My heart was pounding wildly, pushing hot blood through my veins. And I could smell him now, too. The leather of his open jacket. A whiff of something musky and wonderful that might've been cologne, or might just have been his natural scent.

"So how exactly does this go?" I asked, throwing myself completely at his mercy. "I mean, not insofar as what we'd be doing. I get that part. I guess I mean the logistics of everything, and how we'd—"

"Chastity, relax."

His voice was low and manly, but also somewhat kind. He looked comfortable. Casual. Like he'd been here the whole

19

time and it was I who'd just arrived. I took a deep breath and felt my shoulders slump. Seeing him like that somehow relaxed me.

"The whole thing might seem overwhelming at first, but it's actually pretty simple," Senan went on. "First you pay my fee—"

"I already have."

His brows crossed for a moment as he pulled out his phone and punched up his Venmo account. He checked it quickly and smiled.

"So you did," he confirmed. "You paid too much, though."

"I know we discussed an hour," I said quickly, "but I paid your 90-minute rate. Whatever we end up doing, I didn't want to rush."

The handsome man seated across from me nodded, but slowly. "Hmm. You should've asked me."

"What?"

"Well I need to know these things," he shrugged simply. "I have a schedule to keep."

"Oh."

A moment of silence passed. He scratched at his beard, and his smile returned. "Not a big deal, really. So as I was saying, you pay my fee — which you already have, thank you very much — and from there we go to your place." The muscles in his tattooed forearm twitched as he folded his hands together. "From that moment on, I'm all yours."

My eyes met his, and I had to force myself to remain

calm.  It wasn't easy.  Not even close.

*All yours...*

I couldn't begin to fathom what such a thing would mean.  My heart was a jackhammer in my chest.

"Listen," I said hesitantly.  "Before we do that, I have these... three little things."

Senan smiled and nodded.  "Shoot."

"First, we can't go back to my place," I said.  "I uh, no offense, but I don't really *know* you.  I'd much rather—"

"Go someplace neutral," he shook his head in agreement.  "I totally understand."

"Second, I'm still thinking about this," I said.  "I haven't committed to it in my mind yet.  So at any moment, I might back out."

My eyes dropped to the table as I forced myself through the rest of my prepared speech.  "I'm known to do that," I explained.  "And if I bail for whatever reason, obviously that's all on me."

Senan shifted in his seat, the leather of his jacket creaking as he moved.  His expression was all understanding, though.  I couldn't find a hint of judgment.

"Look," he said, "it's okay if—"

"And that's mainly because of the third thing," I interrupted, before I lost my nerve.  "Because although the third thing might seem cataclysmically weird, it's something you definitely need to know."

My guest closed his still-open mouth, and settled back in his seat again.  Although he didn't say a word, I could see in his eyes he was totally intrigued.

"I've never done this before."

Silence. Dead silence. Every second that dragged by was prolonged agony.

"Well it's really not *that* big of a deal," Senan assured me. "You needed companionship, and I happened to need rent money. The stigma associated with the whole thing shouldn't be—"

"No no, not that," I said quickly. "Not the escort part."

He raised an eyebrow.

"I mean..."

*Just say it already.*

"I mean I've never done *anything* before, really. With anyone."

Senan's gorgeous hazel eyes flashed with eventual recognition. Very slowly, he tilted his head.

"You mean—"

"Yes," I said at last. I tried letting out a little laugh, but I only managed a sigh.

"I'm a virgin."

# Four

## SENAN

She wasn't just beautiful, she was absolutely striking. Nerdy good looks, and the smooth curves of a body that matched. She had long blonde hair that framed her girl-next-door face, which was hidden behind glasses consisting of the thickest pair of dark rims I'd ever seen. Except for maybe in movies.

"A virgin," I repeated softly, not really believing it. After what she'd just told me, she could've knocked me over with a single breath.

"Yes," she nodded once.

"*You.*"

"Uh huh."

"Are you sure?"

She laughed, and her laughter was lilting and musical. "Yeah. I'm pretty sure."

All at once it seemed like everything changed. I was

looking at her differently now, like some rare and valuable jewel instead of a pretty cubic zirconia.

"So you've never been with a guy," I clarified one last time, studying her every reaction. "Ever."

"Not in the biblical sense, no," she assured me. "Although I *have* had boyfriends. Two of them in fact. And I have, of course, reached..." she blushed and it was absolutely adorable. "Certain *bases*."

I shook my head in disbelief, caught myself, and stopped.

"Is that a problem for you?" she asked hesitantly. "That I've never had sex?"

"Not for me."

"Because if it freaks you out or something, I'd totally understand," she said. "I've heard some guys are weird when it comes to—"

"Chastity listen," I told her. "It's fine."

As I said the words I leaned forward, dropping my hand reflexively over hers. She looked down at it as I gave it a reassuring squeeze.

"Have you ever... you know..."

"Been with a virgin?" I asked. "No, actually. I haven't."

She seemed almost hesitant now. Somewhat reluctant.

"Does that bother *you?*"

"I guess it should scare me a little," she shrugged, "so maybe. I mean, it would definitely help that you'd know what to expect."

"I'm pretty sure I can handle it," I smirked.

"But actually," she went on, "it doesn't bother me at all. In fact — and this might sound strange — it kind of makes the whole thing a little better for me. It's almost..."

"Endearing?"

"Yes!" she said, excited that I'd picked the right word. "Endearing."

"Sort of like it's the first time for the both of us," I said, relieved that her reluctance was superficial. I caught her eyes again and smiled. "Making it even more special."

"Exactly."

We sat in silence for a moment, reading each other's reactions. She was genuinely adorable. I could tell she was much more relieved now that all the cards were finally on the table.

"So how does something like this even happen?" I asked, hoping the question wasn't offensive.

"What? Getting to twenty-five without having sex?"

"Twenty-*five?*" I swore aloud. I let out a shrill whistle. "I would've guessed twenty one, tops."

She blushed at the complement, then adjusted her glasses. Twenty five. Pretty. No, not pretty. Beautiful.

And somehow she'd called *me.*

"I saved myself all through high school," she began, "though I don't even remember why. In college I was ready to pull the trigger, but school got in the way. I was always studying. Always taking extra classes, to fulfill my double major."

"Nothing wrong with that," I told her.

"While my roommates were out partying, I was busy writing subroutines. While they were off screwing their boyfriends, I was down in the library, surrounded by books."

"You're *still* surrounded by books," I pointed out, jerking my thumb left and right. She chuckled.

"Yeah," she agreed, smiling sheepishly. "Touché."

I watched her settle in, leaning back more comfortably into her chair. She wasn't as tense now. She'd stopped fidgeting with her hands, and crossing and uncrossing her legs.

"Eventually I'd waited so long it became a little uncomfortable," she kept going. "Even after I graduated I was still on campus, acting as a teacher's assistant for certain courses. I was surrounded by twenty-something year-old men who were acting more like boys, really. They were immature. More interested in partying than class."

"Been there done that," I told her. "I was one of those guys, once."

"Yeah," Chastity nodded. "So at that point my maidenhood became less of a novelty and more of an awkward burden. The very idea of telling one of these immature assholes — even the hot, gorgeous ones — something so personal seemed utterly crazy to me."

I blinked, and for a moment or two I could picture the whole thing perfectly in my mind's eye. Those thick-rimmed glasses, reflecting back some complicated equations on a glowing computer screen. That innocent yet womanly body, lying prone on some dorm room bed.

It was all starting to excite me, whether I wanted it to or not.

"I still don't get this," I said. "I mean, look at you. You're gorgeous, Chastity. I mean *really* beautiful."

The color in her face deepened, her expression a strange mixture of embarrassment and gratitude. Could it be she didn't know it? It just didn't make sense.

"You could go on *Tinder*," I continued, "and in less than ten seconds—"

"I'd end up with some random creep who'd ruin the whole experience for me," she countered. "I sought you out because I wanted someone professional. Someone who knew the value of discretion, and who would stay within the parameters of our arrangement."

"You said you've had boyfriends though," I pointed out.

"Two," she nodded. "Both long-term relationships, for the most part."

"And you've never had sex?"

"Actually I've had all kinds of sex," she explained, turning a shade redder. "Except, well... you know."

"Sex sex."

"Yeah."

"How come?"

Chastity let out a long, wistful sigh. "Oh, a whole ton of reasons. None of which, looking back, really made any sense."

"Try me."

She smiled just as the barista came around again, and this time I actually ordered a coffee. When Chastity ordered a tea with lemon, I winced.

"Hey, don't knock it," she chastised me. "They have the best vanilla chi here. It's really good."

"No it's not," I told her dismissively. "But forget about that. Tell me again how you had not one but two long-term boyfriends, and somehow neither one of them screwed you senseless."

I heard a sharp intake of air that could've been mistaken for a small gasp. I leaned in, motioned her forward, and put my mouth as close as I could to her ear.

"Because *I* would've screwed you absolutely senseless," I practically whispered.

The girl across from me turned such a bright shade of red it had me actually worried. Eventually she composed herself, even if her eyes dropped back to the table again.

"Well... first I'd convince myself the time wasn't right," she said. "That the night wasn't 'special' enough, and I couldn't just go through with something *that* big on any old night."

"Okay," I shrugged. "I sorta get that."

"So then I'd *plan* that night, you know? I'd set it all up. Get it all perfect and ready. But..."

"But you'd chicken out last minute."

She nodded sullenly. "Usually, yes. Either that, or the

28

guy would get all goofy. He wouldn't act precisely the way I expected him to act — the way I'd always *imagined* he should act — and it would blow the whole thing for me."

I nodded thoughtfully. "I think I see the problem here."

"You do?"

"Yes."

My stomach did a slow roll as her pretty, blue-green eyes danced with mine.

"Then enlighten me," she smiled.

# Five

## CHASTITY

I was still tingling all over. Covered head to toe in goosebumps, from that spine-tingling moment where he'd whispered into my ear.

I'm sure it also had something to do with *what* he'd whispered.

"Okay," Senan said, leaning back. "Your biggest problem here is you've become your own worst enemy. You've built this whole thing up too much. You put sex on an unreachable pedestal, making it way more important than it actually is."

The barista returned, sliding our beverages in front of us. She got the order backwards, and the moment she turned away he switched them.

"So then you created this flawless, impossible-to-achieve scenario in your mind," he went on. "Probably as a way to guard yourself against let-down, should the whole act not live up to the hype."

He reached out and handed me my tea. I accepted it gratefully as he brought his coffee to his sexy lips.

"Hype?" I asked curiously. "You think I'm hyping it?"

"Over-hyping it, yes."

"But shouldn't it *be* hyped?" I asked. "I mean I've seen sex, and it looks amazing. Shouldn't it be amazing?"

"Yes," he agreed immediately. "It is. It's absolutely amazing."

"So?"

"The problem is you won't let yourself relax and enjoy it," he said. "You're too worried it won't measure up. You missed that awkward-but-fun window, when no one knew anything and we were all just winging it. Now you're a little older, and everyone's had sex but you. You're intimidated and maybe a little bit afraid of that, but you don't have to be."

I set my tea down, suddenly completely disinterested in drinking it. Everything he was saying was dead on. I knew it in my heart.

"If we were to... you know..." I said hesitantly, "how would you make me unafraid?"

"That'd be up to you," he said plainly. "But with me, you wouldn't have to worry about failure. I'm not a boyfriend. I won't be there in the morning. You don't have to impress me, or worry about making everything 'right' between us."

"So you'd be like... practice."

"Exactly," Senan smiled. "We'd take things at your own pace, and no faster. Plus, I'd show you things. Incredible things..."

He stretched, and for a moment I saw the ripple of his abs as his shirt went tight.

"In a way," he finished, "you could consider me your own personal playground."

He rolled forward again, all broad-shouldered and beautiful. His arms were muscle upon muscle. His chest looked like I could get lost in it for days.

*Still need to think about this?* the little voice in my head teased.

"Tell me about yourself," I blurted. "A little, at least."

"Why?"

*Because you're stalling again,* I chastised myself. *Admit it.*

"Because I already feel comfortable with you," I said truthfully. "But somehow... I think it would help."

Senan raised an eyebrow — a single eyebrow, mind you — then shrugged his big shoulders. After a short pause he cupped his big hands around his coffee mug and began telling me his story. Some of it, anyway.

I only half-listened. Just enough to know he was a person and not a psychopath. Enough to put something of a personality behind the scrumptiously hard body I was about to take between my legs.

*Holy shit. You're really going to do this!*

Yes, I probably was. The admission was stark and sobering. It came with the gut-churning excitement of what we were about to do, along with a surprising measure of relief that this long journey would finally be over.

Senan talked, and I listened. Then, all of a sudden, I was talking too. I was telling him about my parents and their unrealistic expectations. About my brother the lawyer, my sister the surgeon. I even talked about *Train Direct*, the failed startup I was a huge part of. How it consumed nearly three years of my life. How I'd worked sixty-hour work weeks for no pay, trading my talents for an ownership stake... in nothing.

Minute by minute we grew more familiar — like two people out on a first date. We laughed at each other's jokes. Sympathized with each other's frustrations. I ended up drinking my tea after all. Eventually I looked down, and the cup was empty. It was now or never.

"So..." I said, the butterflies exploding in my stomach. "I was thinking—"

"That you would tell me your real name?"

The question took me totally by surprise. It left me at a complete loss.

"You know it already," I replied. "Chastity."

"A virgin named *Chastity?*" he smirked. "That's cute. Not very creative, mind you. But definitely cute."

The silence thickened as I stood there, unsure what to do next.

"Oh don't take it wrong," Senan said. "It's not that I blame you for not giving your real name. I just thought... well after all this talking, maybe you might."

"And what about you?" I said defensively.

"What about me?"

"Senan?" I smirked. "That's not your name either."

The smile on his face widened. "Actually, it is."

I laughed. "You're lying! Nobody's really *named* Senan. It's one of those cool baby names you see in a book, but no one ever uses."

"Wanna bet?"

His sudden haughtiness had me wanting to challenge him back.

"Twenty dollars says your name's not Senan," I said smartly. "No, scratch that. Fifty."

"Fifty dollars?" he smiled back at me. "That's the bet?"

"Yes."

"That's not very interesting," he shook his head. "So no thanks."

"See?" I jumped in. "You lied."

"C'mon Chastity," he smirked. "If you're going to bet, make it a *real* bet. Something good. Something better than—"

"Fine," I interjected. "I'll bet you a blowjob your name's not Senan."

In a rush to win, the words just spilled out. Somehow though, I didn't regret them.

"Really?"

"Really."

I kept his gaze, studying those piercing hazel eyes. They were the most amazing green on the outside, fading toward light brown in the middle.

Without breaking our stare, Senan reached behind

himself and produced his wallet. He opened it, pulled out his driver's license, and held it up to me.

*Senan Murillo. 531 Spruce Street.*

Seeing his name, his printed address, it made him all the more real. All the more of a *person* and not just some vague, nameless entity. Our entire transaction suddenly seemed a lot more personal.

"Well... shit."

I could feel myself flushing red, and not just because of the nature of our bet. It was because I'd been wrong. Because I'd assumed.

"I guess I owe you a blowjob then," I shrugged. The little knot of heat in my belly cinched a tiny bit tighter. "I was probably going to give you a blowjob anyway, really," I said. "You know. If we were to..."

"Fuck?"

I was turning so red now I probably looked purple.

"Yeah. That."

"A blowjob from a virgin..." Senan smiled, as if mulling the idea over. "Hmm."

"You ever *had* a blowjob from a virgin?" I asked casually.

"No," he shook his head. "Can't say that I have."

"Well then you're in for a treat," I smirked back at him. "Because we happen to be really, *really* good at it."

The man seated across from me grinned, and his grin was as gorgeous as he was. He looked absolutely delicious. I wanted to eat him alive.

"I'm ready."

The words left my mouth eagerly, breathlessly. Across the table, Senan's eyes flashed.

"You are, huh?"

"Oh yeah," I said definitively. "I am so, so ready."

Pushing his empty coffee mug forward, my guest shook his head sadly. "That's too bad."

For a few seconds, his statement didn't register. When it finally did, I was in shock.

"Wait... why?"

"Because our time is unfortunately over," he said, standing up. His eyes were soft now, his expression apologetic. "And I have somewhere else I need to be."

# Six

## CHASTITY

I stood in the center of the bookstore's cafe, overwhelmed by a flood of mixed emotions. Shock. Disappointment. Hurt.

"I'm sorry Chastity," Senan told me. "I really am."

He laid some cash on the table, then turned and began walking toward the door. The *door!* I couldn't believe it.

"Wait..."

I grabbed my things and quickly caught up with him. By the time I laid my hand on his arm, he stopped.

"Look, maybe we can do this another time," he told me. "If you still want to."

His arm was corded and sexy and impossibly thick. I could feel the muscles flexing beneath my palm as he twisted beneath my grasp.

"Besides, you said you wanted to think about this, didn't you?"

My eyes caught his, and for a brief moment time stopped. I saw my own disappointment there, reflected back in his two penetrating orbs. There was a shift in his expression. A change.

"I *did* say that," I murmured. "I— I mean..."

Suddenly his arms went stiff and Senan was pulling me backward, into the tall, silent world of a row of nearby books. I gasped sharply as he pushed me against the stacks. Then just as abruptly the breath was taken from my lungs, as he slid his magnificent body tightly against mine...

... and covered my mouth with his.

*Oh my Go—*

The kiss was slow, sensual, thunderous — my nostrils filling with musk and leather and steel. In the span of an instant it obliterated my entire world. Every nerve ending in my body surrendered to him, as our lips churned and his tongue pushed past my teeth to swirl against mine.

*—DDDD...*

In an instant I was kissing him back, reveling in the feel of being so thoroughly consumed and dominated by his presence. I was caught between the fiction section and his incredible chest. Sandwiched tightly between the thick wooden bookshelves and the even thicker bulge of his lower torso, pressing high against mine.

Our tongues danced as his hand cupped my face, ever so gently tracing the curve of my jaw. The silence between the stacks was like kissing in the dark. The greatest, most sensuous kiss ever.

And as a virgin, I knew *all* about kissing.

38

Then, just as suddenly as it had started, the whole thing was over. Senan was stepping back, letting go. He left me melted into the shelves, disorientated and breathless. My skirt still half raised on one side, where one of his hands had wandered its way up to the middle of my thigh.

"Well now you have something to think about," he said, as he turned and left.

# Seven

## CHASTITY

My bed was warm, my body warmer. I was flat on my stomach. Stretched out to just the right length, my back arched at just the right angle...

I couldn't help but sigh as my hand slipped down the flat of my belly.

*Mmmmm...*

I was mad. Frustrated. Upset with the roller-coaster of emotions that came with my missed opportunity and even more disappointed in myself. Once again I'd blown a good chance through my own hesitation and inaction.

But damn, I couldn't stop thinking about Senan.

At first I tried letting go of the resentment, but then I realized it was just the tool I needed. Senan was magnificent — the hottest guy I'd ever seen. I wanted him the second I laid eyes on his profile, and even more so once he walked through the door. Even now I could feel the enormity of his body against mine. His soft yet firm lips. The taste of his tongue...

I pushed further, sliding my three fingers between my legs and pressing hard with my hand. Focusing on the anger was much more productive than letting it go. Especially because right now, more than any other time in my life, I *needed* to get off.

*God, he felt so fucking good.*

I grunted softly as the knuckles of my middle finger bumped past my clit. Already I was totally drenched. I had been since our kiss in the bookstore, and that was over two hours ago.

*His arms were like steel bars,* I thought to myself. *And his chest... it was so hard beneath his shirt! So totally and completely—*

BZZZZZT!

I lolled my head to one side of the pillow, still working myself with a tightly-pinned hand. My phone was vibrating on the nightstand — an incoming message or alert. Whoever it was could wait. In fact, whoever it was could fuck right off—

*Oh shit!*

With eyes that were half-lidded I saw the Venmo alert. The user name. The amount.

*What the—*

I bolted upright and pulled the phone from its stand-up charger. Clicking on the app, I realized immediately what had happened.

Senan had sent me my money back.

Well, not all of it. He'd returned almost his entire fee, but it was ten dollars short. Beneath the transaction was a short message:

## The conversation was worth it.
## Coffee's on you, though.

I was stunned.  It was a *lot* of money.  But it was money he was entitled to, because although I hadn't had sex with him I'd taken over an hour of his time just the same.

"I can't believe this..."

Whatever resentment I still had drained quickly away.  It was dark and cold outside and it was getting late.  But wherever Senan was, he was out there thinking about me.

And not just thinking about me, but thinking enough about me that he was refunding my money?

I shook my head and set the phone down.  I could call him.  His number was part of his profile.  I'd emailed him instead because it had felt more formal, which in retrospect was hilarious because our little rendezvous was supposed to be anything but formal.

Calling him didn't seem right though either.  Instead I went to my laptop, got his info, and settled on a text-message:

## You're way too sweet.  Thank you.

I sent it without realizing he didn't even have my number. And considering his line of work, maybe he wouldn't even realize who the message was from.

*Should I... send something else?* The idea seemed a bit stalkerish. *Or maybe—*

I stopped myself and put the phone down. Senan had left me to go somewhere else. Somewhere he 'needed to be'. If that wasn't an indication I should probably leave well enough alone, nothing was.

Still, I couldn't stop thinking about that *kiss!*

My phone buzzed again, and another message came through:

**I'm really not, but that's okay.
Enjoy your evening, Chastity.**

God, even his *texts* were sexy! I felt giddy all over, like a schoolgirl with a crush. Did he really like me? It was a silly question on the surface, yet if he didn't, why would he have refunded me in the first place?

My stomach rolled with conflicting thoughts. I'd never been so attracted before — not to anyone — not even to the guys I'd dated. And yet, how could I be? The connection between us was purely physical, strictly business. He'd refunded me because he felt guilty we never hooked up. His comment was purely a nice one, to make me feel good.

*Or...*

Or he'd actually had a great time.

I swung my legs off the bed and stood up. The heat in my belly was still there. My desire, still unquenched. I'd take care of it in a minute, but I had to do something first.

Turning so that I faced my full-length mirror, I looked myself straight in the eye.

"You're a ridiculous asshole, Chastity."

There, I'd said it. I felt better. Hell, I was even smiling.

*I'm not angry anymore, though.*

I slid back into bed again, this time beneath the sheets. This time I let my legs fall gently to the sides, spreading myself open as my body relaxed.

*God, he smelled fucking amazing. Didn't he?*

I called Senan's image immediately to mind, recalling his touch, his scent, the deep resonance of his voice. Slowly I traced my nipples with my fingertips, pinching them once before my hand wandered south along the flat of my belly again.

My orgasm would be a lot less frenzied and vengeful, but no less explosive when the moment came.

44

# Eight

## CHASTITY

"Your brother is leaving for DC soon," my mother rambled on, as she poked her salad with her fork for the tenth time. So far she hadn't speared a single tomato. "And your sister just got back from Dublin, two nights ago. She was part of a big conference out there. I think she spoke at three different symposiums."

Symposium. I had to laugh, even if it was just to myself. Only my mother would use a word like that. I wasn't even sure what it meant.

"Did she visit any pubs?" I asked.

"Who?"

"Jennifer," I said, shaking my head. It was like talking to the wall. "They have good pubs in Dublin, from what I hear."

"Oh, I don't know. I didn't ask."

"But you asked about the... symposiums."

45

My mother's face contorted a little as she realized what I was doing. "Are you poking fun at me?"

"No mom," I smiled. "Not at all."

"Because if you think I'm going to apologize for being proud of my children and their accomplishments—"

"I'm sorry," I said, laying a hand over hers. "Seriously. I was just being a little bit of a dick."

My mother's stern glare was followed by tight-lipped silence. It wasn't a good look obviously, but at least she was letting the cuss word go.

"Tell Jennifer I said 'Hi'," I told her. "And that I miss the kids."

My mother made a face. "You don't miss your sister?"

"Her too."

"Because she misses you, you know. She wishes you never moved out here, what with all your books and computers and games and whatnot."

"They're not games, mom."

"That stuff you were doing with screens then," she said. "And the videos of people exercising."

I slumped forward on my forearms, sighing so badly I wanted to bang my head into the table. My mother — sweet as she could be at times — was also one of those people who could never understand. I'd told her half a hundred times about *Train Direct*, but she still hadn't caught on. She never knew what the product I'd been trying to develop was, nor did she really care.

Worst of all though, she was still asking me about it as

if it were something I was still doing.  Long months and years after the whole project was dead and buried.

"Are you still making exercise videos?" she went on, twisting the knife.

"No, mom."

"Ah, good.  Then you've come to your senses!"

I rolled my eyes.  "I'm *not* going to medical school, if that's what you were thinking.  Or law school, like Chris."

"Maybe you could just take a few anatomy courses?" she offered hesitantly.  "See if you like it?"

The conversation was always the same, only the restaurants changed.  Sometimes we had Italian food.  Other times, Mediterranean.  Once she grilled me about my apparent 'lack of forward progress' over a flaming pu-pu platter in the back of a Chinese teahouse.  My father had been there for that one, so it was twice as annoying.

"I just don't get it Delaina," she said, adding the requisite resigned sigh.  "You spend all those years learning all this crazy computer stuff, and then you just... *teach* it to other kids?"

*Mom, I'm a professor at Dartmouth!*  I wanted to scream.  Instead I bit my tongue.

"Something like that," I grumbled.

"So that *they* can teach it to other—"

"No," I jumped in immediately.  "So I can do other stuff with it too.  Lots of stuff."

My mind wandered back to the failed startup, and how close we'd come to an actual launch.  We'd gotten beaten to the punch, though. Missed our window for launching something unique and useful, by about three or four months.

"What about your love life, then?"

Ah, so we were onto *that* part of the conversation. My favorite part. The best part of all.

"What about it?"

"Anyone special we should know about?" she asked, as innocently as possible. "A young man maybe?"

For a brief, fleeting instant, an image of Senan popped into my head. Just as quickly I shoved it away.

"No."

She studied me closely. "Or if not a young man, maybe even a—"

"I'm not gay, mom." I speared my own salad with a vengeance now. "I told you that at least half a dozen times."

"Okay, okay," she said placatingly. "I'm just saying sweetheart, you know we'd support you no matter what choice you make."

"Really?" I asked, jumping at her mistake. "So you'll support me *not* having a special someone in my life, then?"

"Well..."

"You'll be fine if I'm still single?" I asked. "Or if I don't want children right now, or—"

"Delaina, you're a Buchanan!" my mother gasped.

"So?"

"So you need to start having heirs!"

I laughed into my glass of water and set it down. "For fuck's sake, why?"

"Language!" she frowned.

"But seriously mom, what's the difference?" I asked. "Jennifer has two children already, and Chris has his first baby on the way. Can't you busy yourself with them?"

"I—"

"You're a wonderful grandmother," I said, buttering her up. "We've seen that already. But don't worry about me. One day I'll settle down. Possibly. Probably."

She finally broke, and her expression went sad. It was the point of the conversation I always regretted.

"Mom, I love you guys. You and dad know that, right?"

"We know," she sniffed.

"Then let me do my thing. Even if it's not the thing you wanted or expected, you've still got a doctor and lawyer and a couple of *really* beautiful grandchildren already."

She half-laughed, half sighed in resignation. A tear threatened to make a break from the corner of one glassy eye but I was already on it, dabbing it with the clean edge of my napkin.

"Besides," I grinned back at her. "Maybe Meatloaf's had it right the whole time."

"Meatloaf?" my mother's brows crossed. "The singer?"

I smiled as I sang the song for her, or at least a small part of the chorus:

"*Two out of three ain't bad.*"

# Nine

## CHASTITY

Lunch with my mother set me back a bit, in terms of work. I had lessons to plan for the upcoming semester. Tests to draw up. I got some of this done in the Baker Library after meeting with Edward; the student I'd promised to help. But even that dragged on, slowing me further in terms of progress.

In reality though, I knew the real anchor keeping me from being productive.

*Senan.*

The gorgeous escort occupied my mind all day and well into the evening, his handsome face racing through my thoughts. His granite-like arms hamstrung my productivity. The vision of his broad shoulders dominated my fantasies, and distracted me from getting anything done.

The more I thought about him, the more excited I became. By nine o'clock I was alone in my apartment, my heart racing. My body warm with the rush of my own heated thoughts, even as a light snow accumulated on the wind-swept windows of my second-story loft.

I poured a large glass of wine, then drank it slowly as I sat on the sofa. The lights were dim. Soft music played in the background, as I heard the tinkle of ice being driven against the glass panes.

It was time. No, forget that. It was *long* past time.

On a whim I grabbed my phone and clicked on the Venmo icon. A few taps later I was sending the same amount as last time, to the exact same account.

*Holy shit.*

My fingers flew, hammering out a single sentence in the message area of the payment form. Before I could even think about balking, I hit the send button:

## Are we doing this or what?

I stared down at the screen for a few long moments, assessing the ramifications of what I'd just done. Then I sat back into the cushions, my heart racing about a million miles an hour.

*Holy shit holy shit holy motherfucking shit!*

A minute went by. Two minutes. Slowly, surely, disappointment set in.

*Damn.*

My analytical mind went to work, trying to rationalize the lack of response as a number of different things. It could be he didn't have his alerts turned on for his Venmo payments. Or maybe Senan just wasn't in front of his phone right now.

*C'mon. Everyone's in front of their phone.*

Or maybe he could be with someone else. Friends maybe, or another client perhaps. Someone who'd Venmo'd him just like I did now, requesting his services. Only they'd done it a little bit earlier...

The thought made my stomach do a tight little barrel roll. What was that emotion just now? Jealousy? *Really?*

I would've laughed if it weren't the truth. And yet—

BZZZZZT!

My phone wasn't buzzing with a message or alert, it was actually ringing. The number was his.

I forced myself to relax as I picked it up.

"About time, no?"

I was being fun. Funny. Hey, it came with the wine.

"I take it from your message you're probably alone?"

God, his *voice!* It was so low and smooth. Not gravelly, but still sexy and raw.

"I'm in need of your services," I said playfully. Glancing down into my empty glass, I suddenly regretted not pouring a second cup of wine. "Tonight, if possible."

"What type of services?" asked Senan, going along.

"Well I'm a damsel in distress," I purred into the phone. "An innocent maiden, in need of rescue from her own virginity."

53

"Ah," he chuckled. "I see."

"Do you charge extra for that?"

"Depends," he said. "I'd have to consult my price chart."

"Please do," I told him, swinging my legs from the couch. I rose and made my way barefoot into the kitchen. All over my body, my skin was on fire from the wine. "What I really need is someone with experience to show me the ins and outs of sex."

On the side of the phone, I heard Senan swear under his breath. "Did you seriously just say that?"

"I'm corny, I know," I admitted. "It's a problem. I'm working on it."

"And where would we be doing this?"

"Right here in my apartment," I blurted. "It's warm. It's toasty. I have music on. And I'm already only half-dressed."

I felt a surge of excitement, followed by a pang of distant panic. Did I really just invite him *over?* My heart was a jackhammer now, thundering away.

"I thought you'd never consider inviting a perfect stranger back to your apartment," Senan pointed out. "Didn't you say it would be too dangerous?"

"No less dangerous than jumping straight into bed with him," I admitted, adding a shrug. "Besides, you're not a stranger anymore. We had coffee together, remember?"

"No, *I* had coffee," he replied. "You had hot water strained through a bunch of bitter, dried up leaves."

I laughed, and the laughter tasted like wine. "That's a matter of opinion."

I had my hand on the bottle of wine already, but decided against more. Instead I put my glass in the sink. If he was coming over, I wanted to be relaxed but sober. If this was actually happening, I wanted to enjoy and remember it.

"It's a little late," I heard Senan say. "And there's a storm outside. Not a terrible one, but..."

My heart sank. My shoulders followed.

"Still, I have to admit I've been thinking about you."

His words struck me so hard, I almost tripped on the way to the fridge.

"Y—You have?"

"Yes, Chastity. I have."

My hand trembled as I unscrewed the cap from a bottle of water. I brought it to my lips, feeling my whole body come alive as the cool liquid slid down my throat.

"Besides," he went on, "maybe the whole blowjob-from-a-virgin thing intrigues me."

My stomach rolled again, this time in a really sexy way.

"It does huh?" I smirked.

"Yes."

"Well I'm not sure I can afford it."

"Afford it?"

"Yeah," I teased. "I'm hiring *you*, right? So I mean under the circumstances, wouldn't I have to pay you for it?"

"Nah," he said. "I'm pretty sure I'd let you do that for free."

"Or maybe I'd charge you for it," I teased back. "A little tit for tat."

Senan huffed. "I see what you did there."

"I told you already, I've got pun problems."

"And a virginity problem too," he countered seamlessly. A second or two of silence went by. When he spoke again, his voice was serious. "Would you like me to come by and take care of that?"

I swallowed hard, holding the half-empty bottle against my heated forehead. I was tingling all over.

"Yes please."

The relief was back again. But right now it was nothing compared to the thrill and excitement.

"Then send me the address," Senan said finally. "And I'll do the rest."

# Ten

## SENAN

Her place was even cozier than she claimed it to be, a pretty little loft apartment at the end of some steep wooden stairs. She took my coat as she closed the door behind me. I watched as she shook it gently, to free it of snow.

"Thanks."

The place was dim but not dark. String lighting near the ceiling cast a warm amber glow, augmented by scented candles that smelled something like butterscotch. The kitchen and living room were all one area. Both were neat and immaculate...

... except for a large area of blankets, pillows, and bedding, arranged in a big square on the living room floor.

"Looks like you mean business this time," I joked, raising an eyebrow.

"Ya think?"

She slid something cold into my hand, and I realized it

was an open beer. Into my other hand she slid something warm, and that something was her ass.

"You're not getting away this time," Chastity told me.

Her body was soft and fragrant and curvy, and now pleasantly pressed against mine. She had one palm on my chest. With the other she reached up and tilted my chin downward, so she could kiss me.

*MMMMmmmm. Nice.*

Nice didn't even begin to describe it. Her lips were even softer than last time, and tasted vaguely of something sweet. Sugar maybe. Or cotton candy. The kissing continued for half a minute, our tongues getting reacquainted until finally she stepped down from her toes and batted her eyes at me.

"You're really taking charge," I noted, finally sipping my beer. "Aren't you?"

The lithe blonde creature attached to my hip shook her pretty little head. "No. I'm really not." She nodded toward the makeshift bed. "Once we get in there, I want you to do everything."

"Everything?" I teased.

She blushed again. I'd forgotten how cute it was.

"Everything within reason," she purred. "But yes, I'd like you to take over. You can have me in all the ways that you want. Maybe you can pretend I'm your girlfriend."

She looked down at her shuffling feet, and her expression went even more adorable. She was planting seeds of how she wanted this to go in my mind. I could feel my arousal growing.

"I want you to make love to me," she said shyly. "I want you to make me *yours.*"

Now it was my turn to place a finger under her chin. Delicately and slowly, I forced her to look into my eyes again.

"Okay."

I kissed her again, setting my beer down so I could get both arms around her. She was wearing a red lace babydoll teddy, short enough that it danced around the tops of her thighs. Cupping her delectable ass in both hands, I inhaled her scent: coconut and vanilla, and maybe salt from the sea. She smelled like the tropics. Like a beautiful stretch of unblemished beach. I was going to leave footprints on that beach — indelible ones, too. But I was going to do it gently.

"You feel amazing."

I slid my palms over the warm, supple expanse of skin, until I found what I was looking for. Chastity's thong was a thin strip of embedded satin, emerging only at the very top of her perfect ass. I followed it downward, through the valley between her thighs. My fingers slid even lower, until her wetness became apparent as she gasped against me.

"Come on," I told her softly. "Let's go."

I took her hand in mine, and led her in the direction of the makeshift bed. Her tiny lips were pursed, her eyes glazed with excitement. Wordlessly I took her glasses off, and laid them on the table beside the couch.

"You blind without these?"

"No," she chuckled softly. "I can see well enough."

"Good," I whispered, kissing her again. "Because you're gonna wanna see this."

We sank to our knees together, on the makeshift bed where everything would go down. It turned me on even more, thinking about her setting this up. Getting it all ready for what would come later. Knowing full well it was a moment she'd been waiting for all her life.

I took her hand and placed it squarely on the bulge in my jeans. Then I pulled my shirt upward, lifted it over my head, and threw it to the floor behind her.

"C'mere."

I pulled her in, bringing her against my bare chest. I felt her mouth seek my skin, as she began planting a series of soft, light kisses all over me.

Her hand was working me slowly, as my own hands wandered her body. Eventually I was wriggling out of my jeans. Sliding up alongside her in nothing but my underwear, as we continued kissing and nuzzling and facing each other.

The music played. The candlelight danced. Chasity's hand found its way through the front of my boxers, still tongue-kissing me as her fingers closed over my warm, quickly-hardening thickness. I let her go on for a while, sliding her palm up and down. Bringing me to near full erection as our mouths churned and our bodies twisted and my own hands wandered dangerously up the insides of her smooth, porcelain thighs.

"Time to pay up," I told her, murmuring playfully into her mouth.

"Hmm?"

60

"The blowjob you owe me."

Her eyes flashed, and her lips curled into a smile. This was something she knew.

"Lay back, then."

Her tiny hands pushed on my chest, trying to force me down. It might as well have been a pair of feathers against a brick.

"I want to see," I told her, leaning back on my elbows. The position flexed my stomach, turning it into a rippled sea of rock-hard abdominals. "I want to watch you do this."

Chastity paused to look at me, her blue-green eyes turning turquoise in the amber half-light. Then, kissing me once more for good measure, she began tracing her way down my body with her hot pink tongue.

*Damn...*

She kissed my neck, my chest, my flat, quivering stomach. And all the while her hands still played, stroking me up and down, getting me nice and ready.

"Lift."

I lifted, and she yanked my boxers all the way off. Then, without even a second's worth of hesitation, she buried her beautiful girl-next-door face between my legs...

"Mmmmm..."

... and pressed my banana-shaped erection right up against one beautiful cheek.

*Fuck.*

It felt enormously powerful, watching her do this.

61

Seeing her eyes follow mine as she showered the sides and head of my manhood with tiny, almost innocent little kisses that were driving me wild. In time she swallowed me, all the way to the root. Never breaking eye-contact. Maintaining the intimacy of our connection the whole time, as she began bobbing up and down the entire length of my glistening shaft.

*God. She's just... perfect.*

It would've been a strange word, if it weren't so suitable. The girl between my legs was gorgeous. Flawless. Wholly unsullied. I'd wanted to make her mine, even before she'd said the words. I'd wanted to take her fully, body and soul, in every possible way.

I hissed my pleasure through clenched teeth, reaching out to sift one big hand through her soft blonde hair. Chastity was blowing me lovingly. Doing her best to make everything slow and soft and sensual. It was what she wanted from me of course, so it seemed only natural. I couldn't wait to give it to her.

But first, this.

*I wonder what her name is?*

I'd wondered lots of things about her over the past few days. Who she was. What kind of life she was leading. It wasn't normal, because I'd never had reflections like this before. I'd never lent more than a few stray thoughts to other clients, preferring to follow my strict rule of keeping business as business.

But this...

This was nothing but pure pleasure.

I let out a groan as Chastity began picking up the pace,

adding her fingers and the tips of her nails to the mix. She began teasing me, dragging them lightly over my scrotum. Stopping on the upstroke to squeeze and play with my balls, before tightening her lips and really sucking me back into her hot little throat.

*Holy fuck.*

My stomach tightened. My hips bucked upward, all on their own.

*She's right. She's good.*

All new shivers of arousal bolted through me, as Chastity added a finger just below my sack. She pushed firmly but gently against my perineum. The pressure there, coupled with the feel of her tongue sliding wetly against me was absolutely delicious.

*No,* I thought to myself. *She's fucking amazing.*

I was sifting her hair with both hands now, and she was shaking her head back and forth. The sensations were unreal. It felt like she was consuming me, tip to base. Swallowing my entire lower body, much less my manhood, into the wonderful heat of her talented mouth.

"You... you need to..."

If she heard me, she didn't listen. Chastity kept stroking me. Blowing me. Rolling my balls gently in one soft palm, while pressing that incredible button I wasn't even aware I had.

"Chastity you have to *stop.*"

I was so used to being in control, I could barely sense my resolve dropping away. It was a slippery slope. Everything was happening so fast.

*FUCKKKK...*

It would be so easy to just let go. For a moment I even considered it. I could explode like a cannon, emptying myself gloriously into her precious, beautiful mouth...

Instead I pulled myself free of her magical grasp, and rolled her onto her back. Her lips were plump and full, her face all flush and glowing. Her eyes flared wide for a second as I hovered over her, and I could feel her trembling nervously as I pressed my hard body against the heat of her own.

"My turn," I growled, before burying my face into her neck.

# Eleven

## CHASTITY

He devoured me inch by wonderful inch, his beard tickling my skin all the way down. I gasped as he stopped briefly at my breasts, pulling them free of my lingerie to lavish them with warmth and attention. His lips closed over my nipples, and I clutched at his head. The gentle pull of his teeth had me dragging him hard against my body, as his hot tongue ran loving circles over my areolae.

*This is going to happen...*

I couldn't believe it. Only I could. Only I still couldn't.

*This is really, really going to—*

I gasped again as his mouth dragged lower, and now he was kissing my stomach. The hand trapped between my thighs the whole time was slowly moving now; two impossibly thick fingers pushing along the edge of my thong.

*Holy shit...*

The thin strip of fabric was my last line of defense. The only thing that separated his hard, eager fingers from the ultimate prize.

*I still can't believ—*

"Lift."

My stomach went tight again as I lifted my ass from the blankets. Two strong, masculine hands went to either side of my trembling thighs. They grasped the tops of my near non-existent panties and rolled them down my legs, all the way to my ankles.

Then they were on the floor... and Senan was between my legs.

*Oh... oh wow.*

He looked at me for a moment, his fingers still moving, sliding, just *barely* penetrating. They glided deliciously up and down through the shallows of my furrow, as he leaned forward to kiss me.

"Look at you," he murmured, kissing my mouth over and over. "You're so drenched you're practically in heat."

I glanced down, to where one tattooed forearm was working me over. It was frightening. Exhilarating. Beyond incredible.

"You've waited way too long for this."

I nodded obediently as he dipped back down, then buried his head between my thighs. When Senan's tongue flicked out I jumped. He made it flat and firm, then dragged it *slowly* upward, centimeter by centimeter, through my dripping, aching entrance.

*Ohhhhhhhh......*

My head lolled sideways on the pillow. I could feel my hair spilling out beneath my face.

"Mmmmmm..." he hummed softly, his lips pressed right up against my entrance. "MmmmMMmmm..."

I was throbbing. Twisting. His tongue lashed again and I gripped the blankets with both hands.

"Here."

He took one arm and placed my hand on his head, then used it to press himself further against my sex. His tongue was probing now, scooping away inside me. His upper lip fluttered against my clit.

*"Oh fuck..."* I breathed.

He played some more and I bucked instinctively, rolling the hand in his hair into a tightly-clenched fist. I pulled tightly on it, as the sensations became too much. He pulled right back.

"Senan..."

He was sucking, eating, devouring me whole. Lapping up my honey as fast as I was making it, while moaning and humming against my swollen button. I couldn't take it anymore. I was desperate to come. But more than that — more than anything else — I was desperate to have him inside of me. To take him into my body. To feel the weight of him finally crushing me into the pillows, as he slowly, carefully, filled me up...

"Fuck me."

They were two little words, gasped from between my

67

parted lips. Two words I hadn't said to anyone. Ever.

"Fuck me *now.*"

"Please?" he teased, still lapping away.

I closed my thighs against the sides of his beautiful face, but the pressure only made things more intense. I was gasping at this point. Panting. Begging.

"*Please.*"

Pushing up on his two big arms, Senan rolled himself forward over my body. I didn't resist as he nudged my thighs apart. I didn't even flinch as I felt him push his way between them, positioning himself for the one last act that would make me whole.

Our eyes met, and we both looked like we were dreaming. Our lids were half closed. Our searching irises looked past each other, into each other's souls.

I wanted to tell him I was ready. That I'd waited for this my whole life — this one perfect, pinnacle of a moment — and I was glad to be sharing it with him.

But I needed one last thing...

# Twelve

## CHASTITY

"Alexa," I breathed out loud, my eyes going temporarily over his shoulder. "Play my playlist *Perfect*."

The current music stopped. The electronic voice told me it understood, and there was a brief moment of silence as it switched over.

Then the familiar keyboards started up, as an all new song began playing.

Senan was looking down at me in disbelief, his eyebrows knitted together.

"What the—"

I went to kiss him, and he kissed me back. But he was distracted.

"*In Your Eyes?*" he asked quizzically, still listening to the song. "By Peter Gabriel?"

"Yes," I smiled.

"From the movie, Say Anything?" he cocked his head.

"The scene where the two of them—"

"Yes," I said again, a little more embarrassed this time. "I know. I'm corny."

He breathed out a chuckle. *"Really?"* he asked incredulously. "Are you telling me you made a 'lose it' mix for yourself?"

"Okay, sue me," I shrugged shyly, pinned snugly beneath him. "I wanted the moment to be special."

I went back to kissing him, and once more our tongues intertwined. The music played on, the lovely harmonics of the song permeating my warm little apartment.

"Alexa," Senan said abruptly, breaking the kiss. I saw a glimmer of mischief in his eye. "Play AC/DC's *Thunderstruck.*"

The song switched and the familiar intro began, along with the screaming of an electric guitar. Senan smiled and began nodding his head to the beat.

"AC/DC?"

"Sure. Why not?"

"A little fast-paced for something like this," I protested smartly. "No?"

Our bodies were melded together, my breasts pressed tightly beneath his surging chest. I was still in heat, so to speak. Still throbbing for completion.

"Fine," Senan murmured, his smile growing even wider. "Alexa, play *Like a Virgin.*"

AC/DC stopped, and Madonna started up. The music was 80's and poppy and wholly familiar. As he grinned down at me, I couldn't help but laugh.

"No."

"No?" he chuckled.

"I'm afraid not."

Senan lowered his lips to mine, kissing me so hard I swooned. I was growing dizzy with want. Giggly with merriment. It was all so perfectly imperfect.

"Alexa," Senan called out again. "Play *Feels Like the First Time.*"

New guitars started up almost immediately. Way before Foreigner's singer began belting out the first lines of the classic song, I was shaking my head.

"You're a tough crowd," he sighed. "Very picky." He kissed my forehead this time, then spoke again.

"Alexa, play *Closer* by Nine Inch Nails."

The repetitive drum-hiss drum-hiss started up, filling the room with its distinctive beat. As he shifted forward to kiss me again, I rolled my eyes.

"I am *not* losing my virginity to Nine Inch Nails."

"But the lyrics are perfect," he smiled.

I laughed bitterly. "Yeah, no. Alexa, shuffle my playlist *Perfect.*"

Another one of my songs came on, this one slow and melodic. I wasn't even sure which one it was, to be honest. I'd been compiling the list since I was a teenager.

"Sorry," said Senan. "I can't let you do this again."

"Can't let me do what?"

"Over-hype this," he said simply. "Chastity, you've planned for this moment down to every last detail, including the *song list*. That's not healthy. There are some things you need to let go."

He looked at me again, but for once the smile on his face wasn't mischievous or judgmental. His expression was actually hopeful. Helpful.

"Alexa," he called out once more. "Play *Fade Into You*."

There was a moment of silence, followed by the gentle strumming of an acoustic guitar. The chords were soft. Graceful. Almost hypnotic. Before I knew it I found myself swaying slowly, as Senan rocked me gently beneath his body.

"What is this?"

"Mazzy Star."

The guitar chords repeated over and over, as he began nuzzling my neck. My body relaxed. A woman eventually began singing, and her voice was that of an angel.

"Wow," I swore in admiration.

"Um-hmm."

Slowly Senan's mouth worked up to my ear, where he traced my earlobe with the tip of his tongue. Goosebumps exploded down that side of my body.

"I—"

In the meantime, the lyrics kept coming. The woman singing the song seemed heartbroken, her words haunting. The melody itself was soft and exquisite.

"This is amazing," I gasped, pulling his face to mine. I kissed him slowly, sensuously, as the heat rose between us. He nestled even further between my legs as our hands found each other's, and our fingers intertwined.

"My sister played this song on her guitar all the time," he murmured, lost in my lips. "She used to, anyway."

"Senan, it's beautiful."

Holding my gaze in his, he nodded solemnly.

"So was she."

My brow furrowed, but only as long as it took for him to lean forward again. Our foreheads touched, as our lips brushed in one last gentle kiss. Every breath he took was mine. Every subtle movement, we were sharing together.

"You ready?"

Somewhere between my legs I could feel something heavy and thick and warm. I knew damned well what it was. By the way my hips bucked forward, my body knew too.

"*So* ready."

Senan smiled as he dragged the bulbous head up and down through my warm, wet entrance. Satisfied, he shifted forward just enough that it was pressing against me.

"I'll go slow," he promised. "You tell me if—"

"I will."

He shifted again, surging forward, pushing his way inside. My legs spread even wider, and I felt him parting me like a flower. Opening me up, to take him into my world.

*Yesss...*

I breathed out in a grateful sigh, feeling the pressure build as he disappeared inside me. There was a brief moment of discomfort — a razor-sharp knife's edge between pleasure and pain — and then I felt it; that one last push. That last band of physical resistance finally giving way, and then he was sliding *all* the way in, filling me up, making me whole.

Leaving the very last of my innocence behind.

# Thirteen

## CHASTITY

The songs played, the candles burned, the snow fell outside. All of those things added to the moment. Every one of them contributed to the ambiance in its own special way.

That said, I would've screwed this man in broad daylight, or in a raging thunderstorm, or on the fifty-yard line of a football stadium, with fifty thousand people watching.

It was really just *that* good.

Senan took me slow at first, just as he promised. I clawed his back as he rocked into my body. Gasped into the warm flesh of his neck, even biting his shoulder as he dug his way deeper and deeper inside me.

There were no boundaries between us. No hesitation. Every reservation I ever had had somehow melted away, dissolving instantly in the wake of his gentleness, his compassion, his sensitivity. He made love to me exactly as he said he would, and there was definitely no other word for it. Again and again our bodies rocked, sliding against each other as we lost ourselves in a molten hot sea of kissing, licking, and touching.

But there was another side to our lovemaking, too. The side that came later, after he'd made me come so hard around his magnificent thickness I felt my vision go blurry at the edges. It was the side of command. Of control. Of dominance.

*My God...*

It was the other side of the coin when it came to Senan's abilities; maybe even the darker side, although it didn't seem dark to me. Because after making me come, after bringing me off so fully and completely that my endorphin-addled brain was still spinning with rapture, Senan flipped me onto my stomach, grabbed me by the hips, and then *really* took charge.

*Mmmmmmmm...*

I wasn't the least bit frightened as he slid into me from behind. It stung a little, but in a good way, and the feeling of fullness superseded everything else. His hands felt incredible on my ass. Domineering and possessive as his fingers flexed tightly, pulling my body against his with every wave of his own arousal.

My whole body shivered as he pumped me slowly, gliding in and out in a way that made me feel deliciously used. His rippled stomach pressed itself tightly against my back. I felt one hand leave my ass, to roll into my hair..

"You're mine now."

He whispered the words just an inch from my ear, his breath so hot it made me gasp. Somehow I was able to nod. I

Corrupting Chastity - Krista Wolf

breathed the word 'yes' even as he picked up the pace, slamming into me faster and deeper, rolling my head back so he could lay his face against mine.

*Oh my God, YES.*

The whole thing was dirty as all fuck.

In time I was rocked backwards, onto my hands and knees. Screwed doggie-style from behind, with my head pushed into the nearest pillow. I let him move me, manipulate me, take me however he wanted. His pleasure was my pleasure, through every delirious push and pull.

We fucked through song after song, kissing so deeply our bodies became one. Screwed each other straight through the storm, our eyes locked so soulfully it made my heart ache. I came hard with my legs pinned back, my hands grasping at the two iron-like pillars of his massive arms. And again after that, screaming silently into a pillow as he plowed me face-down.

I kept thinking how foolish I was, how crazy I'd been. How my lover had been right the whole time, that I'd psyched myself out on far too many occasions. That I'd denied myself years of pleasure, all over nothing.

He was wrong about one thing though: I hadn't over-hyped this at all. If anything it exceeded even my wildest, most optimistic of expectations.

But maybe that was all because of *him*.

Senan took me on a roller-coaster of slow and soft, then fast and hard again, our bodies writhing together over every blanketed surface of my living room floor. In the end he pulled me carefully on top of him, positioning me by the hips.

77

I gasped sharply and then sighed, as he pierced me to my very core.

*Ohhhhhhh...*

Locking eyes again, his hands moved up to my breasts. He played with them gently, rubbing his palms tantalizingly over my nipples as my own hands found the hard, broad expanse of his naked, tattooed chest...

Then we rocked together gently, as I rode him for the very first time.

*This is...*

Shifting back and forth, his manhood buried achingly deep inside of me, I never felt more *whole.*

*This is amazing.*

My hair fell into my eyes, and Senan reached out to brush it away gently. I took the back of his hand. Pinned it lovingly against the side of my face. Our eyes locked one final time, and I could sense his control faltering. His expression was glassy and far away. Saturated with lust.

"It's time."

He murmured the words sexily, barely holding on. I smiled and nodded.

"Do it."

We'd talked about this at the bookstore – how I wanted my first time to be safe, natural. I'd been on the pill forever, more for medical than sexual reasons. Now there was nothing holding me back.

"*Come* in me."

The words came breathlessly, almost silently. And holy shit, they *really* turned me on.

"Let it go, just let it—"

I gasped and bit down on my lip, my eyes flaring wide as he erupted inside me. It felt like a molten volcano. Like jet after jet of lava, splashing hotly against my innermost of places.

*Oh my God...*

They were places that were beautiful yet still foreign to me. Newly-unlocked places only Senan had been.

Over and over he spasmed, twitching and thumping as he emptied himself inside me. It was the very last of a long list of taboo acts. The final piece of the overarching puzzle that initiated me into womanhood.

"Holy *fuck*, Chastity."

A hand found my face, and suddenly he was pulling me down against him. He kissed me as a lover now, with an intimacy and familiarity I knew only came with such a union. Down below he was still contracting inside me. Riding out the last throbs and pulses that made up his orgasm, as my hair spilled down around us like a shimmering blonde waterfall.

And that was it. Just like that, I was no longer a maiden.

*Just like that... huh?*

Senan shifted again, this time rolling me onto my side. Face to face, still buried inside me, he kissed my lips and smiled.

"You get what you wanted?"

I flexed my legs, squeezing him internally. I felt

exhilarated. Numb. Pleasantly sore. I traced his skin with my fingertips, as our bodies stayed wrapped tightly together.

"I'll tell you after we do it *again*," I purred.

We kissed and laughed, then kissed some more, until the playfulness faded and the arousal grew. The snow fell, the candles burned. Our bodies eventually uncoiled, refilling with a familiar sexual tension.

"Alexa!" Senan called loudly, rolling me onto my belly. I was already laughing before he even finished.

"Play *Closer* by Nine Inch Nails."

# Fourteen

## CHASTITY

He stayed late into the night, holding me. Cuddling me. Sleeping beside me, with his giant arms wrapped securely around my naked body. I woke once near morning, to watch the rising and falling of his chest. To trace every outline of his tattoos with my sleepy gaze, and to stare at his beautiful, tranquil face.

We made love again once more, in the dead of night. It was slow and heated, short and sweet. It ended with Senan spending himself deep inside me, shortly after I'd clawed him through another toe-curling climax of my own. Then we fell asleep still wrapped around each other, physically and emotionally wiped out.

When I awoke to the sunlight he was gone.

The candles were still burning, the music still playing so softly I could barely hear it. But those things were there. Remnants of last night. Fading memories of our ultimate evening, which had turned out so perfect I could barely contain myself.

*God...*

I lay there for a while beneath the blankets, burning the memories into my brain. I could still feel his body against mine. Still smell the musky, manly scent of him, or perhaps that part actually *did* linger on my sex-soaked bedding.

I stretched, feeling the oxygen surge through my tired arms and legs. My thighs still hurt, maybe from a recent workout, maybe from something else. But the feeling of completion was still there. The sense of fullness I'd felt in my belly was as real as the distant soreness between my thighs, which I welcomed and embraced along with the memories I was tucking away forever.

After a good fifteen or twenty minutes of staring at the ceiling I rolled out of the makeshift bed and showered, then went about getting ready for my day. By the time I pulled my phone off the charger, there was already an alert on the screen.

It was from my Venmo account. Apparently, Senan had returned my payment again. Minus ten dollars, of course.

*What the—*

I punched the messenger icon and fired off a text:

## You know you're really bad at this whole getting paid for sex thing.

Almost immediately he wrote back, the little ellipsis flashing as he typed:

> Sorry, can't take anything for last night.
> It was too much fun.

I felt my heart swell with gratitude. By taking away the transaction aspect of what we'd done last night, he'd just made my perfect moment even more perfect.

*He knows that, too.*

It was an interesting idea. On meeting him at the bookstore I'd pegged Senan as all business. But now there was a different side to him. A softer, sweeter side — echoes of our evening together.

> What's the ten dollars for this time?
> I'm curious.

Without missing a beat he typed back:

> Gas, probably. Or maybe the trauma
> of being subjected to your
> devirginization playlist.

83

I laughed so hard I almost dropped the phone.

> Devirginization, huh?
> My spellcheck tells me that's
> not even a word.

A moment passed. Then:

> Yeah, well your spellcheck never
> devirginized anyone before.
> I have.

The smile on my face was so wide it almost hurt. Apparently this guy had the gift of being funny and sarcastic and sweet, all at once.

A little more seriously, I typed some more:

> Honestly I should be paying you double.
> You were amazing.

This time a full minute went by, and I started

wondering if I'd gone too far. That maybe I was pushing too much, too soon. Then:

## Amazing doesn't begin to describe it. But I broke my biggest rule: I stayed over.

## Actually I broke lots of rules last night.

I didn't know whether the message was good or bad. Whether he was angry or bitter or—

## But can I tell you something? Honestly?

Somewhere in my chest, the beating of my heart picked up a little.

## Of course!

The next message that appeared on screen made me melt.

# I loved breaking my rules with you.

I sat there for several long moments, tingling all over. It was the single most incredible thing anyone had ever written to me. And it had come from a morning-after text message, sent by an escort I'd hired to take my virginity.

*Is he really an escort though, Delaina?* The little voice in my head asked. *If you didn't pay him?*

Of course he was. That's how I'd found him, of course. Hell, he didn't even know my name.

*Still...*

I sent back a simple heart-emoji, then tucked my phone away. It was sweet and non-committal. A good conversation-ender, when you didn't know how to end a conversation.

"Work..."

Tucking away the butterflies in my stomach, I focused on the long list of tasks ahead of me. With the new semester starting up I had tons to do, both on campus and off. The holidays were over. It was a brand new year, a fresh start. In more ways than I expected to count.

Just thinking about that brought a smile to my face.

# Fifteen

## CHASTITY

"We still have to decide what to do with the source code," I said for the third time this week. "We've worked too long on the whole thing to just scrap it entirely."

At the other end of the Zoom call, my three colleagues still looked totally bored. Evan's attention was drawn off-screen, presumably to one or both of his three-year old twin girls. Claudia was looking down at her nails. Jaime was scratching his head.

"We've been shopping it around for a couple months now," said Claudia, "with no real takers. I've got some postings up on some forums, but most people want to see a finished product rather than a bunch of disjointed routines."

"Which we obviously don't have," Jaime chimed in, a little annoyed.

Evan left the frame for half a minute, then returned to the sound of an additional television in the background. It was certainly distracting, but at least the twins had both stopped screaming.

"I know it sucks," he apologized eventually. "But give it some time. We have a few more places we can try, if it's not something we can sell to—"

"Why aren't we trying those places now?" interrupted Jaime.

I crossed my arms purposefully in front of my laptop's camera. It was a good question.

"Honest answer?" asked Evan. "Because we're too busy on the new project."

"We..." I scoffed. The new project — whatever it was at this point — was something Evan had run off with Claudia to work on. They hadn't looped Jaime or I in yet. At this point we doubted they ever would.

I tried my best to stay positive, but it wasn't working. Our bi-weekly meetings used to be several hours long. They were filled with excited chatter about where we'd take *Train Direct* next, and how each of us were doing on our own parts of the project.

Then other platforms started popping up — mirroring the exact thing we were trying to do. Face-to-face training sessions, attached to spin bikes, treadmills, elliptical machines. They gave the user the freedom to interact with entire rooms full of other spinners and joggers, all from the comfort of their own living rooms. And there weren't one or two of them, there were *five*. Three really good ones. One of them was actually excellent.

In other words, we'd missed the boat.

Right now the project that once involved over a dozen

people only just four of us left. Our animated bi-weekly Zoom chats were now fifteen-minute doom-and-gloom checkup sessions, to see if we could salvage any money at all from all our apparently wasted time and effort.

"If you want," Evan offered awkwardly, "maybe we could—"

My phone buzzed, flashing my friend Naomi's number. I smiled, grateful for something positive. I considered sending it to voicemail, then stopped myself.

"Guys I've gotta run," I said, more apologetically than I actually felt. "Shoot me an email if anything else comes up."

"Will do," Claudia said. Evan nodded.

I fake-smiled and severed the connection, grateful to be rid of the same meeting I used to look so forward to.

*Things change*, I sighed to myself. *And not always for the better.*

It took less than three seconds to let go of that bullshit and pick up Naomi's call. I braced for the sarcasm I knew would be coming, especially since I was picking her up on the fourth or fifth ring.

"About fucking time," she growled in her best mock-angry voice. "You burying a body, or what?"

"No," I laughed. "Not yet, anyway."

"Better not be," she swore. "Not without me, anyway. You know that right? That I'd bury a body with you?"

"Oh I know," I smiled. "You've said it before."

"Anytime, any day," Naomi confirmed. "Gotta have *someone* I can call when I need a favor like that cashed in.

Body bury buddies are for life, you know? The kind of secrecy you can only get from—"

"What the hell do you want?" I laughed.

"Well I want lots of things," Naomi said without missing a beat. "Bigger tits. Zero calorie ice cream. A man who makes good money *and* can hold it down in the sack." She paused to consider her own made-up list. "That would be a good one, actually. A man's man. A *real* man."

"Doesn't sound too unreasonable," I smiled.

Naomi swore viciously under her breath. "Do you know the last guy I dated couldn't even jump-start a car?"

"Lots of people have triple-A these days," I shrugged. "Maybe it's a lost art?"

"A *lost art?*" she sneered. "Maybe it's two fucking cables you attach to each battery, red and black. It's not rocket science, Delaina."

"Solid point."

"Shit," she went on. "The last asshole who took me out didn't have a pair. His battery died while we were in the restaurant, and when I asked if he had jumper-cables he looked at me like I asked him to solve the Riemann Hypothesis."

"God you're such a nerd," I laughed. "You know that, right?"

"Nerd's offensive. We prefer the term Geek now."

"As if anything could actually offend you."

"Who the fuck doesn't stuff a simple set of jumper-cables into the trunk?" my friend swore. She still couldn't let it go. "Or under the seat, or—"

"What is it you wanted again?"

This time *she* laughed, and her laughter reminded me of how much I loved her. Other than the fact she was socially extroverted and completely unafraid of men, Naomi was a lot like me. We'd met in a cybersecurity class, toward the end of my college career. She'd been taking it for the company she worked at. I'd needed it for my masters. Pairing up for projects had us hanging out off campus, and before long we were friends. It was easy to make friends with someone like Naomi.

"You get your dress yet, bitch?"

At first the question didn't register. "Dress for what?"

"Uhhh... the wedding?"

My brows crossed. "The wedd—" Suddenly it hit me. "OH SHIT. Heather's wedding!"

"There we go," she chuckled. "I just jump-started your brain."

Panicked, my mind began racing through my mental calendar. My friend Heather had invited me to her wedding, and to stave off boredom I was using Naomi as my plus one. That had been ages ago. I'd totally forgotten.

"Oh wow," I said. "I... I totally—"

"It's not *this* weekend," said Naomi, putting me out of my misery. "It's still about a month away."

I breathed a huge sigh of relief. "Thank God."

"Yeah."

"Did you still want to go dress shopping?"

"Nope, I already took care of it," she said proudly. "For once I'm ahead of the game."

"Oh."

"But I figured I'd remind *you*," she said. "Because you know... scatterbrain."

"Scatterbrain?" I said in my own mock-offended tone. "Look who's talking! More like busy as hell, and—"

"Busy," laughed Naomi. "Sure."

Damn, I *really* needed to go to lunch with Naomi — especially since she was one of the only people I could actually tell what happened. My geeky computer friend was many things, but the one thing she wasn't was judgmental.

"Shop with me anyway?" I offered. "I'll buy lunch."

"Sounds good," she said. "Except I'm not in town. I'm actually in Irvine."

"California?"

"Yeah. Tech conference. Nerd stuff."

"You mean geek," I teased.

"Whatever," Naomi chuckled. "You should fly out here, crash my room with me. The weather's fucking fantastic. And all this nerd shit would be right up your alley."

"Tempting but I can't," I sighed. "New semester is starting up. And they gave me three classes to teach instead of two."

Somewhere on the opposite side of the country, my friend sighed. "Gonna have to wait until the wedding then," she said. "We'll catch up then."

"Definitely," I said, my face breaking into a smile just thinking about it. "I... have a lot of stuff to tell you about."

"Good," declared Naomi, "I could use some girl time. The nerd world's come a long way, but it's still predominantly male."

"Not jumper-cable male though," I teased.

"No," my friend sighed all the way from California. "Unfortunately not."

# Sixteen

## CHASTITY

It had taken every ounce of willpower not to call Senan the next day, and the evening was even harder still. I wanted to give him space, though. To let the memory of a good thing lay unblemished, in case I needed to call upon him again, which of course I did.

The worst part was thinking about how *his* night was going.

I could imagine how it was for most girls, sleeping with a guy for the very first time. Picturing and re-picturing it in your head. Wondering when the two of you would be able to make it happen again, and whether or not it would be even more magical than the first time.

With Senan though, the situation was a little different. And that's because he wasn't even close to being mine.

No, the unfortunate part about falling for an escort was exactly that — he was an escort. He had other clients, other customers. Other women he likely saw — and yes, slept with —

when he wasn't with me.

That made me jealous whether I liked it or not. Because for all I knew, he could belong to someone else at the very moment I was thinking about him.

*Don't be silly. It's not like you're falling for him.*

Maybe not, but it sure felt that way. I'd fallen for guys before that hadn't wanted me back. Unrequited crushes. Even a relationship that should've never been, because the guy had been only borderline interested in me to begin with. We'd hung out more like friends than lovers, which was fine because my virginity was always the elephant in the room. Even kissing him seemed wrong somehow.

With Senan though, it was so totally different. There had been fire on both sides. An undeniable chemistry that made everything that happened between us incredibly natural. At first I'd convinced myself that it was all part of his job. That he was just good at making his clients feel welcome and happy, in an effort to drum up new and repeat business.

Only I wasn't a client. And since he'd returned my money, I wasn't his customer. I was merely a lover. Someone he'd played and had fun with.

But also someone he'd broken rules with, too.

I focused on thinking about that part, and that part alone. It put me in a fantastic mood when I called him the next morning, and an even *better* mood when he finally answered the phone.

"Hello gorgeous."

Just the sound of his voice sent me reeling with memories of our night together. Already I was tingling all over.

"Well hello yourself," I said past the lump in my throat. God, why was this so difficult? I spoke to fifty, sometimes sixty students at once sometimes. But here...

"I'm in need of your services again," I went on.

"Oh really?"

"Yes. But much different services than last time."

I could tell by the pause at the other end I had him at a disadvantage.

"Okayyy," Senan admitted. "Now you've got me curious."

I smiled, enjoying the moment for a second or two before continuing.

"More specifically I need your shopping services," I told him succinctly. Another second or two of silence followed.

"Funny. I don't remember that being part of my profile."

"It's not," I admitted. "But I need a new dress, and I'll pay you for your time."

More silence. This time it was borderline awkward.

"I, uh... I really could use a guy's opinion," I said truthfully. "I figured we could hit the mall. Have lunch. I'd try on a few things, and you'd tell me what you thought of them."

"No sex?" he asked plainly. "Just shopping?"

"S—Sure."

My confidence wavered. Suddenly the whole thing

seemed tremendously silly to me. Almost childish.

"If it's not your thing I get it," I said apologetically. "No big deal. I guess I was just hoping that—"

"Which mall?"

My heart — which had just sank into the pit of my stomach — rose back up a couple of inches. I told him.

"Could we do it today?" Senan asked.

"Um. Sure."

"Tonight's bad. Tomorrow too."

"It's okay," I answered. "Today's fine."

I felt the sharp stab of jealousy just thinking about Senan's plans. What would he be doing tonight that he was so busy? And tomorrow too?

*More like* who *would he be doing...*

I shoved the unwanted emotions away. Some anger still lingered, but not for Senan.

"One o'clock sound good?" he asked. "Meet at the food court?"

I nodded mechanically. "Sure."

"I'll give you my honest opinions," he warned. "But I'm gonna tell you right now, I might be a little jealous."

"You? Jealous?"

"Yes."

My heart pounded. "Why?"

"Because you'll be going to a strange wedding in a hot dress. With someone else."

"It's just a friend," I reasoned.

"Always starts that way," he said smugly.

"No, I'm serious," I protested. "Actually I'm going with a girlfriend."

The voice at the other end of the phone changed. It sounded suddenly much more interested. "Oh *really?*"

I laughed. "No, it's not like that either."

"Uh huh," Senan said.

"Sorry."

"Too bad."

"You guys and your lesbian fantasies," I sighed. "If I had a dime for every—"

"Make it twelve-thirty," Senan said abruptly. "I'm already kinda hungry."

I looked over at the time. It was past ten o'clock. I'd be seeing him in under two hours.

The nervousness was starting already. "O—Okay."

"Oh, and *Chastity?*" he asked, drawing out my not-so-real name teasingly.

"Yes?"

"Don't be late."

# Seventeen

## SENAN

"Are you ready?" she called out from the dressing room corridor.

"As ready as I've been the last twelve times."

I'd found her in front of Panda Express, between Jamba Juice and the gourmet pretzel place. We'd had Nathan's for lunch, then hit a half dozen dress shops. Right now we were at the ass-end of a big box department store, all the way in the back. I was sitting in the Chair of Pain. The same chair thousands of poor guys had sat in for countless hours, waiting patiently as their wives and girlfriends tried on clothing.

"Yeah," giggled Chastity. "But this might be *it*."

"*It* it?" I asked cautiously. "Or 'it' as in the same 'it' from ten outfits ago?"

"You tell me."

She pushed her way through the swinging doors, and stepped out in a sleek, body-hugging dress. The color was a stunning, shimmering red, the material alternating as she moved between light and dark.

"Wow."

The material was soft, and for some reason made me want to touch it. It probably didn't hurt that it clung to every last curve of her hips and ass, and there were plenty of delicious curves involved in both those places.

"Is that a good wow or a bad wow?" she asked.

"Is there such a thing as a bad wow?"

"Yes."

"Well it's a good one then," I shrugged. "A *really* good one. Now turn around."

Turning around was my favorite part, of course. I'd gotten to ogle her beautiful ass in every color of the rainbow so far, except white. That color being reserved for the bride of course.

"What exactly do you like about it?" she asked excitedly.

"That it shows off your body," I told her. "Also that it hugs all your good places."

"Is there such a thing as bad places?"

"Naughty places, yes. But not bad places. Not on you."

Her eyes flashed at the complement as she spun around in the mirror. I could tell she liked the dress as much as I did. Thankfully, this might actually be 'it.'

"What kind of wedding is this anyway?" I asked. "That

you're bringing your girlfriend instead of a date?"

"Just a friend," she called over her shoulder. "Hey, what kind of shoes do you think would go best with this?"

"I didn't sign on for shoes," I laughed.

"Oh no?" She was engrossed in the mirror. "And what if I paid you extra?"

I folded my arms across my chest. "How would you pay me?"

"I'd just Venmo you a little more."

"I already refunded your payment," I said. "The second we got here."

Now Chastity finally turned my way. She frowned, making that pouty face she didn't even realize was cute.

"Senan, listen..."

"You really want to pay me a little extra?" I interjected.

I raised my eyebrow at her. She nodded.

"Fine," I said, standing up. After a quick glance left and right, I took her hand and pulled her back through the swinging doors. "Come."

Down the little hall we went, passing doors on either side. None of them actually looked occupied, but it was difficult to tell.

"This is the *woman's* dressing room," she hissed softly.

"Yeah. So?"

"So!" she looked alarmed. "You can't be in here!"

"No one knows I'm even here," I countered, lowering

my voice. "Besides, I won't be dressing. Now which stall is yours?"

She pointed apprehensively, and I yanked her into the last stall on the right. With a quick flip of my wrist, the tiny silver latch clacked into place, locking us in.

"Take that dress off," I told her sternly.

Chastity gulped. Already her alabaster skin looked flush and pink.

"Why?"

"Because if you don't, we're gonna get it dirty."

She looked up at me, and I actually saw the internal battle as it raged in her eyes. The devil on one shoulder fought the angel on the other. In the end, caution lost as I knew it would. Arousal won handily.

"O—Okay."

Chastity peeled the dress from her body, revealing acre after acre of warm, smooth skin. A pair of sleek, sky-blue panties matched the satin bra on top. Both ended in a sexy lace border.

All of these things, I realized, she probably put on for me.

"Nice."

I pulled her into me, kissing her so hard she actually whimpered. In the meantime, my hands explored the lower expanse of her naked back. They slipped slowly downward, cupping her ass possessively, pulling her even further against me.

"*Senan...*"

She whispered my name into my mouth, but never stopped kissing me. There was nothing to say, really. She just wanted to say it.

"*Fuck* you feel good."

I growled the words lustily, nibbling her lip as I worked a hand between our bodies. My fingers slid into the precious valley of her thigh gap. Her panties were already soaked through.

"I... I need to tell you something," Chastity whimpered.

"What?"

She seemed hesitant. Tentative. Her eyes were apologetic.

"I'm still *really* sore."

Moving ever so slowly, I dragged a gentle finger through her furrow. It came back full of heat and coated with wetness.

"It's okay," I told her. "I'm not going to fuck you."

She seemed both disappointed and relieved by the same statement. "Y—You're *not?*"

"Not in the way you think, anyway."

Her hand was already on me, stroking me through my jeans. I yanked them down. Boxers too.

"Here."

Chastity's breath caught in her throat as I placed her hand back on my manhood. Her fingers closed around it this time. She began stroking it slowly, getting it nice and hard. It

103

felt like a million fucking dollars.

"That's my girl," I told her, savoring the feel, her touch, the very scent of her. "Now, hop up here."

Reaching out with my heel, I kicked a small footstool over to where she stood. Before she could even step onto it, I was lifting her by the waist.

"That's better."

Standing on the footstool, she was just about my height. We were eye to eye, toe to toe. Face to face.

Mouth against wet, searching mouth.

*Damn, she tastes amazing.*

We kissed for a long time in the silence, hyper-aware of our surroundings. Listening to the sounds of approaching chatter from outside the changing room's outdated saloon doors.

"Shhh."

I shushed her, then rolled her panties partly down her thighs. I only moved them a few inches, though. Just enough that they lay poised there: a damp piece of satin fabric stretched out beneath her dripping, golden treasure.

"Now don't move."

# Eighteen

## CHASTITY

I was breathless and trembling, every one of my senses heightened and alive. Senan's kisses were molten, and I couldn't get enough of them. But my hand...

The hand I was gripping him with had me so, so fucking *hot*.

"Shhh."

I stiffened as voices floated in distantly from outside the dressing room area. Senan was all the way hard now, and almost as thick as my wrist. My whole body was vibrating as he rolled my panties down...

"Don't move."

He stepped forward and took control of his erection, stroking it a few times as I watched in awe. Then he pushed forward, guiding it between my legs. Sliding it through the tiny gap between my thighs, where the top of his shaft pushed through the very bottom of my glistening folds.

*Ohhhh... wow.*

I'd never seen anything like it before. Senan began thrusting forward and back, pushing himself through my tight little gap. Trapping himself between the warm flesh of my inner thighs, while dragging himself against my dripping, throbbing entrance.

"Oh my God..."

I whispered the words as his hands slid up my body, shoving my bra aside to cup my full, naked breasts. He bent to take one in his mouth, and I grabbed his head and pulled him in tightly. But all throughout he kept sawing away between my legs. Slowly fucking my thigh gap with his warm, pulsating thickness, until the friction of his shaft against my folds began teasing my swollen clit.

The whole thing was incredible, made even more so by the knowledge we could be caught at any time. Someone entered the dressing area, chose a booth, then locked the door behind them. I could hear the clatter of plastic hangers being hung on a metal hook. The softer sounds of mild exertion, followed by the faint whoosh of shedding clothes...

*She's in the next booth!*

Maybe. Maybe not. With Senan's mouth moving hotly over my breasts, it was difficult to concentrate on anything.

"Stand still," my lover whispered. "Now flex your legs. Make them tight."

I did, and suddenly the sensations were even more powerful. My thighs were soaked, and Senan was plunging in and out down there, screwing his way between them. He grabbed his shaft and held himself upward, increasing the pressure against my button. The added pleasure made me gasp, and his hand went over my mouth.

"Don't come."

It was an order. And a stern one at that.

"You don't *get* to come."

His words were strangely powerful, and they only turned me on even more. I was being fucked but not fucked. Screwed to the point where I was ready to explode, but still not penetrated the way I had been the other night.

The whole thing was making me crazy with want. His member, pinned tightly between my thighs. Plunging in and out as he fondled my breasts with one hand, while still holding one rough palm over my mouth.

*Holy—*

His hand screwed even tighter against my lips, as more voices drifted in from outside. I was being driven out of my fucking mind. Conflicted with the need to remain absolutely silent, while barely able to control my desire to explode all over him.

"Get ready."

I whimpered into his hand as his thrusts came faster, harder, his look more determined than ever. I clenched my thighs even tighter. Pushed down even harder against his throbbing, sawing manhood, until the look in his eyes became abruptly dreamy and far away.

*Holy shit, he's going to...*

At the last second he pulled out, still holding himself

between my legs. His shaft looked incredible. It was magnificently hard, all thick and throbbing and covered in wetness.

"Senan..."

I whispered his name once, before he shushed me with a finger. We were both looking down. Both watching as he finished himself hotly.

Then he jerked himself off... right into the open stretch of my satin panties.

*Oh.*

*My.*

*God.*

It was the hottest thing in the whole fucking world, watching a man come. Seeing him twitch and pulse, his thickness jumping in his big, masculine hand.

"Fuckkkk..."

My lover growled as he continued to stroke through his climax, spraying hot, rhythmic jets of his thick, pearlescent seed straight into the crotch of my panties. I couldn't stop staring. I could barely even breathe as he finished himself off, filling my already-drenched underwear with his own warmth and wetness. Wordlessly he wiped the last few drops against the inside of my thigh, dragging the head hotly against my skin in a way I'd never forget. Then he stepped back, reached down, and rolled my panties back into position.

"There."

Senan patted my crotch, which was an absolute *mess.* The front of my powder-blue satin thong had more dark spots than light — a tribute to how much he'd deposited there.

"Now get dressed."

I was so weak at the knees, it took me a moment to regain my senses. When I did, he was already handing me my jeans and helping me into my sweater.

"What..."

The words got stuck in my throat. I was too turned on. Too choked up to get them out all at once.

"What the hell am I supposed to do now?"

Senan shrugged as if nothing had happened. As if the throbbing, frustrated heat between my legs wasn't already soaking through my jeans.

"Now you walk out," he said simply. "Shopping's over."

# Nineteen

## CHASTITY

"Please..." I gasped softly, screwing my ass into the leather seat. "Please..."

"Please what?"

"Please don't stop!"

Senan's hand moved a tiny bit faster, the 'V' of his fingers pushing down with that much pressure. He had one hand down my jeans, wedged tightly between my come-soaked panties and my *very* wet opening. With the other, he was playing with my lips. Feeding me one of his thick fingers, as I gasped into the interior of my own car.

"You want to come?" he asked for the tenth time.

"Yes."

"You sure?"

"Yes!" I gasped in frustration. "*God* yes..."

"Then show me."

I howled again, my hips bucking upward to meet his touch. I was so close. So tantalizingly fucking close to my own release, I could practically taste the delicious dopamine ready to flood my brain.

"Senan..."

His fingers thrummed against my clit, his palm sliding wetly through the shallows he'd so thoroughly fucked. Walking out of the mall had been quite an experience. I was sure everyone and their mother could sense my wetness, as the dark stains of my lover's melting seed began bleeding through the fabric of my jeans.

Apparently no one had looked. Not the women we passed on the way out of the dressing room, and not the sales clerk who sold me the dress as I crossed my legs and tried to keep a straight face throughout the transaction.

No, no one said anything at all actually. Not even as we crossed the parking lot, as Senan walked me back to my car.

But damn, wearing him against me like that had been *so fucking hot.*

"Come then," he whispered, finally giving me what I wanted. His hand went rigid, as his mouth moved to my neck. He kissed me in that secret spot just behind my ear, and slid his fingers rapidly up and down.

At the penultimate moment I closed my hand over his, applying just the right amount of pressure. I exploded hard against his palm, lifting my ass from the seat and grinding myself upward against his fingers.

*Ohhhhhh...*

My well-earned orgasm was blinding whiteness and

111

pure euphoric oblivion. I let it consume me, taking me to screaming new heights of pleasure. Somehow I knew Senan's denial back in the dressing room — as well as my ensuing walk of shame — had made the whole experience even more explosive for me. Holding back for so long had made everything that much more intense.

*He knows exactly what he's doing.*

He did, and that part excited me. His experience, his willingness to take command — these were things I'd always needed from a man, though maybe I never knew it. Somehow, especially with the guys I dated, they'd always been lacking.

More than anything else though, I trusted Senan. And that went a long way toward my feelings for him.

Eventually I came down, chest heaving, my eyes darting left and right through my windows for fear anyone had seen us. No one had. The back half of the parking lot was thankfully empty, especially since — in the throes of my orgasm — I'd been no stranger to making noise.

"That... was too fucking hot," I breathed at last.

"No such thing," Senan grinned.

"Seriously," I smiled weakly, my eyes drawing him in. "Best mall trip ever."

He sat in the driver's seat, his handsome face locked on mine as I wound slowly down. I wanted to kiss him some more. To bring him some of the same pleasure he'd just bought me. I reached for him again, but he stopped me.

"I can't, baby," he smiled, reading my thoughts. "Another time though."

Something inside me melted as he called me 'baby'. It had come so easily to his lips. So naturally to my ears.

"Can you come over on Friday night?"

The words came from him, not me. I was astonished to hear them.

"Wait, what?"

"I said—"

"To *your* place?"

"Yes," Senan chuckled. "As I was about to say, my roommates and I are having a little homecoming party for one of our friends. He's getting out of the Navy."

My heart soared. I couldn't say yes fast enough.

"Good," he smiled, as I nodded back at him. He reached out and tucked an errant lock of hair over my ear. "I'll send you the address. It's not too far from your place, actually."

I was still lost in a post-orgasmic haze as he popped the door open. Before stepping out, Senan leaned in and gave me the hottest, wettest, open-mouthed kiss.

"See you then."

Still dizzy I watched him go, clearing a spot on my steamed-up windshield with the back of one forearm. Senan was looking down at his phone as he walked back through the parking lot. Checking his emails, maybe. Or his text-messages. Or—

*BZZZZZT.*

I glanced down at my own phone, not sure whether to

frown or smile. Once more he'd Venmo'd me back his fee. This time though, he even *added* ten dollars, as well as a message:

*Pick up something for dessert on Friday night.*

# Twenty

## CHASTITY

It was the worst week and the best week, all rolled into one. A slow-moving series of days during which nothing went right, and every project I worked on seemed to expand exponentially rather than wrap itself up.

For one, the two-million record database for my second most profitable client had somehow fucked itself during a table purge. And since their IT guy was apparently skipping the duty of making backup tapes, it became my job to unfuck it.

That took most of the week, especially because I had to do it alone. I could've used the help of said IT guy, but they'd fired him so fast his desk was all packed up by the time he returned to it. By Thursday morning I finally had things in order again. I was bleary-eyed and exhausted from consecutive late nights, but they were paying me triple time for additional hours so I couldn't complain.

This left me little room to work on my lesson plans, and with school starting up Monday that wasn't a good thing. I'd have to dedicate my weekend to working through everything, including creating assignments for three different classes and laying out the schedule for the entire semester.

But Friday...

Friday was mine, and mine alone. Or rather mine and Senan's, and anyone else who happened to be at his friend's homecoming party.

My mind couldn't help but wander, every time I thought about him. I kept playing and replaying our night together, and now I was even more distracted by what we'd done at the mall. I couldn't *believe* the things this man had me doing, and yet it all came so easily and naturally for me, despite my inexperience.

*Experience. That's what you need.*

That was for sure. And I intended on getting as much as possible, as soon as the party wound down.

By Friday morning I was practically vibrating with excitement. I'd already cyber-stalked the address he sent me earlier in the week; a nice-looking craftsman-style home, in a neighborhood not far away. I finished work on time, slammed my laptop shut, then took a life-changing shower. As the near-scalding hot water washed over my body, I scrubbed every inch of skin with my favorite body wash while using my best loofah.

I'd decided on a sexy skirt and semi-high heels, so I could at least kiss him without having to stand on my tippy toes. Beneath that I wore a brand new set of lacy silk underwear, cut high on my hip to make my legs look longer.

Well, they'd make my legs look longer once my skirt was off, anyway. And I intended on that happening as soon as possible.

Finally dressed, I made my way into the kitchen to put the icing on the cake — literally. Rather than stop to pick up dessert, I'd baked the best triple-chocolate cake in the universe. From a recipe I'd of course picked up by Googling 'best triple-chocolate cake in the universe'.

*Have you* seen *his body?* the little voice in my head chided me. *He didn't get that by eating cake.*

No, maybe not. But the man had asked for dessert, and that made me determined to blow his socks off. Among other things.

*BZZZZZT!*

My phone rattled with a new text message from Senan. I picked it up all smiles, but almost immediately my heart dropped:

Sorry hon, but the party's off. Our buddy redeployed yesterday. Last-minute thing.

My shoulders slumped like I was holding the weight of the world in each fist. I put down the spatula, then licked my finger clean before typing back:

Ah crap. I understand, though.

As disappointing as it was, I'd have to be a jerk not to understand. The military was the military. Circumstances were circumstances.

We're still hanging though, if you want to come over and help us eat some of this food. You'll need to drink some of this liquor too, come to think of it.

A glimmer of hope. My smile returned.

Is that okay? I don't want to interrupt anything else you guys might have going on.

Senan typed back almost immediately:

It's more than okay. Gonna be a low key night, though. Just the roommates and me. And you. And a bunch of beer and ice.

I felt bad for his party, but good that he still wanted

me over.  After waiting all week, I  don't think I could've stayed away if I'd wanted to.


## Beer and ice I can deal with.
## See ya in a bit.

# Twenty-One

## CHASTITY

Senan's place would've been a beautiful home for a beautiful family... if three twenty-something year old guys didn't live there. As it was, it was a bachelor's paradise. There were many more mirrors than normal, and much less in the way of decor and decorations. The latter included a collection of movie posters, a pool table, even a fully-stocked bar, all complete with a sound system that filled the house with rich, resonant music that seemed to come from everywhere at once.

Not that I saw that much so far. The second I got there I made Senan tell me which room was his. Then I pulled him inside and literally jumped him, barely taking the time to set the cake down on a nearby table and close the door.

"Whoa."

I was kissing him all over. His lips, his face, his cologne-scented shoulder... I tasted the salt on his skin as I dragged my tongue over his neck and began nibbling hungrily on his ear.

"Hello to you too," he laughed.

120

"Hellos can come later," I growled, sliding my hands all over him. "Right now I need *this*."

I whispered the last sentence directly into his ear, as my hand closed over his thickening bulge.

"Really?"

"Really."

It was obviously the most forward thing I'd ever done. But I'd decided it during the week, in the heated throes of bringing myself to orgasm. Rubbing myself in exactly the places he had, while thinking about doing this the whole time.

"I want to *fuck*," I told him wantonly, shamelessly. Already I could feel him nice and hard. "Then I want you to show me around your house."

"Can you do it quietly?" he asked.

"No. Probably not."

One of his hands found its way beneath my skirt. It slid past my ass, all the way down between my legs.

"Because if you're gonna be loud," he said, "maybe we should wait until my roommates—"

I bit his lip, just hard enough to draw his full attention. Senan shoved me back on his bed. I fell with my legs spread, my skirt floating up near my waist. My panties were already damp, and I'd been there less than two minutes.

"Looks like I created a monster," he chuckled.

"Yeah," I agreed. "You did. Maybe you should put a warning in your profile."

The mere mention of the escort website seemed to

throw him back a little. I, on the other hand, was fully prepared to deal with it. Dismissing jealous thoughts, I'd told myself time and again that I couldn't get attached. That what we were doing was little more than a friendly transaction, even if so far he hadn't let me pay him for it.

"You got lucky when you picked me," he said, pulling his shirt over his head. For a moment I sat practically mesmerized, motionless and daydreaming. Lost in the hard, muscle-bound valley of his broad, flawless chest.

"Actually you were the one who got lucky," I giggled. "Coin-flip lucky."

Senan raised an eyebrow. "Coin flip?"

"Yeah," I went on, leaning back on my elbows. I had it narrowed down to two of you, actually."

"On the website?"

I nodded, letting my flat-ironed hair fall intentionally over my eyes. "It was between you and some other profile, listed directly next to yours." I paused, remembering. "Lighter hair. Slimmer build. Some really ripped guy named Ander."

Senan's entire expression changed. Was that... *jealousy?*

"*Ander?*"

"Yes."

"That was his name?" he asked needlessly. "Are you sure?"

"Yeah," I shrugged. "It was you or him. I picked you."

His body bounced gently as he let out a little laugh. "You tossed a coin."

I shrugged guiltily. "So? I couldn't make up my—"

Abruptly Senan turned, pulled open the door, and stormed out. He did it so suddenly I couldn't even tell if he was angry or not.

*Uh oh.*

It didn't make sense for him to get jealous. Did it? I mean... considering his own line of work, how could he be? And besides, it's not like I went with the competition anyway. I'd ended up picking him, coin or no coin.

Outside in the hall I heard voices. Deep ones.

Shit, maybe I'd fucked this up.

"Senan?"

I suddenly stopped. My lover was in the doorway now, and still moving forward. He stepped through and crossed his arms, as another man came in after him.

Senan's arms folded causally across his chest. Thankfully he was smiling, though. Grinning wryly from ear to ear.

"What?" I asked.

He shifted to one side, and the man behind him stepped into view. Light brown hair. Tight, muscular build. A bright, beautiful smile.

*Oh my God...*

It was a familiar smile. A smile I'd probably stared at a hundred times, while lying on my belly, looking into my computer screen.

"Chastity, meet Ander."

123

Corrupting Chastity - Krista Wolf

# Twenty-Two

## CHASTITY

Sometimes you stumble into situations where you're so stunned, so utterly shocked, you really don't know what to say. This was one of those times where I felt like I actually swallowed my tongue.

"So this is her?"

Ander elbowed Senan, who only nodded. Apparently I'd been talked about.

"Nice to meet you, Chastity."

The ripped, beautiful hunk across from me extended his hand. I knew he was ripped because I'd seen him with his shirt off in almost a dozen profile photos, each one hotter and more revealing than the last.

"This is the part where you say 'nice to meet you' back," smiled Ander. "Or else things get awkward."

Things were already awkward, and way more than he even knew. Eventually my brain told my arm to move, and I found my hand enveloped in his. He shook it gently but firmly.

"She already knows you, by the way," said Senan.

"Oh?"

He shot his friend a sideways glance and grinned. "Wanna guess how?"

Ander's expression went from amused confusion to sudden recognition — all in the time it took to blink. I saw him flush a shade redder, but only for a moment. He regained control quickly, but I could see in his body language that he was still at a disadvantage.

"Well... shit," Ander laughed nervously. "Guess that's embarrassing."

"Is it though?" I countered. "I mean, look where *I* was when I found you."

"Browsing the site," Senan nodded. "And then calling me."

Ander cleared his throat. Now it was my turn to figuratively shuffle my feet.

"Turns out she had it narrowed down to the both of us," said Senan. "Your profile shows up right after mine, because they sort potential meetups by distance."

"That makes sense," Ander smiled.

"So in the end she flipped a coin," Senan went on. "Was I heads or tails?"

The old Delaina would've been too humiliated to speak. But for some reason, I felt somewhat confident. I was Chastity now. A name which, in retrospect, didn't make much sense at this point.

"You were, uh... heads, I think."

Strangely enough, I considered myself a different person. Physically and emotionally changed.

"Lucky me," said Senan.

"Yeah. Lucky you."

Ander winked at me, and I melted a little on the spot. He was breathtakingly gorgeous. His arms filled out his casual T-shirt to the point of bursting, and I could see the incredible 'V' of his back as it tapered down to a slender, well-toned waist.

*And his abs...*

His abs had been even tighter than Senan's, and that was saying something. That and his soft brown eyes, offset by his high cheekbones, had been two of his best features.

"Want me to turn around?" he joked.

Now I did flush red, because I couldn't believe I was still staring. Yet I was. In front of Senan and everything.

"That's not really necessary," I countered, adding a smirk of my own. "I've seen you from the back *lots* of times."

"I'll bet you have."

The guys let out a short laugh together, in unison. It was the same laugh you shared with close friends, or roommates.

*Or co-workers.*

Holy shit, I couldn't believe they were *both* escorts! And they lived together, too. The knot somewhere in my belly tightened a little, reminding me of the fire that was burning there only a few minutes ago.

"He brought me in by the way," said Ander, "in case you were wondering." He elbowed his friend again playfully. "So even if the coin came up tails, you still could've blamed him."

I nodded mechanically, wondering why he felt the need to explain himself. It was a little cute though, I had to admit.

"You don't need to—"

"I'm a physical trainer at a couple of local gyms," Ander went on. "Decent money. Lots of running around, though. But then Senan told me how much he was making for a few hours of work, and well..." he shrugged.

"It was sort of a no-brainer?" I smiled.

"Yeah," Ander conceded. "Especially since a big chunk of it goes to such a good cause."

He followed up the mysterious statement with a nod toward Senan, who only looked down at the floor. Now it was his turn to look disadvantaged. My brow furrowed, as I wondered what he could mean.

"Anyway, there's a six-foot hero in the kitchen that's not getting any fresher," said Ander. "Brett's in there now, working on it already."

"He's home?" asked Senan.

"Been home all day," Ander confirmed. "He's been sleeping days and staying up nights, doing all his nerdy computer stuff."

"Nerdy computer stuff?" I chimed in quickly, my voice

showing signs of sudden interest.

Ander looked me over, his smile widening. "Oh no," he said coyly. "You're not one of those—"

"Nerdy computer girls?" I laughed.

Reaching into my purse, I pulled out my glasses and slipped them on. It was astounding how much it really changed my whole look. Even Senan laughed.

"Nerd's offensive by the way," I joked, putting on my cutest smile. "We prefer the term geek now."

# Twenty-Three

## BRETT

"Yo!"

Ander's yo was more of a head's up than a call for
attention, as he and Senan filed into the kitchen. Over the
years I'd gotten to know his yos well. There was the "I'm
home" yo, the "hey let me ask you something" yo, and the
"holy shit, what the fuck did you do" yo, which was a bit lower
and more staccato than the rest.

This particular yo meant someone else was here, and I
needed to be on my best behavior. And since Senan had
already informed us he was bringing "her" over, I'd actually put
on a clean shirt and some decent shorts.

"Brett, this is Chastity."

I put down my section of hero, licked my fingers, then
quickly wiped them on the nearest napkin. But the girl who
filed in behind them made me do an instant double-take.

*Holy shit.*

For one, she was absolutely stunning. Blonde hair. Blue-green eyes. She had a pretty face, accented perfectly by a pair of black, thick-rimmed glasses pinned over a pair of perfectly formed ears. Even her lips, which were full and pouty for such a triangular face, were utterly beautiful.

"Hi."

It was the best I could manage. As I held my hand out to her, I couldn't help but wonder if she'd seen me lick my fingers.

"Hello Brett," she said sweetly. Her eyes lingered on me for a second, sizing me up. "Nice to meet you."

"Chastity's a nerd like you," said Ander.

"Geek," she corrected him with a cute chuckle. "Remember?"

"Oh yeah. Sorry."

"It's alright," she told him. "We geeks and nerds are easy to mix up."

She shook my hand, and her fingers were soft and delicate. Senan had described her well. Which made sense really, because he'd also described her often.

"Beer?" I asked, popping open the fridge.

"Sure."

I pulled out three, handing one to everyone. I twisted the cap from hers though.

"There's uh... hero here," I laughed, nodding toward the giant, partially-eaten sandwich that dominated our kitchen table. So far about three pieces had been taken out of thirty. "Help yourself."

131

Chastity looked at me again, smiling as she tipped her beer back. I watched as the liquid slid down her slender, porcelain throat.

*No wonder why he keeps talking about her.*

It made sense now, all the stuff Senan had been telling us. How he'd lucked into a client so special, so perfect, he was actually refusing to take money from her.

"So what makes you a geek?" I asked, as Ander handed her a plate.

"Computer stuff mostly," she said.

Instantly my eyebrows went up. She was suddenly three times as attractive.

"What kind of—"

"Webportals, shell scripts, database management..." Chastity started in. "I've dabbled lately in app development, but the bulk of my business comes from freelance programming."

My pulse quickened. Actually quickened.

"You're a coder?" I asked.

"Uh huh. C++, Python, Java..."

"Php?" I butted in excitedly.

"Oh yeah," she smiled dismissively. "A little Ruby, a little Perl. I do a lot of SQL, too. It's not as much fun of course, but—"

"Alright, alright," laughed Ander. "Enough with the geek-speak. The two of you can stop talking dirty to each other already."

"Yeah," Senan agreed. "It's not fair if we can't join in."

"Oh you could join in," I chuckled. "If only you knew geek-speak."

"Yeah, except that we don't."

Senan slid a possessive arm around her, which made me suddenly and inexplicably jealous.

*Inexplicably?*

Okay, maybe not that inexplicably. For one he'd been talking her up all week, and quite honestly I was looking forward to this girl *not* being anywhere near as good as he'd made her out to be. When in fact, she was even better.

But even more explainable, my attraction stemmed from our common interests. My field wasn't exactly buzzing with the fairer sex, which meant opportunities to find women like this were limited. But this one...

This one was so beautiful she actually made my heart ache.

"So Brett, what exactly do *you* do?" Chastity was asking me.

"Well I'm in the process of getting my masters in electronic engineering," I said proudly. "But for now I work for a—"

"Blah blah blah," Ander cut in. He scooped some potato salad on his plate and sighed. "Forget all that nerdy talk. Let's dig in."

Together we sat down in our kitchen, which I feared was a little more bacheloresque than a girl like Chastity might be used to. For example, we had a roll of paper towels instead of napkins. Ketchup and mustard in packets rather than bottles, and salt and pepper in disposable plastic shakers rather than anything permanent. The latter looked stolen from the nearest McDonald's or Wendy's, but I wasn't accusing my friends of anything.

"Sorry," I apologized, as Chastity reached across the table for something to eat her macaroni salad with. "Only thing clean right now are plastic utensils."

Chastity picked up the plastic fork and laughed. Even her laugh was adorable. "No problemo."

Ander transferred the giant sandwich from the table to the counter, and together we ate. There was a half-tray of chicken wings still untouched, as well as something else that might've been fried mozzarella sticks. I wasn't exactly sure. I hadn't ordered the food, I'd only picked it up.

"So when are we playing cards?" asked Ander.

"Umm, bad news on that," I told him hesitantly.

His shoulders slumped. So did Senan's.

"What?"

"Curtis can't make it. Which means JD can't make it either, since Curtis was his ride."

Ander sighed so heavily it actually weighed him down. "So we're forced to eat and drink all this stuff by ourselves... and now we can't play poker either?"

I shrugged, my eyes eventually drifting back to Chastity. An idea formed.

"Not unless *she* wants in," I said.

Chastity looked up as all eyes went to her. She could

sense the hope. I could see the wheels turning.

"Poker?" she asked. "Is that what you said?"

"Yup. Texas hold 'em."

The pretty blonde set down her sandwich and lifted the bottle to her full pink lips. She smiled around her next sip of beer.

"I was hoping you'd say that."

# Twenty-Four

## CHASTITY

"You're bluffing."

Ander squinted back at me from across the table. He had one hand stroking his stubbled jaw, and a half-smile fixed on his face that he'd refused to change through the turn and the river.

"Go ahead," I grinned. "Try me."

He sniffed, grabbed half his chip stack, and moved to push the pile forward. Then, with a disgruntled sigh he abandoned the action and dropped his cards.

"Take it."

The others laughed as I stood up and gleefully swept the pile in the center of the table in my direction. I counted out a stack of four green chips, and shoved them out of play.

"You..." I said, with my eyes still locked on Ander. At the last second however, I turned and pointed to Brett. "Strip."

Brett looked a little surprised but definitely not

136

unhappy about my choice. He peeled the Battlestar Galactica T-shirt from his body — original series, not the newer one — and tossed it over one handsome shoulder.

"So did you have it?" Ander asked, staring at my pair of face-down cards.

I was too busy ogling Brett's body to answer. Unlike the others, it was the first time I'd seen him with his shirt off.

"Maybe," I said, pushing the cards toward Senan. He shuffled them in without looking at them. "Maybe not."

I smiled and winked at Brett, and he grinned right back. For a geek, he was fantastically built. A bit taller than his friends, he had the same musculature and body type of someone who worked out daily.

*And he can code*, my brain reminded me sharply. *And he likes Battlestar Galactica.*

I chuckled inwardly at that last part. Brett liked lots of the same things I did. Like cosplay, for example, or sci-fi movies and online role-playing games. He'd been to Comic Con in San Diego only twice, though. If he wanted to keep up with me on *that* level, it was something he'd have to work on.

"Everyone get your chips in," said Senan, dealing the next hand. "Big blind and little blind."

I settled back in my chair, pleasantly buzzed, feeling relaxed and loose. We'd been playing poker for almost two hours now. At first just with chips, because the guys hadn't planned on taking each other's money. When Ander declared that boring, Senan asked him what else he wanted to play for. And that's when I came up with an all-new version of strip poker that allowed us to 'buy' each other's clothes off with a certain amount of chips.

"You'd actually *do* that?" Senan asked incredulously.

"Sure," I'd answered. "What, you don't think I've played strip poker before?"

"Well..."

"As a virgin," I'd bumped his leg under the table, "you usually have to get pretty creative. And you'd be surprised at how close I threaded the needle sometimes," I winked, "when I wanted to keep from rounding third base."

That much was true, although I'd never played the version we were playing now. And I'd never played strip poker as the only girl at the table, of course. To offset the obvious fact that the odds were stacked against me, it only cost me $100 in chips to strip someone of an article of clothing rather than $300.

Right now I had the guys down to their boxers, and Senan still had his shirt and socks as well. I had only my bra left, having lost my panties two hands ago. The guys were a little surprised when I'd laid them on the table, but I figured the move was strategic since everything below the waist was pretty much out of view. For now, anyway.

"I still can't believe you're doing this," Brett grinned.

"Why?"

"Because Senan told us you were shy," Ander chimed in.

I laughed, feeling better than awesome. I'd switched to wine for a little while, then to water to maintain my buzz while still keeping my wits about me.

"I am shy," I shrugged. "Usually."

"Why not now?" asked Brett.

I looked over at the hot, handsome programmer with the big strapping arms. It still seemed so strange to me. So out of place.

"Maybe because you guys are good company?" I shrugged, pushing my bet forward.

Ander cackled. "First time we heard that before."

"You guys are fun," I admitted. "Funny. You make me comfortable."

The flop showed me nothing as I sat on a pair of threes. Everyone but Ander passed, betting the pot up before the next card.

"How comfortable?" Brett asked boldly.

I twirled my hair and locked eyes with him. To go along with his broad shoulders and chiseled jawline, he had the most beautiful cerulean blue irises I'd ever seen.

"It's strange that you don't wear glasses," I said without answering his question. "For a geek, I mean."

"Contact lenses," he said simply.

"Ah."

I saw those irises shift downward, as his gaze crawled my body. It was fun, knowing the whole thing was permissible. After all, we *were* stripping our clothes off for each other.

"You gonna go," Senan prodded me. "Or..."

I folded my pair of threes on the turn, then watched the guys go at each other for the final card. The river was pulled, and Ander won the hand. He very promptly counted out three hundred dollars' worth of chips and nodded my way.

"Let's see em'."

A thrill of exhilaration shot through me as I reached back and unclasped my bra. I paused dramatically, letting the fabric hang over my breasts for an extra moment or two before Senan finally reached in and did the honors.

And then suddenly that was it: I was sitting buck naked before three gorgeous men. On a whim I stood up for them and did a slow, deliberate turn.

"Holy fuck..." I heard Brett say.

As I turned my back on them, Ander whistled like a wolf. My skin felt flush as they devoured my body with their eyes. Even Senan, who'd experienced this all before, seemed lost in a trance.

"Well that's it," Ander lamented with a sigh. "Game over."

I frowned immediately. "Why?"

"Because you've got nothing left to give up," he smirked. "And we're sure as hell not going to play to strip each *other*."

"No," laughed Senan, pushing his cards away. 'We're certainly not."

I placed my hands on my hips, thinking about how fast the night had gone from simple to complicated. It was a good complicated, though.

"Well what if I offered something else?" I asked coyly.

For once the guys were finally speechless. They stared

back at me as an idea formed in my head.

"Like what?" asked Ander.

My heart pounded as I stared back at these three perfect men. My skin felt like it was on fire.

"Well, maybe one of you should win the next hand," I said, sitting back down in my spot. "And you'll see."

# Twenty-Five

## CHASTITY

The kisses were slow, searching, soulful... and oh so totally *hot*. For a minute or so they drowned out everything else: the clearing of the other guys' throats, the shuffling of the cards...

But damn, I just couldn't stop.

"Ten seconds left."

Our lips still crashed against each other's, our tongues swirling in slow, lazy circles. The hands on my hips were firm and wonderful. They held me squarely in my paramour's mostly-naked lap, as I felt the rising bulge of something big and thick straining beneath me.

"Time's up!"

Those hands finally released me, but not before sliding intentionally down my thighs. I broke the kiss, as my lids fluttered open. I was left staring into Brett's crystal blue eyes, the both of us still lost in the same lust-fueled haze.

"Alright, I gotta admit," breathed Ander. "That was *definitely* hot."

I smiled dreamily on the way back to my seat. To my right Senan was watching me. Staring on with something that was half excitement, half approval. My eyes met his, and I asked a silent question.

*You sure this is okay?*

He smiled and sipped his beer, telling me all I needed to know. Trading kisses in lieu of clothing had been my own idea, of course. But actually *making out* with them... And doing it from the comfort of their own half-naked laps?

Well, that part had been suggested by them.

"My turn," said Ander. He pushed half his chips forward and reached out for me. "C'mon, let's go."

"But we haven't even played another hand," I protested. "I thought—"

"Do we really *need* to?"

The question hung in the air for a moment, as the rest of the guys considered it. They had more than enough chips to buy kisses from me already. And I had enough chips to—

"Strip," I said, pointing to my own colorful stacks.

"Who?" asked Brett.

I whirled on him and laughed. "Are you kidding? All of you."

The guys stood, glanced at each other shyly, then shrugged. I gasped as they both dropped their boxers at the same time, as if on a dare. Everyone but Senan, anyway. He was watching the whole thing from his end of the table, his

143

mouth set firmly in a half-grin.

"You alright with this?" I asked over my shoulder.

"Who, me?"

"Yes."

Senan set down his empty bottle and wiped his mouth with the back of a big forearm. He looked at his friends, then back to me again.

"Yeah," he said finally. "I'm just as good with it as you are."

My eyes flared, my pulse pounding even faster as the last of the walls came down. I strutted over and straddled him as a reward. Sliding my arms over his shoulders I kissed him so slowly, so hotly, I actually felt the fabric of his boxers tenting against my naked ass.

"Get those off," I told him, giving him a gentle squeeze as I left his lap. "You're not going to need them for the rest of the night."

I turned and Ander was already there, pressing his body against me like it was some sort of prize. Which it was, too. In every possible way.

"Been waiting all night to do this..."

He took my face in his hands, then planted his mouth against mine. Our lips rolled and our tongues played hotly in the space between us.

*I'm in trouble...*

Sometime during the kiss we fell back into a sitting position. Ander took my hand and placed it on something big and warm and impossibly hard. Before I knew it I was stroking it up and down. Still kissing him sensuously, my thoughts spinning, while marveling at the strength and thickness of his growing manhood.

*Big trouble.*

The whole thing had progressed in steps, throughout the night. Little steps, like playing poker. Then playing *strip* poker. Than trading kisses that turned into lapdances that were now turning into—

*Ohhhhhhh!*

Another mouth closed over my neck, this time from the side. I reached back and grabbed a handful of thick dark hair — Senan's hair — as I pulled his lips even tighter against me.

*Holy shit...*

I felt like a victim in one of those vampire movies, surrendering to the inevitable. Clawing these men against my neck, my shoulder, even my breasts, as they circled around and kissed me from three directions at once.

I WANT this.

The decision came plainly, easily, definitively. There was no second-guessing. No hesitation.

"Go on," I heard Senan say, his voice muffled against my neck. "Tell them."

His tongue was liquid heat. It sent shivers everywhere it touched.

"T—Tell them what?"

"Tell them what you told me earlier," he said. "In my room. Tell them what you want to d—"

"I want to *fuck*."

I said the words breathlessly, tasting them as they left my lips. They sounded fantastic, so I said them again.

"I want you to FUCK me," I cried more specifically. My voice was louder now, the inflection more desperate. The wine had made me hornier if possible, as well as brave. Make no mistake though, I was still in total control.

The mouths on my body were joined by hands — six of them, in fact. They grew bolder as they kissed me. Every time I turned my head I encountered a new set of lips, moaning softly into three separate mouths as countless fingertips traced their way over my skin.

"Senan told us a little about your... initiation," Ander whispered softly.

I couldn't move, couldn't speak. I could only coo, and whimper, and nod.

"Seems to us, you probably need to make up for lost time."

Reaching out, my hand found Senan's. I squeezed him possessively, gazing at him past Brett's head, which was busy kissing my shoulder. There was a look in my eye that I knew was there, and I could tell he saw it too. It was an expression of love perhaps, of connection, of desire. But it was also something else.

I was seeking permission.

"You want this?" he asked, mouthing the words.

My eyes fluttered for a moment as Ander's mouth closed over my breast. I gasped sharply. Brett's tongue was hot on my neck.

*Yes,* I mouthed back, adding a desperate nod.

He smiled, squeezing my hand back. Then, leaning over his friend, he kissed me so tenderly it made my entire body convulse with a wave of heat.

"Then let's go."

# Twenty-Six

## CHASTITY

The journey from the kitchen to the bedroom was a complete blur. It was filled with kisses and touching and hard, muscular flesh. A feeling of weightlessness as I was carried against Senan's tattooed chest, then deposited gently across the soft blankets of his bed.

*Are you really going to do this?*

The voice of reason was more a voice of sanity at this point. But I didn't want it. I didn't want any distractions from what I was about to do, from what was about to happen to me. And that's because I wanted it with every last fiber of my being.

I wanted them *all*.

"Lay back," whispered Ander, bringing his face to mine. His smile was gentle. "Relax."

It was a little surreal actually seeing him in the flesh, mostly because I'd poured over his photos countless times. Ander's profile had included his face, and he was so good-looking it was almost criminal. It was that face I often went to whenever I lay back in my own bed. The face I'd imagined ravaging me, over and over again, as I let my fingers wander.

Now the very same man was kissing his way down my body. I watched as his mouth closed over my breast, his rather long tongue flicking out to tease my stippled areola. In the meantime, Brett had both hands on my thighs. He was sliding down between them, grinning up at me. His mouth lowered. His lips parted...

*H—Holy fuck...*

I squeaked like a mouse as he went down on me, clutching the sheets in my fists. Ander's tongue swirled harder against my nipple. Brett's lips bumped wonderfully against my button, as he began devouring me with long, broad strokes of his apparently talented tongue.

*Ohhhh....*

I stretched out across the bed, all buzzed and happy, warm and safe. My body felt more amazing than it ever had in my life, floating happily between four roving hands, two eager mouths...

"Hey..."

Senan's bearded face hung over me. His hazel eyes sparkled with something strange and dynamic. Something I'd never seen before.

"Are you ready to get fucked again?"

I nodded eagerly and smiled, even as I sifted both hands through Brett's hair. I lifted my neck from the mattress to kiss Senan, but he pulled back just enough.

"And what about my friends?"

The way he said the word sounded dirty. Taboo. Wrong. But wrong in all the right ways.

"Are you ready to fuck them too?"

My GOD! To hear him talking like this! It was so crazy, but also so dirty and intimate. Such a turn-on.

"I'll make them go slow," Senan whispered. His lips were so close I wanted to scream. "I'll make them be careful..."

I squirmed as the tongue inside me fluttered over something magical. But my eyes stayed locked on Senan's.

"We're going to take *turns* on you," he murmured. "All three of us."

His beard tickled my lips now. His mouth was a cool glass of water, and I was dying of thirst.

"But we're going to tag-team you," he went on. "Spit roast you back and forth between us. We're going to worship your body with our hands and mouths, and then screw you until you can't see straight."

The words quite literally took my breath away. For a few moments I went without oxygen, and almost panicked.

"Nothing's off limits," he whispered, his hand sliding over one hot cheek. "Nothing at all... unless you say so. Understand?"

Oh my *God* did I understand! I nodded helplessly, giving myself over. At this point I would've agreed with anything.

"Good," Senan smiled. "That's what I needed to hear."

He finally kissed me, and my whole world was complete. I felt my body relax. I felt the pleasure flow in from down below, unhindered by thought or consequence or reservation.

"Did you plan this?"

I'd asked the question on a whim, but Senan just laughed.

"Can you ever really plan something like this?" he asked before kissing me again.

I shrugged shyly. "I— I don't know."

Somewhere down below I felt Brett lifting my legs over his big, not very nerd-like shoulders. He leaned forward, pushing his two corded arms against the flesh on the bottoms of my thighs. A second later, he was poised at my entrance.

*Do you want this?*

The question was entirely silent. It was spoken only by his beautiful blue eyes as he hovered against me, the bulbous head of his pulsating manhood pressed against my folds. He waited there patiently, devouring me with his eyes. Seeking that final permission.

I nodded almost imperceptibly, giving it to him.

*OHHHHHhhhhhHHHHHHhhhh...*

Unlike Senan, Brett filled me completely in a single, glorious stroke. It would've been impossible, if not for how wet I was. If not for the near-orgasm I'd already achieved while he went down on me, his face still glazed from my own excitement.

*Wow!*

151

Brett felt so very different inside me, but also the same. He gave me that same wonderful feeling of fullness and completion, but the weight of his body, the angle of penetration — it was all just a little dissimilar. Even the timing of his thrusts contrasted with the way Senan had taken me.

*You've only had two lovers, remember?*

Sure, but two in the same week? Soon to be three? No matter how you sliced it, that seemed pretty exceptional.

"Mmmm... oh my *God* she feels good!"

Brett was talking to Senan, not me. Just that little fact alone turned me on.

"Uhh, I mean you feel *ridiculously* good," he smiled bashfully, shifting his attention my way. "I didn't mean to—"

"Not a problem," I interrupted him with a little gasp. "You feel..." his thrusts were forcing the air from my lungs. "... pretty fucking amazing yourself."

Brett's smile widened as he began really sawing away, screwing me deeply every time our bodies came together. Something brushed my face, and I realized it was Senan's already-hard member. He was kneeling beside my head. Thrusting himself past my eager lips, as I turned my head and opened my throat to accommodate him.

*Two guys at once.*

It was that easy, that simple. A moment later I was pinned between them, being pumped hotly from both front and back.

*Holy shit, Delaina.*

The craziness of it hadn't hit me yet, especially

considering my circumstances. And this wasn't exactly a threesome either, because there was *another* man waiting in the wings. Another amazing-looking guy holding my legs back for better leverage, so his friend could really put the screws to me.

"I love these fucking *legs*." Brett grunted, wrapping his arms around my upper thighs. "So smooth. So perfect."

Our movements had become one now, each rock of our bodies a constant, steady rhythm that kept all three of us deeply happy. I rose up on my elbows, assuming more control. Taking Senan even deeper, until Ander worked his body up to take his place as well. His thickness was inches from my face, but this time on the other side. Senan took my free hand and guided it toward his friend.

"Go ahead," he breathed. "Him too."

Closing my fist around Ander — while still blowing Senan — was unimaginably hot, especially with Brett buried so perfectly inside me. It took only a moment to switch between them. To roll my head left instead of right. To pull Senan's length from my sucking, churning throat...

... and to take Ander all the way down instead.

"Ohhh *FUCK,"* Ander grunted.

Having sex was still new to me, but blowjobs were something I knew well. It was all a matter of getting the timing right. Of swallowing one hard dick while stroking the other, while giving the rest of my body over to Brett's breathtakingly deep thrusts.

There were hands on my face, touching and caressing. Hands on my body, taking control. I surrendered willingly, letting these three strong men pierce me to the core. Spreading my legs for each new lover in turn, as they rotated patiently around me, feeding me, using me...

Eventually it was Ander's turn, and I looked up at him dreamily as he nudged my knees apart. There was a moment of eye contact. The heat of a connection forged between us, as he positioned himself in that penultimate moment.

"I still can't believe this," he sighed as he sank into me, his thickness stretching me in ways that were both shocking and thrilling. "It's just... so..."

"Crazy?" I sighed happily, as his head slid over my shoulder. I wrapped my arms and legs tightly around him, digging my nails in as I felt the full extent of his raw strength and power. His ass began churning and rolling, the muscles of his glutes going deliciously tight as he began pumping away.

"I was going to say 'perfect'," he sighed, his lips pressing into my neck. "But yeah. Crazy works too."

# Twenty-Seven

## ANDER

She was the girl Senan had been talking about for days, nonstop. The nerdy little blonde who'd called him as a potential client, but who he'd somehow refused to take in that way.

And yet he *had* taken her. According to him, he'd even taken her virginity! Brett and I had laughed at him at first, for believing such a bunch of bullshit. Only now...

Now it seemed more and more obvious it was the truth.

Somehow this girl — no, this beautiful *woman* — had made it to this point in her life without ever having had sex. She wasn't shy. She wasn't introverted. Hell, from what we'd heard she was even a college professor! But the fear of intimacy thing made perfect sense, especially when you considered her long-term relationships had morphed into friendships rather than romances.

Senan had totally lucked out, in the most literal sense

155

there was. By the flip of a coin, he was the one who got her first instead of me.

But that was then. And this was *now*.

"Ohhhhh..."

Chastity — the name itself was hilarious — lay moaning beneath me, raking her nails down my back as I continued burying myself inside her. I bottomed out, grinding her hard into the sheets. Driving her perfect little ass deep into Senan's bed; a bed which had seen more than its fair share of ass, if we were being honest. But none *this* hot. This tight. This...

*Crazy.*

She'd said it herself, the very moment we became lovers. A woman who'd gone a quarter-century without a man inside her, and now suddenly, three men in as many days.

"H—holy *fuck...*"

Even her grunts were adorable, tiny moans and whimpers punctuated by phrases like 'oh God' and 'holy shit' or a random combination of both. My own dialogue was similar, even if it was internalized. My own thought process interrupted by a steady stream of brain-numbing pleasure, as her tight little channel milked me for everything I was worth on every stroke.

"You're big..."

She murmured the words into my mouth as I kissed her, sliding my tongue against hers. She tasted sweet, like wine and strawberries. Like something fresh and new and delicious that I wanted to eat forever.

"You feel so... so— *OH!*"

Chastity gasped as I drove myself home, rolling my hips in a big deep circle as she clawed at my ass for dear life. I could've emptied myself inside her at any time. It was a tribute to how excited she made me, how hard and full and ready I was.

But I also wasn't ready, because I needed more from her. I needed the visual of her body in the prone position, her round little ass pointing high in the air. I wanted to be behind that ass, plowing away. I wanted to be *inside* her, while pulling back on that long blonde hair.

In other words, I wanted to dog the daylights out of her. Make her scream and whimper as I held her wrists, locking her arms back as I took her in a way that was rough *and* sexy. A way that turned me on even more than it did for my lovers, and that was saying a lot.

Still... she wasn't mine. She was Senan's if anything, and I wasn't about to—

"Turn her over," Senan grunted, his hands on her shoulders. "She deserves it harder than this."

His words were music to my ears. It was like he was speaking my language.

"Ooohh—*Oh!*"

Chastity shouldn't have been surprised when she was flipped onto her stomach, then entered almost immediately from both ends. Senan had her face in his hands, cupping it gently as she took him down her tender little throat. I knew that mouth well already. It was a talented mouth, whether you were kissing it or—

"Mmmppffhh!"

She groaned again around Senan's manhood as I drilled myself home, bouncing her steadily and deliberately off the end of my rock-hard dick. I had one of those erections that would never go down on its own. The ones that felt like you could hammer nails with, or cut diamonds. The ones where the girl you woke up next to took one look at before knowing exactly what came next.

"Ander..."

Chastity popped my friend from her mouth just long enough to sigh my name. I figured it must've been important.

"Yes?"

"Ander, please *fuck* me."

Senan's body was curled down around her churning blonde head. He was feeding her eagerly, murmuring instructions. But she'd turned to look over her shoulder at me, while gasping the request.

I took hold of her hips and gave her exactly what she wanted.

"OhhhHHHhhh..."

Chastity might've still been a maiden until this week, but her body was certainly made to be fucked. Her shapely hips had this amazing, sexy flare. It lent perfect handholds to whoever was lucky enough to be behind her, and right now that lucky asshole was me.

*FUUUUCK.*

As incredible as her body was, she was better from the inside. Her womanhood gripped me desperately on every stroke. The harder I screwed her, the more it seemed to milk

158

me back, and the more desperate I became to unload inside it.

"Bro..."

I was looking at Senan, my expression serious. Desperate. Almost pained, it felt so good.

"I know," he acknowledged.

"If I don't..." I grunted. "Soon..."

"*I know*," he reiterated, and his voice sounded just as thick with lust as mine was. He was sifting his hands through her hair. He bunched it into a rough ponytail and handed it off to me.

"Go ahead and finish inside her if you need to," Senan told me. "That's what she wants, anyway."

I took her by the hair and pulled. The noise she made was something between a whimper and a cry.

*Holy fucking shit.*

Chastity's eyes flared in what I thought at first was alarm, but was actually excitement. Her head was still moving steadily, her lips sliding tightly along the full length of my friend's shaft.

"We could go all night like this," I told her, leaning over her back. "Trade you off, over and over again. Make you *ours*."

She winced in pleasure, still bouncing, still fucking me back. Only now she was screwing her ass tightly against my abdomen. Pushing hard to gain that extra inch or so at the end of every thrust.

"Damn."

It was totally unreal, how good it all felt. How natural it came to be doing something like this, with not just one of my friends but two.

"You like being shared with my friends," Senan was whispering just loud enough to be heard. "Don't you?"

She nodded, but never stopped. Her body kept on going.

"You love having the three of us, all to yourself."

He pulled himself free, and motioned Brett back into the mix. Chastity's mouth closed over him as she sucked him down, without missing a beat.

As for me I was dying to let go, holding on for dear life. Ordinarily I'd exhibit much more control, but the sights and sounds of this beautiful creature had me at the point of no return. I loved hearing her whimpers. Seeing her body twist, as she writhed beneath us...

"Senan..."

He nodded my way, understanding immediately. At the last minute though, he leaned in and whispered something directly into her ear. Chastity's eyes went glassy, her face contorting in heat and ecstasy as she nodded back at him from all fours.

A moment later I was erupting inside her, roaring out loud as my hands clenched and my fingers flexed and I poured my soul into her hot, willing body.

# Twenty-Eight

## CHASTITY

No arrangement of words could ever do the night justice. Description failed in light of the thoughts, the feelings, the butterfly-inducing explosion of emotions that wracked my body, even as it was physically taken, over and over again, by not one but *three* gorgeous, incredible men.

I woke in the dead of night, drenched to the core. Warm and cozy beneath the blankets of Senan's sex-soaked bed, above which the scent of our lovemaking still hung cloyingly in the air.

I was *sore.* Sated. Shell-shocked by the night's events.

But still deliriously, wondrously happy.

It was a simple thing to sneak out — to gather up my clothes and belongings, clutching my keys tightly to keep them from jangling as I saw myself out of the guys' house. After a quick stop at the bathroom, I could hear snoring coming from further down the hall. I envisioned Ander or Brett in their own bedrooms, slumbering away after spending themselves so fully and completely inside of me.

*Good God, Delaina.*

Not that I had much to compare it to, but it was the single hottest night of my life.

It seemed almost unreal, looking back at it. Drinking, laughing, playing cards. Picking at my triple-chocolate cake with three different forks, without realizing the symbolism it would represent in Senan's bed later on.

*Senan...*

If last night had an architect, it was certainly him. My tattooed lover had facilitated me going to bed with all three roommates, who then proceeded to share my body in every possible way. Oddly enough, that part seemed relatively believable. The guys had gotten along like brothers from the very moment I met them, sharing everything from food to money to living arrangements, and now, also *me.*

Still, it was the lack of jealousy I found the most shocking. Senan had willingly and unhesitatingly given me over to his friends without batting an eye.

*Wait, that's not right.*

No, he hadn't given me to his friends at all. He'd *shared me* with them. He'd joined in and even quarterbacked the entire affair, from the moment I was carried into his bedroom until the moment his friends ultimately left to crash out on their own.

Senan hadn't hesitated. He hadn't been jealous. He'd participated fully in everything; kissing me, holding me, guiding me through every new adventure and change of position. He'd whispered hot, dirty things in my ear. Things that made me dripping wet. Things that made me gasp with the anticipation of actually doing them, and then he'd held me throughout that too.

In the end I'd been made whole, taking on all three men until they'd exploded inside me. That part had been unspeakably hot, making them come one by one. Spreading my legs and watching their faces as they enjoyed me all the way to orgasm, then studying their expressions, their sounds, their own unique ways of expressing that climactic moment.

They filled me to overflowing, leaving me lying there, panting, basking in the glory of my own climax until their heat ran back out of me. Then they left, kissing me goodbye. Whispering still other things in my ear — forbidden promises, maybe — that caused my belly to flutter and my toes to curl.

I remembered the door closing, leaving Senan and I alone. He smiled back at me before cuddling up. The last thing I remembered him saying before pulling the covers over us both:

"Well, you did say you wanted to do *everything*."

I fell asleep almost instantly, and woke up feeling safe and secure behind his slumbering bulk. Outside, the weather was freezing. Hanover was a frozen wasteland of ice crystals and crunchy residual snow; a far cry from the warmth and safety of sleeping in Senan's arms. But I had to get home. With classes starting up, I had all kinds of work to do.

*Work...*

That part of my life seemed so pedantic now, so very far removed. For as long as I could remember, it had consumed every minute of every day. Work and academia were practically all I had the time for. Up until now at least, when

163

I'd finally taken some time for myself.

And boy had I *ever.*

I thought about all of these things on the short ride back to my place, my breath making little puffs of white smoke in the crisp winter air. By the time my heat kicked on I was already home. Already climbing the stairs to my loft apartment, while going over and over the events of last night in my mind.

*Probably just making up for lost time.*

Ander's words made me laugh now, in retrospect. But what wasn't funny was how much I'd actually missed out on, all these years. How many times I could've been sexually fulfilled rather than sexually frustrated, if I'd only known then what I know now.

Then again, maybe I wouldn't have met Senan. Or Ander. Or Brett. Maybe then I wouldn't have starred in the Super bowl of all possible fantasies, leaving me still hungry and wanting more.

Not that I *wasn't* still hungry and wanting more.

Locking the door behind me, I threw my keys on the table and flipped open my laptop. There were no fewer than sixty-two new messages in my inbox, patiently waiting for me.

At the very least they'd have to wait the duration of a long, hot shower.

# Twenty-Nine

## CHASTITY

With the new week dawned a new semester, and new responsibilities. Two new classes I'd never taught, and a third I already knew very well.

Programming theory was easy to teach, but a little harder to master. Since the long-lost days of 1's and 0's, writing code has been the same general series of loops and subroutines. A simple matter of receiving data via user input, and then processing that data for whatever output format might be necessary. This went for any computer language at any time in history, regardless of how or when it had been invented.

But that was the key: being able to learn today's cutting-edge languages on the fly, while putting the old ones to pasture. Figuring out how to interface with today's GUI-driven software was a constant battle of keeping up with the Joneses, which meant some of the classes I'd taught — and been taught — in the past were already borderline obsolete.

For this reason I'd spent the rest of the weekend

working solely on tests and lesson plans. I had outlines to make. Quizzes to draw up. A list of assignments that would teach students all new terminology and programming commands, while still maintaining the origins of loop logic and compartmentalized routines, all streamlined for maximum speed and effectiveness.

In other words, big-time nerd stuff.

Striding across Dartmouth's campus was always like taking a trip through the past; both through my own history as well as those who'd gone before me. I walked by the new smart classrooms of Kemeny Hall. Passed beneath lines of 200 year-old ivy-league elms, all the way down to the new Center for Engineering and Computer Science.

The stark white corridors seemed especially bright against the clear blue January skies, which beamed in through long glass windows and filtered through overhead skylights. I took the stairs instead of the elevator. Enjoyed the familiar burn in my calves as I stepped up to my classroom's level, then continued down the ramp and into my assigned lecture hall.

There, several tiers of desks lay spread out before me like a Roman amphitheater. For a moment, like always, I let my imagination run wild. I was the gladiator, and they were the bloodthirsty crowd. I held their collective attention captive, under penalty of bad grades. The lectures would be my battles, their questions my opponents. The assignments would be... would be...

*Holy shit.*

I stopped halfway through my introduction, having already written my name on the board. As always, I allowed my eyes to scan the rows. To visually absorb and take in the faces of the students I didn't know, but whose names I would hopefully, by the end of the semester, be able to recite by memory.

All except the one I *already* knew.

*Just... just WOW.*

In the third row, two seats away from the right-hand aisle, Brett stared back at me with his piercing blue eyes. He had his laptop already open. A pencil twirled slowly between two thick fingers, one side of his mouth already curled into a wolfish grin.

I faltered in the middle of my opening speech, a well-rehearsed yet concise group of paragraphs outlining what we'd be going over for the next few months. I didn't realize my heart had begun racing until I finished the last line. I was already perspiring beneath my sweater. The big lecture hall seemed abruptly smaller than it had before.

*Figures. Doesn't it?*

Of all the students in all the classes, somehow I'd gotten *him*. And yet in the back of my mind, for some odd reason, I wasn't at all surprised.

*Karma?*

Had he mentioned which school he attended? I honestly didn't remember. Only that his studies coincided with mine, and he was still working on his masters.

*A cosmic joke?*

I let out a short laugh under my breath, and Brett caught it. I could tell by the way his smirk widened, just a tiny bit more.

*Stop looking at him!*

For the rest of the class I made a conscious effort *not* to look his way, which of course was impossible. I found myself wholly distracted by him. I paced back and forth across the front end of the hall, going through the motions of my first lecture. I did my best to keep on track, intentionally trying not to make eye contact while handing out the small stack of printed materials I'd prepped for the class.

And of course, that didn't work either.

I kept checking the time and pulling at the collar of my grey turtleneck sweater. After what seemed like a thousand years, I reached the end of my lecture. I let the students go five minutes early, watching as they slowly filed out of the hall.

All of them of course, except Brett.

"You have *got* to be kidding me."

It was all I could think of to say as he approached the lectern. Slinging his backpack over his shoulder, he rubbed at his stubbled chin.

"Hey teach," he smiled merrily.

"Did you know?"

Brett shook his head slowly back and forth. "I mean, I suspected I *might* see you. After all, Senan told me this is where you—"

"Why didn't you tell me you attended class here!" I asked, my heart still racing. Grinning broadly, my lover looked back at me and shrugged his big collegiate shoulders.

"You never asked."

# Thirty

## CHASTITY

Brett moved closer, then closer still, until his body was less than a foot from mine. The scent of him reached my nostrils, and instinctively my body remembered it. Reacted to it...

"Not here."

I turned and fled through a door behind the lectern, into a hallway leading to a series of smaller rooms. They were reserved for professors who wanted to prep early for class, or stay late to help students. Right now, thankfully, they were empty.

"Listen, I–"

We weren't in the room two seconds before Brett already had me pinned to a wall. I gasped as he swept me up in his arms, crushing me against his hard, rippled body. His lips easily found mine, and before I knew it we were kissing like star-crossed lovers.

*Oh my GOD...*

169

Alarm bells flashed through my head. I was in a scary place — a dangerous place — where someone could walk in on us at any moment. A teacher, kissing her student. And that's just for starters.

"Brett..."

I could barely utter the word between deep, soulful kisses. And it wasn't just him, either. It was me, kissing him back. Clutching the back of his head with one eager hand, while whimpering softly into his churning, searching mouth.

"We can't," I gasped again. "Not here."

*Not here.*

Those words again. They weren't denial, they were postponement. They told the story of 'yes', but under different circumstances, in a different place.

They also made me wet between the legs.

I kissed him some more, enjoying the weight of his body pressed tightly against mine. We'd picked up right where we left off. There hadn't been any words, any actions between us. Only the understanding of... this.

Whatever *this* was.

Eventually I gathered my wits enough to pull back. My glasses were crooked. I straightened them by pushing them higher on the bridge of my nose, my lips still wet and heated from being pressed so forcefully against his.

"Come with me," Brett said.

"Where?"

"Coffee."

The word was both a relief and a disappointment. Part of me knew following anywhere on campus was a bad idea, but coffee was innocent. The other part...

The other part would've done just about anything he wanted.

"I have another class," he said. "In an hour and a half."

"Oh."

"But I want to see you," he smiled. "I want to talk to you."

He stepped in again, his blue eyes searing their way through mine. This student — no, this *man* — he towered over me. This man who'd kissed me like I belonged to him. This man who'd been *inside* me.

"I've been wanting to see and talk to you for days now," he said, lowering his gaze timidly. "Ever since—"

"I know."

I took his hand briefly, pulling him from the room and back into the hallway. There I let go, and we became teacher and student again. Nothing more than two people following each other through the Computer Science building.

"Do you know where Lou's is?" I asked.

Brett made a face like I'd just asked him if he knew the sun were yellow.

"Alright, dumb question," I smiled. "Meet me there in fifteen. I need to drop this stuff off first."

We parted ways, and I made the brisk walk to my car. My blood was pumping as I crossed the lower part of the

171

campus. My mind racing with a thousand different thoughts, ranging from bad to good to downright filthy.

*So... what about this being a one-time thing?*

The little voice in my head had a distinctly mocking tone. Over the past few days I'd convinced myself of this idea. That I'd had my fun with the guys — and of course, they with me — and that was pretty much where things would land. Senan had text-messaged me a few times, checking to see if I was 'all good.' When I told him I was better than good, he'd sent me a smiley face followed by the devil emoji followed by a thumb's up.

From there it was all work, all school. But in the back of my mind...

In the back of my mind was what my heart wanted.

*And what exactly would that be?*

Of course I didn't know. I was a woman who thought she'd been in love two times already, but was thoroughly hopelessly wrong. A woman who'd just recently been introduced to a whole new world of sex and heat and pleasure, and the last thing I wanted was to confuse that world with what I thought I knew about 'love.'

*Yet here you are, about to have 'coffee.'*

I sighed. The voice wasn't exactly wrong.

*With a man who doesn't even know your name.*

My brows crossed. I was two seconds away from telling the voice to shut the fuck up.

*A student, no less. From one of your own classes.*

Now I did tell the voice to shut up. Not that it

listened.

*A guy you actually* screwed... *within a few hours of knowing him.*

Lou's came into view, the striped green-and-white awning dutifully cleared of snow. Behind the glass-paned windows the light was yellow and orange, warm and inviting. The perfect place for a warm cup of tea, and maybe a frosted pastry on a cold winter's day.

The perfect place to get into trouble.

# Thirty-One

## CHASTITY

"And you've played Dungeons and Dragons," Brett continued excitedly.

"Since the fourth edition," I confirmed. "Yes."

"As a dungeon master?" he continued. "Or as a player?"

"Both, actually," I said. "When most girls were planning their sweet sixteen I was world-building, designing my own campaign from scratch. I found it lots more fun than using existing modules, although some of the older ones can be great, especially—"

"And you go to Comic Con..."

"Four out of the last five years," I laughed. "Yes."

"*And* you cosplay?"

I put down my cup and pulled out my phone, as Brett stared incredulously at me across our little table. He was drinking a cappuccino. He'd even put extra sugar in it.

"Here," I said, grinning as I passed it over to him. "Scroll left."

For the full minute I sipped my tea in silence, as Brett scrolled through the folder of cosplay outfits I'd worn over the years. The early ones were rudimentary, but the last two years had included some of my best work. Most of my costumes were homemade. Put together by hand and glue-gun, rather than bought online or in some random store.

"Harley Quinn?" he breathed.

"Yeah," I laughed. "That was an easy one."

"Not on your ass," he smirked, still staring into my phone. "Those shorts are *short.*"

I chuckled as he tapped the screen, then pinched his fingers to zoom in on what I could only assume was my ass. Most of my outfits were rated PG, but I had to admit the Harley costume had been exceptionally slutty.

"You done?" I smirked. I put my hand out, pretending to be annoyed.

"Not yet."

He punched a few buttons, and I heard the sound of a text-message being fired off. Somewhere in his pocket, his phone dinged. I tilted my head as Brett laughed.

"Sorry not sorry," he said. "I had to have that one."

"Yeah, yeah."

"Seriously though," he said leaning back. "I need to tell you something important, so brace yourself."

I raised an eyebrow, intrigued. Sipping my tea again, I cupped it in both hands. "Okay. Braced."

"You're the perfect girl," Brett blurted immediately. "The girl of my dreams. The girl I've been looking for all my life."

"Is that so?"

"You play games. You dress up. You go to Cons..." he said. "Right there you're almost a ten."

"Almost?"

"But then you code, too! You know Perl. You write Php scripts. You make most of your living online, doing the things you love." He threw up his hands. "The things *I* love."

"I play a mean game of Zelda too," I chimed in. "If that helps push me towards that elusive ten."

"See?"

"I'm halfway through my replay of the Ocarina of Time," I smiled. "Still stuck at the lake. Haven't caught the Hylian loach yet."

Brett folded his hands together, his big arms flexing as he set them on the table. The combination of biceps and triceps stretched the sleeves of his shirt all the way to the max.

"Maybe you should invite me over," he said slyly. "and we'll catch it together."

I looked down at the table for a moment, blushing shyly. Picking at one of the flaky, delicious donuts that Lou's always baked daily.

"I— I want to, but..."

"Senan?"

A strange silence settled over our table, amplifying the

background noise around us. We could hear people talking, chatting excitedly. The clatter of silverware against plates. Eventually I just nodded and shrugged.

"I could always bring him," Brett said, his smile turning a little wicked. "That would be fun, especially for you. But when it comes to playing Nintendo, I'm pretty sure—"

"Tell me about his sister?"

The words just sort of tumbled past my lips. I blurted them more as a question than a statement, although I immediately regretted it. Brett looked suddenly uncomfortable.

"What's wrong?"

"You should probably ask him about that," he said evenly. "About Kylie, I mean."

*Kylie.*

"O—Okay."

"I mean, it's not like it's a secret," Brett stumbled. "But it's, well..."

"I get it," I said. "It's personal. And I want to ask him. He mentioned her, although not by name. And he sort of, well..."

"Well what?"

"He sort of used the past tense."

Brett nodded thoughtfully, without saying anything. It only deepened the mystery.

"Is she..."

"No," Brett said. "She's still very much alive. He sees her just about every day, actually. Ander and I do our best, too."

Relief flooded through me, for a girl I didn't even know. My mind wandered to Senan, and the choice of words he'd used. All of a sudden I wanted to speak with him very badly.

"I'll talk to him," I said at last. "Tonight, maybe."

"Well don't wait too long," winked Brett. "I want to hang out with you. No, scratch that. We're *going to* hang out."

I laughed softly. "Okay."

"Promise?"

I nodded solemnly. "I promise."

"Good enough," he said, standing up. I watched as he slung his backpack over his shoulder, then stopped.

"By the way," he said. "About your class..."

I glanced up at him from my seat, my tea still unfinished. "What about it?"

"Is it tough?"

My eyes dropped from his face to his chest, then down over the flat of his stomach. They lingered at his belt for a moment, then dropped lower still.

"I have a strong feeling you're going to do *really* well," I smirked, then sipped my tea again.

# Thirty-Two

## SENAN

The whole thing played out in slow-motion, as it always did, whenever I remembered it. There was no recollection otherwise. Almost like it had actually happened that way, instead of real-time.

*"Look out!"*

I remembered my sister's scream, so loud and piercing it felt like it should shatter the windows outward. The slow shift of gravity. The feeling of weightlessness as the car drifted out from under us, followed by the thump of three sets of hands, bracing against the doors, the dashboard, the inside of the roof...

The crash was an explosion of light and sound. It came from every direction, although the impact had come from high up on the passenger side. Glass flew. Metal groaned. There was a sudden rush of wind, followed by an icy blast of cold as all the warm air was blown from the car. The windows were gone. The silence was shattered.

*"SENAN!"*

My mother's shout came during the roll, the first of many times we were upside-down. It felt like the car would go on rolling forever, tumbling down the embankment into infinity. Never stopping. Never coming to rest.

When it finally did, I remembered the pain first. My wrists were both broken from bracing against the roof, my ankle was fractured. My mother's cheek was bleeding, and I knew right away the cut was deep. A steady stream of red dripped from the lowest point of her jaw, dribbling thickly down over her ivory-colored shirt.

*Her favorite shirt.*

My jaw clenched. My heart ached.

*The one she usually wore when we went out somewhere special.*

The car came to rest as it always did, on the driver's side. My mother was trapped, her door pinned against the frozen mud. But my sister...

My sister hung limply from her seat, her arms dangling like a lifeless mannequin. She was still belted in, still attached to her seat. Her eyes were open but she wasn't conscious. Or rather, she was conscious but she wasn't there.

*"Kylie!"*

I scrambled to stand, to reach her, and that's when I saw the blood on the glass next to my sister's head. A whole spiderweb of cracks in concentric circles, that looked both horrifying and beautiful.

*"Kylie wake UP!"*

Silence. It faded from the past into the present. Transported me from the frozen world of our car, lying at the base of that embankment, to the midnight stillness of my bedroom, some eight years later.

"Senan..."

The voice at the other end of the phone wasn't just sympathetic, it was absolutely gutted. I could hear the sorrow in Chastity's voice. Feel the heartbroken thickness in her throat, as she struggled to speak.

"Senan I'm so, so sorry."

I'd told the story as I remembered it, in every last detail. It was a story only the closest people in the world knew. Ander. Brett. And now, now...

*Now this girl you hardly know.*

Fuck that. I knew this girl inside and out. I took pride in my judge of character, and Chastity's heart was pure. When she asked about Kylie, I hadn't hesitated to tell her. Not for an instant.

I'd told her everything.

"Intracranial hematoma," I said miserably. "That was the diagnosis. The truck T-boned us from the passenger side, jerking her head sideways and into the glass."

Chastity sat in silence, wallowing in her own misery. I wished absently that she were in the bed with me. That I could slide my arms around her and squeeze her tight.

"And she's... she's still suffering from..."

"She hasn't talked since the accident," I explained somberly. "Too much bleeding on the brain. Two weeks after the accident they transferred her from the ICU and changed her meds. When her alarms went off the next morning they found her standing in the corner of the room, staring out the window."

"Oh my God," Chastity breathed.

"She'd pulled out her tubes and all the leads, and just stood up," I went on. "At first we were thrilled. But then we realized she wasn't all there. I mean, she's there, but there's a part of her that's missing. A part of her that seems... just..."

*Just gone.*

I wanted to say it, but I couldn't. It still hurt way too much.

"Senan that's horrible. I– I can't even imagine..."

"No," I agreed. "You can't. But that's not your fault. No one could ever understand."

The ceiling seemed lower than before, like it was closing in on me. I rolled onto my stomach, staring down at the phone. The speaker button was engaged. The timer said we'd been talking nearly an hour, but with her, it felt like nothing.

"The accident was eight years ago, but I still blame myself a lot," I admitted. "We were only going out that evening because of me. Because of my eighteenth birthday."

"Senan, *no.*"

"It's true," I went on. "Sometimes I wonder how things would be right now if I'd spent that night with my friends. If I'd just gone out and left my mom and sister home, instead of–"

"But you had no way of knowing!" Chastity pleaded. "It couldn't possibly have been—"

"Or even if I'd sat in the front seat, instead of her," I went on. "She called shotgun. Can you believe that? It was one of the last things she said to me. 'Shotgun!' And then she smiled that beautiful seventeen-year old smile, and she jumped in the—"

"I'm coming over."

Her words stopped me mid-sentence.

"Chastity, it's after midnight."

"I'm coming over right now."

"No," I said. "You really don't have to—"

There was a click, followed by silence. When I looked down at the phone again, the timer had blinked off and I was talking to no one.

# Thirty-Three

## CHASTITY

When the door opened I flung myself into his arms, wrapping myself tightly around his body. It felt good, right, perfect. Like I could stay there forever.

Instead we went back to his bedroom, where I held him all night long.

Senan melted into me, and I could feel the pain and sorrow slowly drain away. In the hour before we drifted off to sleep we didn't talk about Kylie at all. Instead we discussed everything and anything else, including Brett showing up as a student in one of my classes... as well as his invitation to come over and play Zelda with me.

"He invited you too, you know," I smiled, spooning into him.

"Yeah?"

"He said you don't really play video games but it would be fun."

"It sure would," he joked. "For you anyway."

"I know," I chuckled, feeling that familiar knot of excitement cinch a little bit tighter, somewhere below my navel. "He said that too."

Senan sighed, clutching me against his wonderfully naked chest. He was in boxers only, and I in my G-string. We'd stripped down together, to sleep in our underwear.

"I wish I could this week," he said, "but I'm going to be busy every night with work. Too many bills to pay. Not enough hours to pay them."

I felt a sharp stab of jealousy, just picturing him working extra hours. Taking on additional clients. Sleeping with other women...

"Definitely take Brett up on it though," he said nonchalantly. "You guys should hang out. Have fun."

His words put a knot in my throat. For conflicting reasons.

"Y—You'd be okay with that?"

"Sure," he shrugged. "Why wouldn't I be?"

"Well, I guess... because..."

"Because you don't want to 'cheat' on me?"

There. The cat wasn't just out of the bag, it was chained beneath a spotlight.

"That's cute and all," Senan went on, "but I really wouldn't look at it that way. Not if you did it with Brett, or Ander."

"Why?" I asked. "Just because I've been with them

185

already?"

"That, yes," he admitted, "but mostly because they're my *friends*. My brothers, really."

"And you share everything with your friends?"

"Not everything, no," he chuckled. "But this? You?" He spun me around, turning me so that I faced him on the pillow. In the dim light filtering in through the window I could see his lips, his mouth. The hard curve of his bearded, masculine jaw as he spoke.

"For some reason sharing you seemed natural," he shrugged. "It seemed right to me, and to them."

"You've talked to *them* about it?"

"Of course. And believe me, they loved it just as much as I did. Not only in a sexual way, either — any guy would love *that*. But in all the same emotional ways, too."

My stomach did a slow somersault. It woke the butterflies up again.

"*Emotional* ways?"

"Yes," said Senan. He reached out gently to stroke my cheek. "The guys got a little — how do I say this? 'Attached' to you the other night. After you left they couldn't stop talking about you. And they talked about you as a person — someone who was funny and perfect and cool. They talked about those things way more than they talked about what we actually did."

My body was on fire, and not just because we were beneath the blankets. It was an internal heat. One that came from feeling warm and fuzzy inside.

"What exactly did they say?"

Senan smiled and kissed me softly, briefly, before crushing me tightly against him. My face was buried in his tattooed chest. His mighty legs, wrapped around me in a cocoon of smooth, hard flesh.

"They said lots of things," he replied, "but so did I. And after we finished talking about how great you are, they both told me they wanted to see you again. With or without me."

There should've been alarm bells. There should've been shock, surprise, maybe even some outrage.

Instead there were only goosebumps. They erupted unbidden over every surface of my body, despite the heat.

"Is that something you'd be interested in?" Senan asked.

My heart was hammering out of my chest! I was absolutely sure he could feel it, pressed up against his.

"I..."

"You don't have to say anything right now," Senan told me. "Sleep on it. The decision is entirely yours, but I wanted you to know I'm okay with it."

A hand touched my chin, gently tilting my face upward.

"And not just okay with it," Senan said, his eyes gleaming. "I'm *excited* by it, too."

# Thirty-Four

## CHASTITY

"Eggs?"

Ander's voice was way too cheerful for this early in the morning. It wasn't even six o'clock. I'd barely slept four hours.

Yet when I'd woken up, Senan was already gone.

"Umm... sure."

I hadn't expected him to slip quietly out of his own bed, but that's exactly what happened. I found the sheets still warm. The shower dry, as I washed the exhaustion from my sleep-gummed eyes.

"I've got bacon coming too," Ander nodded, pointing to the oven. He looked deliciously casual in a pair of cutoff sweat shorts and a way too-tight T-shirt. "If you could just grab us some plates–"

I turned toward the cabinets, just as Brett appeared in the doorway. He wore a similar outfit, plus a pair of ragged jogging sneakers. He was also out of breath, and covered head to toe in sweat.

"Whoa!" he gasped, his look of surprise quickly turning into a grin. "When'd you get here?"

"Last night," I replied. "Around midnight."

"Ah."

"Senan had a sleepover," Ander chuckled.

"Didn't get much sleeping done though," I groaned, opening cabinets. I found a stack of paper plates on the third try and stopped myself. "Wait. That didn't come out right."

"Uh huh," smirked Ander.

"No, seriously," I said. "We talked for hours, then fell asleep. When I woke up he was—"

"Gone, yeah," said Brett. "He had an early shift."

My eyebrows came together. "Shift?"

"At the warehouse."

"He works at a *warehouse?*" I asked in surprise.

"Of course," said Brett. "Just about every day."

Ander took the stack of paper plates from my frozen hand. He separated three of them and began dividing up the eggs. While he did that, Brett poured three cups of coffee. He pushed one my way and I shook my head.

"What? Milk and sugar's over there."

"I don't drink coffee."

He and Ander looked at each other like I'd just grown a third arm.

"What the hell do you mean you don't drink coff—"

"Got any tea?"

Ander sighed dramatically, then reached into some faded metal canister. After rooting around for a bit he tossed me a wrinkled, naked teabag.

"She's a self-employed college professor with a double major and a masters degree," Brett chuckled, "and somehow she's accomplished all of this without coffee." He turned his smile on me, still sweating from his run. "What are you a genie or something?"

"Or something," I grinned back. "You sure this teabag is still good?"

"Did you check the expiration date?"

"Funny."

"Give it a squeeze then," said Ander. "If it doesn't disintegrate, it's probably good."

I glanced down at the teabag again, wholly disappointed. For a moment I actually considered coffee, but it was a brief moment.

"Nuke me some hot water?"

Ander pointed again, this time with a crispy piece of bacon. "Microwave's over there."

It should've been strange, going to bed with a guy and waking up with his two roommates instead. But oddly enough it felt weirdly natural. Totally casual, as if the three of us were having breakfast for the hundredth time instead of the first.

I nuked some tea and found the sugar where Brett had indicated earlier. I didn't even dare ask for lemon.

"So..." I inquired, trying to pry a little without being too nosy. "What does Senan do at this warehouse?"

"Packaging and shipping mostly," said Ander. "Sometimes they let him deliver for a route here and there, but only when they're short-staffed."

"Or when they're absolutely desperate," Brett laughed. "Because Senan can't drive for shit."

I sipped my tea, which was every bit as stale as it looked. The eggs were overcooked also, but I couldn't complain. I preferred that to runny.

"When does he... um..."

*God, I can't believe you're even asking this!*

"Do the other thing?" asked Brett.

"Yeah."

"Mostly on the weekends," Ander said through a mouthful of bacon. "Sometimes on the weeknights, too, but that's rare."

"Ah."

"He hasn't lately though," Ander continued. "Come to think of it, neither have I."

An image came to mind: Senan and Ander's profiles, side by side, splashed across the screen of my laptop. And me, reaching for a coin.

"So the site's been slow I guess?" I tried forcing a smile.

"My phone's been ringing," Ander shrugged. "I just haven't taken those calls lately. Been focusing more on other stuff."

"Like what?"

"Like scurrying like a rat between three different gyms," smiled Brett, as he needled his roommate. "Sometimes for clients that don't even show up."

I glanced back at Ander. "Clients?"

He nodded, still chewing. "I'm a personal trainer. I do hour long sessions at all different places, depending on the date and time."

"Wow, that's pretty cool," I said admiringly.

"It would be if the gyms weren't such fuckups," Ander growled. "Half of them won't let me make appointments directly, I have to go through them. They usually screw up a date or a time, and I end up going there for no reason or I miss out on training sessions because their booking systems suck."

"Funny," I said. "I was working on an exercise system called Train Direct. "It linked trainers directly to people looking to hire them, plus it had meal-plan spreadsheets, a calorie counter, a nutrition-based forum..."

Ander put down his fork. "That doesn't sound funny, that sounds amazing."

"Yeah," I said wistfully. "It was."

"What happened to it?"

"The project stalled because my colleagues insisted on linking a peer-to-peer video system to the entire product," I explained. "I warned them other companies bigger than ours were already working on that. That we should just go with Skype, or Zoom, or whatever it took to get people connected with an outside piece of software. But no," I shook my head.

"They didn't want to pay those licenses. They wanted control of everything."

"And so you missed your window," said Brett, understanding everything in greater detail. "Your product was obsolete before you brought it to market."

I grunted bitterly. "It was obsolete before we even finished it. Which we really didn't."

The anger inside me was rising, so I directed my attention elsewhere. I dug into my eggs, and together we finished breakfast. Ander called first shower, and Brett didn't fight him on it. While they were throwing their plates away, I headed to the sink to clean up.

"She's alright," Ander nodded my way, on his way through into the hallway. He laughed and winked. "Maybe we'll keep her."

"Maybe don't use all the hot water this time," Brett warned.

I washed the pans, and Brett dried them. Somewhere in the back of the house the shower kicked on, leaving the two of us alone.

"So what time am I coming over tonight?"

So bold, I thought to myself. So straightforward too, and unlike any of the guys I'd dated before.

*So refreshing.*

"Tonight, huh?"

"Yup."

"Dinner or no dinner?" I asked.

193

"Dinner. I'll bring it."

His biceps flexed as he ran the dishtowel in tight circles over the last pan. I wanted to peel his shirt off and see the rest, sweat or no sweat.

"Then be at my place at six," I said. "Any later and I'll be starving."

"Shoot me your address then," Brett said. "I'm looking forward to seeing your place."

I stepped back to the table and reached for my phone, still without taking my eyes off him.

"And don't worry," he added with a wry grin. "You'll definitely be getting *fed.*"

# Thirty-Five

## CHASTITY

"You're running out of Rupees!" I exclaimed from my couch. "If you don't catch it soon, you're gonna have to go back and—"

"No way," Brett protested. He held the joystick firmly in both hands, tilting it forward. "I *got* this."

He'd arrived promptly at six, with some of the best Chinese food I'd ever put in my mouth. Our feast consisted of boneless spare ribs, black pepper chicken, and two crunchy egg rolls. Forgoing the waters he brought with him, we washed it down with a couple of imported beers I had in the back of my fridge.

After that, I gave him the grand tour.

Brett was much more impressed by my place than Senan had been, and that's because he appreciated my many little shrines to geekdom. I had sci-fi movie posters, professionally framed. Shelves of limited-edition figurines for all different comic book universes, some of them exclusive to

Comic Con only. There were my Harry Potter bookends. My scale replica of the Sulaco. A few more subtle nods to different genres were peppered throughout my decor, but somehow Brett found them all.

Eventually, our bellies full, we finally curled up on the couch. He'd invited himself here under the pretense of playing Legend of Zelda, but I expected it was simply an excuse to get into my shorts. Which, since getting the green light from Senan, was more than fine with me.

Right now, however... he was *actually* playing Legend of Zelda.

"Make sure you cast into the lily pads," I said, pointing at one side of the screen. "That's where the loach strikes the lure."

Brett laughed and looked my way. "Are you serious?"

"What?"

"Do you think I'm a *rookie?*"

I laughed back. "No, but—"

"Honey I've caught the loach before. *Lots* of times. In fact—"

The fish hit his lure mid-sentence, and immediately he started reeling. On-screen Link was fighting hard, his pole bending all the way down to the surface of lake Hylian. The loach was roughing him up. Shaking its head back and forth as the controller's rumble-pack kept making a deep, vibrating sound.

"You sure you can handle it?" I teased, putting my lips near his ear.

"Uh huh."

"Because if you can't, it might be easier to just—"

He turned again and I kissed him, fully and deeply on his perfect mouth. For a second or two he just sat there, still pressing buttons. Still trying to reel in the imaginary fish from the imaginary lake, as my tongue slowly searched his mouth.

Then Brett dropped the controller, and his hands went straight to me.

*Thank God!*

He pushed me back into the couch, stretching his body alongside me. Our kisses grew stronger, hotter, more insistent. Just as his hands slipped beneath my T-shirt, the fish broke off the line and I laughed into his mouth.

"Told you you couldn't handle it."

Brett's eyes flared in mock anger as he shifted forward to bury his face in my neck. I laughed as his stubble tickled my skin. Laughed some more as his hands joined in, tickling me around the waist as he blew a raspberry against my skin.

"*Now* you're in for it."

His hands shifted lower, sliding over my ass. He took my shorts down with them, then slid to the floor so that he was kneeling between my legs. Before I knew it he was kissing my chest, my stomach, the insides of my thighs. Then he slid lower still, pushing my knees apart...

*Mmmm...*

Brett's eyes found mine, totally holding me prisoner as he slowly slid a finger inside me. I was already wet, already eager. But the sensation of that single finger, gliding slowly in

197

and out of me, had me gasping with all new levels of arousal.

"God, you're beautiful."

One finger became two. I knew this only because it felt twice as good, twice as hot. My eyes however, were still locked on his.

"Have I told you you're perfect?"

I nodded slowly, solemnly, watching him finger me. "The girl of your dreams, I believe you said."

He lowered his mouth and kissed me, right on my flower. As his lips dragged lightly over my clit, my legs quivered involuntarily.

"I'm going to need to see that Harley Quinn outfit," he murmured, planting tiny kisses all along my sex.

"W—Why?"

"So I can get you all dressed up in it," he said softly, "and screw you stupid."

He drove his fingers deeper and my body convulsed around his hand. The heat inside me was rising. My breath was coming in shorter, more ragged gasps.

"In fact, I'll need to see all your cosplay outfits. The sexy ones, anyway. Hell, even the non-sexy ones. I'll fuck you in all of them."

Brief but heated images flashed through my mind: my Wonder Woman outfit, ravaged beyond recognition. Me dressed as Supergirl, with my little red skirt hiked over my ass. I had a fantastic steampunk costume that might or might not be a turn-on for him. But Brett would *definitely* have fun plundering me in my first-ever cosplay effort: dressed up as a female Link.

"But not tonight," he murmured, nudging his way downward. He was nosing his way along my entrance, now. Dragging his tongue along the outer edges of my heat and wetness.

"Tonight you're not making it past this couch," he breathed. His fingers still churned inside me, driving me wild. Making me crazy with the need to be—

"I'm too fucking hot for you," he said. "And you're too fucking *wet*..."

With that he buried his face between my legs, plunging his tongue inside me. I squealed with joy, squirming my ass into the couch cushions. Rolling my head back to stare dazedly at the ceiling, as my lover continued going to work on me with his hands and mouth.

*This is crazy, this is nuts, this is—*

A hand shot up, cupping my breasts one by one. Brett squeezed them firmly beneath my T-shirt as he went expertly down on me. My mouth dropped open in ecstasy. My glasses fell from my face.

*Oh my GODDDDD...*

Then everything else was forgotten, as the first of several monster orgasms came screaming up from my core.

# Thirty-Six

## BRETT

I devoured her beautiful flower, sliding my tongue up and down through her entrance as I fingered her through a blistering orgasm. Chastity bucked and screamed as she came. I used my elbows to pin her shapely thighs against the soft leather couch and just kept going, burying myself in her wetness, reveling in the violent explosion that wracked her body.

"Oh... Oh GOD..."

My fingers told the tale of her climax; a sharp internal squeeze, so tight it was better than anything I'd felt before, and then I was thumbing her button as well. Swirling my tongue around it as she convulsed and shuddered, stopping now and then to flutter over it with just the right amount of contact and pressure.

Her hands were claws for a good half minute, scraping the sides of my head. Eventually though, she came down. Her body relaxed and her stomach flattened and her breathing, though still rapid, became more regulated again.

"My God, Brett..."

Now her fingers were moving, sifting through my own blond hair. I let her pull me upward, into her face. There she kissed me, over and over again, her tongue sliding hungrily through my mouth as she tasted her own honey on my lips.

"Mmmmm..."

I could tell she liked it. No, *loved* it was more accurate. Her starry eyes were all glassy, and glazed with lust. But they still glowed with an arctic blue fire.

"I need you *in* me."

She was pinned into the couch now, legs spread wide. Her arms pulled me in as I divested myself of the rest of my clothing.

"Oh wow..."

Her surprise came as my manhood sprang free, long and hard and aching to see some action. It had been hotter than hell, watching her come. Now, as a reward for straining so hard against my boxers, I glided easily into her smooth, eager hands.

"Let me do it."

Chastity smiled as she guided me inside her, stopping first to look down at what was about to happen. Gripping my manhood commandingly, she dragged the head through her own dripping folds. We watched together, as she dragged it back and forth, until it became absolutely coated and glistening.

"I love this fucking thing," she murmured, like I wasn't even there.

I couldn't help but chuckle. "In case you haven't noticed, it loves you too."

"Prove it."

It took nothing to shift forward, pushing the head inside her. It slid in with a cute little 'pop', and she bit her lip adorably as the shaft followed.

"Oh my God this feels so fucking *good...*" she cooed, spreading her legs even wider. Her hands found my sides. They ran tantalizingly over the muscles of my flanks, then curled to pull me in. "I'll never stop wanting this," she gasped. "I'll never stop needing you to—"

The rest of her sentence was lost in a hiss of hot air, as I shoved the full length of myself inside her. Chastity groaned as I took her deep. Whimpered softly, as I plunged in and out of her body. At first I took her slowly, so we could both watch as she got used to me. Then faster and more frantically, as the heat of our connection grew.

*I could do this forever.*

I lifted my head for a moment, to look around. To gain a sense of my surroundings, and to enjoy where I was — and not just because I was between this incredible woman's legs.

*Look at this place...* I told myself. *She's the female version of* me.

She really was, and in every possible way. Chastity was the kind of woman a nerd like me would build for himself, if you could actually build a woman. The movie *Real Science* flashed briefly into my head, and I had to shake the fond image away.

*Look at her!*

I did, and it only made me hotter. Chastity's beautiful face was flush with sex, her lips full, her mouth slightly open. Already she was grunting toward another climax. She came quickly and easily we'd found out, as the three of us had taken her in so many different ways that first night.

"Kiss me."

Her request came through half-lidded eyes, and I couldn't refuse. I buried myself all the way to the hilt and kissed her again, and for once it felt like I might lose control. She was just too hot, too pretty, too exquisitely tight. Too totally perfect.

*Oh man...*

I screwed her harder, faster, driving her deep into the couch. When I couldn't take a single stroke more, I pulled out and shifted forward so that my knees were on the cushions.

"Here."

Grabbing her wrist, I shoved her hand downward and between her legs. She was drenched — a total mess.

It didn't take anything for her to begin playing with it.

"Make yourself come for me."

Her lips parted as she began rubbing up and down, stopping to dip her middle finger deep inside. The rhythm was wholly familiar. It was obvious she'd been doing it so long she knew exactly what she needed.

"Now... tell me when."

She reached for me with her free hand, but I pushed it away. Squatting over her body, I was stroking myself instead.

My erection was heavy and thick in my hand, still glistening from her arousal. I squeezed on the upstroke, in the sensitive spot just beneath the glans. Keeping myself at the very edge. Ready to explode any moment I wanted.

"Say it," I breathed. Our eyes were locked now, blue on blue-green. Our souls entwined. Our combined arousal, a single interconnected thing. "Tell me when you're going to come."

I saw her expression change. She went from paying attention to lost in her own moment, her eyes still looking at me but not even seeing me. Down below, the hand between her legs was gliding faster and faster.

*Holy shit...*

It was the hottest thing in the world, watching her eyes roll back. Seeing her body tense, as her lips came together to form a single, breathless word:

"Now."

I squeezed again, and three strokes later I was rewarded with my release. I guided myself precisely over her face and mouth, rolling my own chin upward in pure euphoria as thick ropes of hot seed rained down all over her lips, her face, her pink, flushed cheeks.

Chastity moaned through her orgasm, squinting hard but keeping those beautiful eyes still locked on mine. She shuddered beneath me, gasping as my come rained down all over her.

*Holy—*

It splashed her chin and her nose, dribbling into her open mouth. She took it all without flinching. Without swallowing. I watched as she lay there in pure unedited rapture, gasping breathlessly through each powerful wave of her own climax. Her gaze completely and utterly unwavering, as the raw heat of the moment seared the memory forever into our respective brains.

*Ohhhhhh FUCKKK.*

It took a long time before I was done — a full minute of draining every ounce of myself onto her beautiful, upturned face. Then I leaned down, used my thumb to push my own seed away, and planted a gentle kiss on her forehead.

"*Now* let's see your bedroom," I told her, reaching down to take her hand.

# Thirty-Seven

## CHASTITY

I lay in bed long after Brett left. At least an hour after his silhouette kissed me a tender goodbye, his tall form a buff, hulking outline against the backdrop of a yellow-orange sky.

We'd made love in my bed. We'd screwed slowly and hotly at first, enjoying the rebirth of our arousal, but over time Brett took the reins and *really* put in some work.

And God did he *ever* put in work.

The first couple of times I'd had sex I was still afraid I might break. This time however, the gloves were off. Brett hammered me home, nailing me against my headboard with my hair pulled back and my ass in the air, screaming his name as I came. He showed me reverse cowgirl, which I'd known about, but also the sidekick, the lotus blossom, and the triumph arch. The names weren't as important as the positions of course, but it was fun to learn there were names after all.

One of my favorites included having sex standing up, with my legs spread wide and my back pinned tightly against my bedroom wall. I marveled at the strength of his back and body. At the sheer length of time he could hold me cradled in his arms, his hardness buried deep inside me, screwing me with his legs locked tight and his mouth searching the nape of my neck for that one special spot that made me shiver all over.

Best of all, he held me all night. After the lovemaking was over, well after we'd screwed our socks off, Brett held me snugly and securely in his two big arms. He fell asleep almost instantly after we'd wrapped our bodies together like a pair of pretzels, and I drifted off happily to the sound of his light but adorable snores.

*Is this weird, though?*

It was a question I had to ask myself, even if I didn't want to. The question I had to face, because it was too big to ignore.

*Maybe. Maybe not.*

I pulled up the covers, determined to give myself at least an hour of reflection before getting up. I spent half the time convincing myself that what I was doing was wrong. That I was somehow cheating the system, and there was no possibility what I was doing could end up in any other way than total disaster.

*Still...*

Still there was a part of me that normalized everything in some very creative ways. After all, lots of girls dated two or three guys without being exclusive. At least for a little while. No one had made any commitments between us. The word commitment was never even mentioned.

Besides, I thought to myself, the guys had wanted this.

Senan had even encouraged it. Ander and Brett both didn't seem to mind, and so far they'd gone out of their way not to show me anything other than respect, attention, and love.

*And they all live together.*

So?

*Yeah... that's going to work out.*

Wouldn't it? It wasn't like I was hiding anything from anyone. In fact, the beauty of them living together was that they all *knew*. There couldn't be any secrets. Any jealousy would reveal itself almost immediately, at which point—

*You're rationalizing.*

I sat up in bed, for once forgetting how good my body felt. Forgetting the satiation of my physical needs, and focusing on the emotional.

*You want a relationship. Someone to care about.*

Staring through the window, I swallowed dryly. Those parts I couldn't deny. I couldn't argue with myself that I was lonely, and that I craved the type of deep connection I'd seen in my friends, my family, my coworkers and colleagues. I wanted a mate. A partner. A boyfriend.

I just didn't expect *three.*

*But what do they want?*

That of course, was the million-dollar question. In the end they were guys, and I was a willing girl. In all likelihood they were in it for the sex and the sex alone, and I was merely a shiny new toy for the three of them to play with.

Whether I liked it or not, that part left me with a knot in my stomach.

I threw off the covers, letting the first light of day filter in over my soft, naked body. I didn't look any different than I did a week ago, but somehow I felt different. Somehow everything had changed.

"Go to work, Chastity."

I said the words as an affirmation, hopping off the bed and letting my feet hit the smooth planks of the wooden floor. Then I stopped.

*Chastity?*

Had I really just said that? If so I'd done it without even thinking. As if I enjoyed playing the role, because so far Chastity had led a far more interesting life than Delaina ever had.

I stepped toward the mirror, where I got a glance of my sleep-lined face. My sex-tangled hair. My warm, still-sleepy body that Brett had encapsulated in his rock-hard arms for most of the night.

*Mmmmmm...*

"Get in the shower *Delaina*," I abruptly told my reflection in the mirror. Then, under my breath I added: "and stop buying into your own bullshit."

# Thirty-Eight

## CHASTITY

I spent the morning on campus, teaching about cascading style-sheets and web-based formatting. The afternoon and evening I spent at home, working diligently on a few different projects I'd fallen behind on. I turned my phone off, so there would be no distractions. Not outside ones, anyway.

Inside my mind though, a storm of conflicting thoughts raged.

I ate shitty frozen pizza. Washed it down with half a bottle of warm Gatorade. I should've gone out for a proper meal, but I wanted to stay in, to finish something. To get the image of my three lovers out of my head, no matter how hot or funny or compatible they were with me, not to mention incredibly talented in bed.

I'd just finished clearing the table when my phone rang. I swiped it open before realizing who it even was.

"Chastity?"

The voice was deep and strong but buffeted by wind.

Whoever it was was obviously outside.

"*Ander?*"

Static. More wind.

"Am I on speakerphone?"

"Hang on."

I heard the unmistakable sound of a car door opening and closing. The wind stopped. Ander was suddenly loud and clear.

"Sorry, it's crazy outside. Where are you right now?"

"Me? Home."

"I need you to get over here right away," he said. "I'm sharing my location with you."

"Ander, what—"

"I've got a cat problem."

My eyebrows knitted together. "A *cat* problem? What the hell is a—"

An alert popped up on my phone, showing his location on the digital map. It wasn't far. According to the display, only twelve minutes away.

"The others told me they saw cat stuff in your apartment," Ander went on. "That you had a cat."

"*Had*," I said, trying my best not to feel sad. "Not anymore."

"Well you know about cats, right?"

"Yes. Of course."

"Well I've got a stuck cat and I need help luring it out.

So bring whatever a cat eats. Or maybe a toy, or—"

"A cat's not going to come to a stranger's toy," I chastised him. "Wait, where's it stuck?"

"Outside. Sort of."

I felt a stab panic. "In the *cold?*"

"Did you get the location?"

"Yes, but—"

"I have to get back out there."

The car door opened. The wind started up again, and my phone's speaker was mostly static.

"Chastity?"

I barely caught my name over the wind, and I knew he could hardly hear me again. I shouted into the microphone, just in case.

"YES?"

"Hurry."

# Thirty-Nine

## CHASTITY

The dot at the end of my digital map was a gym, and the parking lot was a frozen wasteland swirling with snow. I spotted Ander's car at the far end of a long stretch of asphalt. He was parked up against a wooded area, behind which a stretch of power lines ran through the city.

*What the hell?*

He was outside, standing in the front of his car with the hood open. Staring down into the engine, like he was trying to figure out why it wouldn't start. Either that, or—

*Oh NO.*

I parked quickly alongside him and stepped out into the howling wind. The air was pregnant with frost and frozen moisture. It bit at every patch of exposed skin, and considering how quickly I'd gotten dressed I still had a lot of those.

"Thanks for coming," he said, reaching out for me. "I didn't know who else to call."

213

I hugged him quickly and looked down into the open hood. "Where?"

"Right there," he pointed. "Under the engine cowling."

I peered into the darkness, past the steadily falling snow. Ander pointed with one arm. With the other, he guided a flashlight.

"Oh my *God!*" I squealed. "Ander that's not a cat, it's a *kitten!*"

The tiniest, most adorable pair of bright green eyes stared back at me from a small opening between two pieces of dark metal. It was an orange tabby. It couldn't have been more than five weeks old.

"It's a baby!" I cried over the wind. "It got separated from its mother, and it climbed up against your engine for warmth."

I looked at it again, and the smallest, faintest meow somehow carried over the wind. My heart melted.

"We have to get it out of there!"

Beside me, Ander nodded. "Believe me, I know. I've been working on it for almost an hour."

I reached in, but the opening was far too narrow. Even for my smaller hands, there was just no way.

"I tried luring it out with everything in my car," Ander went on, "including a half-eaten Power Bar, plus a few cheese doodles one of my asshole friends left in the back seat."

"Cats don't eat those things!" I called loudly.

"I thought they liked cheese?"

"*Actual* cheese yes," I told him. "Not the orange chemical dust they sprinkle over a U-shaped piece of puffed rice."

Ander wrinkled his nose, as if he'd just now made the connection. His physique alone told me he wasn't the type of guy who would eat cheese doodles to begin with, but still.

"So what now?"

Reaching into my jacket pocket, I pulled out a small, single-serving pouch of tuna fish. I ripped the top away, then positioned it as close as I could to the opening.

"It's too far away," Ander called. "Move it closer."

"No, give it a minute."

If there was one thing I knew well, it was how skittish cats could be. Athena would never come when called. Hell, she barely came when it was dinner time! Yet there were other times when I'd be lying on the couch and she'd curl up right into my lap. With cats, you usually had to let them come to *you*.

"Think it smells it with all this wind?" shouted Ander. "Or should we—"

He stopped mid-sentence, as the little tabby poked its head through the opening. We waited together, our bodies shivering from the cold, until a single tiny paw emerged.

"Do you thin—"

I shushed Ander with a swift kick to the ankle, probably a little harder than intended. I heard him grunt, then swear.

Slowly, surely, a second paw popped up. A body

followed, so, so thin and tiny. So adorably cute, even covered with dirt and grease.

*Oh.*

*My.*

*GOD.*

The cat sniffed the air, then stepped fully out from his little nest. The animal on Ander's engine cowling was hands down the cutest kitten on the planet. Maybe even the universe.

*Look at him!*

I waited until it had tasted the tuna. Sat there patiently, until most of its beautiful kitten head was rooting around in the foil pouch.

Then I leaned in very slowly... and reached out in one smooth motion to scoop it up.

"NICE!" Ander shouted.

The cat didn't even flinch as I grabbed it. It seemed more interested in where the tuna had gone, than in the fact I was now holding it. I reached down and grabbed the tuna as well.

"Quick, get it inside," said Ander. "It's freezing out here!"

He opened the passenger door for me, ushering us into the front seat. Then he closed the hood, jumped back in, and started the engine.

"Thank *God* you didn't start the engine while it was still in there," I gasped.

"I know."

"How did you even know it was—"

"I was walking back to my car after a training session," Ander said, "and I actually heard it." He shrugged. "That thing's got a tiny little meow, but it's a *loud* meow."

I picked the cat up gingerly, holding the tuna pouch with my other hand. From what I could tell, beneath all the grease and grime, the kitten was a *he.*

"He's a hungry little bugger," I laughed.

The cat kept eating, driving his face deeper into the pouch. My heart kept melting. Eventually the heat kicked on, blowing blessedly warm air against our faces. The smell of tuna permeated the interior of the car.

"I *knew* you'd come through," Ander grinned. "You did good. Real good."

He reached out to scratch the cat behind the ears, and it actually leaned into him. My heart started melting again, only this time for different reasons.

"Where do you think he's from?" he asked.

I shrugged. "A stray for sure, probably wandered out of the woods behind those power lines."

Ander nodded. "They go on for miles. I'd imagine there are all kinds of feral animals back there."

We glanced through the windshield, past the swirling snow. Past the darkness of the distant treeline, and the unknown beyond it.

"Well one thing's for sure," my lover said matter-of-factly.

I looked back into his handsome face, his chestnut-colored hair plastered over his forehead. He was still petting the cat. It was purring now, too.

"And what's that?"

"Seems to me you've got yourself a kitten," smiled Ander.

# Forty

## CHASTITY

"A little higher, I think. Way back there. Behind the waffle-iron."

Ander reached back, easily rummaging through the section of the pantry that would normally require a chair for me. Eventually his hand closed around something, and he came back with a lime green bowl.

I couldn't help but lower my eyes a little, as I felt a pang of sorrow.

"Athena?" Ander scratched his chin as he read the name printed across the plastic surface. "I think we're gonna need to change that."

He handed me the bowl, and I filled it with one of the cans of kitten food we'd bought at the 7-11 on the way home. The little orange tabby was still at our feet, gliding back and forth between our legs. Rubbing its now-clean body happily against our shins.

"Here you go little guy."

I slid him the bowl, and the cat immediately began eating. For such a tiny thing he looked absolutely ravenous. But after scrubbing him carefully with dish-washing detergent to get the engine grease off, at least he was clean.

"Damn he eats fast. Maybe we should call him 'Greedy.'"

I chuckled at Ander. He was being cute — *really* cute, actually. And the cat seemed to love him. A lot.

"Your old cat's name was Athena, eh? After the Greek goddess?"

I nodded somberly. "Yes."

"How about Ares, then?"

I blinked in surprise. It actually wasn't half bad.

"Ares is the god of War, right?" asked Ander. "Ruled by Mars. Fire sign. That's badass." He shrugged. "Plus the cat's so orange it's practically red."

I folded my arms and tried the name out. The little kitten licked its nose and actually looked up.

"Holy shit," I smiled. "I think you just named my cat."

"Damn right I did. Plus the name honors me also, as the guy who found the cat."

"And how do you figure that?"

Ander thumped his own thick chest. "Because I'm an Aries."

We watched the cat eat for a little while longer, as Ander ransacked my fridge and freezer. Not that I had much to begin with, but he eventually came up with a pair of ice-cream sandwiches.

"Too late for ice-cream?"

I laughed as he unwrapped both, and handed me one. "Never."

Together we retreated to the living room, and sank into the softness of my sofa. It was colder than cold outside, but toasty warm in my little apartment. A quick glance at the clock told me Ander was probably sleeping over. It was a proposition that was already waking up the butterflies that lived in my stomach.

"So... tell me what it's like," I said, kicking my feet up over his legs.

"What what's like?"

I looked down my nose at him and smirked wryly. "*You* know."

Ander stretched his own legs straight, then dragged his tongue up the side of his ice-cream sandwich. It might've been intentional, or it might've been something he'd been doing since childhood. Either way, I couldn't take my eyes off him.

"Well I haven't been escorting long," he said, "so really there isn't much to tell. Most of my clients have been on the older side: women who have money but no companionship. Introverts not interested in the dating scene." He paused, considering. "A few divorcees, looking to dip their toes back in the water. Women who married young and missed their playtime — that sort of thing."

He bit into the ice-cream sandwich, looking thoughtful. For a moment I wasn't sure he'd go on.

"I've also had clients who just wanted to be taken out on a *date,* and nothing more. Women who'd wanted nothing more than to go out, and for me to hold their hand."

"Wow," I reasoned. "That's an expensive date."

"Yeah, no kidding."

"Why do you think they do that?"

"For the same reason you didn't go to *Tinder* to lose your virginity," Ander said. "Quality of the experience. Guaranteed discretion." He shrugged casually. "They're usually looking for an escape from something more than anything else."

He finished his ice-cream sandwich and licked two of his fingers. When he caught me watching, he laughed.

"What?"

"Nothing," I said, settling back into the couch. "Just... I think it's wild, that's all."

"Don't judge," he smirked. "Remember, you called *us.*"

"I know," I smiled. "No judgment here."

Ander's hands dropped to my feet. He began kneading and massaging them, rubbing them between his two strong hands.

*Oh my GOD...*

I was afraid to even groan, for fear he might stop, but my brain flooded with instant pleasure.

"Besides," he went on, "it wasn't my idea originally. Senan brought it up, and I started doing it purely for Kylie."

I had to pry myself away from my own rapture for a moment. "W—Wait, what?"

"Kylie," Ander repeated. "Senan's sister." He squinted back at me. "You *do* know about Kylie—"

"Yes," I interjected. "I do."

He nodded solemnly. "Well there's this new treatment that was helping her, recently. Has to do with electricity. Jump-starting the brain."

When he saw my mouth drop open, he backtracked a little.

"It's not like shock-treatments or anything," Ander explained quickly. "More like micro-pulses. Small currents that trigger dozens of tiny seizures, but somehow these seizures can reset parts of the brain."

"That's amazing!" I swore. "And these treatments? They're helping her?"

"They were, yes. They're very expensive though. Brett and I took care of the rent for a while, so Senan could dump all his cash into helping Kylie. But then he threw my profile up on the escort site, enabling me to give even more."

Ares came over when he was finished eating, and leapt nimbly into my lap. I started petting him, similar to the way Ander was rubbing my feet.

"Brett helps too," Ander finished, "wherever he can. We all pitch in. Like I said, the electroconvulsive therapy is expensive."

It was all so innocent, so compassionate, too good to be true. My heart ached as I pictured the three of them,

223

working hard to pay for Kylie's treatments.

But then I remembered Senan refunding my payments. Sending back all the money he could've so desperately used.

I felt like total shit.

"So that's why he works so much," I said mechanically. "That's why he's doing all those extra shifts at the warehouse."

"Yes," said Ander. "Partly."

I couldn't hide my confusion. "Partly?"

Ander squeezed my left foot, cracking my toes. It sent a wave of satisfaction up my left leg, as he struggled to find the wording.

"Yeah, well... the other reason for all the shifts is because Senan's not escorting anymore."

It was like time froze. Everything in the room went perfectly still.

"He's *not?*"

"No," said Ander. "And neither am I. Haven't been for more than a week now."

I felt elation, then guilt. An abrupt happiness, but it was tinged with regret.

"Why not?" I asked hesitantly.

Ander turned his square jaw my way, his handsome mouth curling into half a smile.

"You know why," he said simply.

The apartment fell deathly silent. Ares slept soundly, curled up in a ball in my lap.

Corrupting Chastity - Krista Wolf

"A week ago is when we met you."

# Forty-One

## ANDER

She led me into her bedroom, taking me gently by the hand. Our connection was wordless, noiseless. As silent as the heat and warmth that filled her apartment, as she undressed slowly before me.

*God, she's gorgeous.*

I watched serenely as Chastity slipped her clothes off, piece by glorious piece. In the end she rolled her tiny panties down her flawless thighs, then stepped out of them with an innocence she still hadn't shaken. She was no longer a maiden thanks to Senan, but she still had sinless mannerisms about her that I absolutely adored.

And then she undressed *me.*

It ended with her on her knees, sliding my boxers down as she went face to face with my crotch. My nearly full erection sprang upward, bouncing heavily against the side of her beautiful face. Chastity's expression was all business as she reached out and pinned it there, holding it against her cheek.

Her eyes fluttered closed. Her lips brushed its surface as she stroked it a few times in her two soft hands, before finally opening her mouth and swallowing me whole.

*This is crazy.*

I'd never felt like this before, not even with girlfriends I'd had in the past. I knew this woman a week — a week that seemed like a year. And yet somehow I was struggling with feelings that ran so deep it made my heart ache just to see her, even when she was showering every last bit of her energy and attention on me.

I dropped one hand delicately on the back of her head as Chastity went down on me. I left it hanging there, hovering back and forth. Allowing it to move up and down with every delicious push and pull, as her lips went tight and her mouth grew hot and the silky blonde hair against my palm slipped back and forth between my fingers...

*She's incredible.*

I no longer cared that Senan had her first. The only thing that mattered was I had her now. And the way the others had been talking lately, we — the three of us — would have her for a long time afterward, too.

*For as long as she wants it,* I told myself carefully. *And as long as you don't all scare her away.*

I couldn't think about that now, though. Everything was much too early. All I knew was everything we were doing felt like an actual relationship, and not just... just...

"Come for me."

Chastity murmured the words from her knees. She squeezed my thickness in her hand and nuzzled her face against my warm, heavy sack.

"I want to taste you."

The words alone made me want to explode. Her pretty blue-green eyes, staring up at me so innocently, sealed the deal.

Almost, anyway.

"Let me show you something."

I pulled her onto the bed, lifting her lithe, curvy body directly onto mine. We were face to face, chest to chest. Thighs against thighs, when I sat her upright and forced myself between her legs.

"*Ohhhh...*"

She gasped as I pierced her wetness, gliding all the way into her in a single stroke. My hands shifted her into position, as she straddled me to the core.

*So. Fucking. Tight.*

Cowgirl was something Chastity was familiar with. She moved to ride me, shifting her hips forward and back, when I suddenly stopped her.

"Stay still," I whispered. "Don't move at all."

Silence settled over her bedroom as she obeyed dutifully. The windows were frosted over with condensation, the thin panes of glass the only things separating our bubble of stillness and warmth from the roaring wind and bitter cold.

"Now... look at me."

She did, and her turquoise blue eyes were already glassed with heat. Her body was on fire from the inside out. She was dying to move. Dying to get going...

Instead I slid my hands down over her breasts, tracing her nipples gently before settling my palms on her thighs. I was *rock* hard — harder than I'd ever been in my whole fucking life. Buried as deep as possible in the tightest, most beautiful woman I'd ever had the pleasure of knowing in such an intimate way.

Our gazes were locked every bit as tightly as our bodies, as Chastity waited for me to make my move. And then I did, slowly raising my thumb to her lips. She opened slowly, taking it in. Without looking away she sucked it greedily, getting it all wet, all glistening...

Then I took it back, and slid it right over her clit.

*Bump.*

Her body jolted, and I felt it quiver. My hands were locked on her thighs now, keeping them tight. My ass was clenched, keeping myself buried so fully and completely inside her.

Slowly, tantalizingly, I began running the ball of my thumb over her swollen button. There was no other movement. No shifting, no pushing, nothing other than the deep penetration that already bound us together, as my thumb continued circling and re-circling the wet, swollen epicenter of her sex.

Her eyes gleamed, and information passed between us. Chastity knew enough that she wasn't to move. She also conveyed silently that this wasn't fair. I continued on anyway, teasing but *not* fucking her. Just thumbing her clit, rubbing it, playing with it as my member strained upward, seeking something more.

*Holy shit.*

229

My ass hovered off the surface of her bed as I stretched her from the inside. It protested not being able to move and fuck every bit as much as she wanted to buck and churn and screw back and forth over the entire length my achingly hard shaft.

Her eyes softened, as my thumb moved quicker. Slowly Chastity's body relaxed. Her nipples went impossibly hard, her skin erupting with goosebumps as I moved her closer and closer to manual release. To her credit, she didn't move a muscle. Never shifted an inch. The only exception was a slight, almost imperceptible shift backward as she got even closer to climax, and the adorable biting of her bottom lip.

*Holy fucking shi—*

I exploded a full second before she did, pumping her deep from within. My shaft pulsed and thumped, moving inside her with a life of its own. Her eyes flared as I sprayed her insides with thick, rhythmic jets of my hot seed, boiling all the way up from my balls and delivered straight into her womb.

"Oh my GOD."

Chastity's hands curled into talons, raking my rippled stomach as I thumped again and again. My fingers clamped tight on her thighs, holding her against me. Watching her through lust-crazed eyes as I kept coming and coming, filling her up.

*FUUUUUC—*

I thrashed on her pillow, my brain suddenly awash in a whole new ocean of euphoria. As planned my orgasm had triggered her own, and now she was squeezing me internally. Her inner convulsions triggered a whole storm of aftershocks, doubling, tripling, quadrupling my pleasure.

But nothing was better than the eye-contact.

Through it all we'd stayed wholly silent, almost like a staring contest where we'd both been declared the winner. It was liberating, really. The deep, unbreakable connection formed by saying and doing absolutely *nothing*... except coming our brains out all over each other.

By the time I was empty we were fused together, soaked through and through by a combination of our own sex. Neither of us minded. Neither of us wanted that part of the intimacy to be over.

*Look at her. She's just... just so fucking...*

I couldn't think. I couldn't speak. I could only wallow in what had just happened.

In the end she collapsed forward, bending at the waist. Pressing her warm breasts against my chest so she could crush her lips against mine. Kissing me like a *girlfriend*, or perhaps even more, instead of merely a lover.

"Jesus, Ander..." she murmured, snuggling into my neck.

# Forty-Two

## CHASTITY

Work.  Sleep.  Play.  It was a pretty standard balance for any healthy lifestyle, yet mine had been twisted beyond all normal recognition.  Not that mine had been normal to begin with, really.  But after a lifetime of putting in work and sacrificing any sort of social life, I couldn't really feel guilty for all the play.

And right now I was playing like crazy.

I woke up mid-dream: a swarm of butterflies were tickling my face, swirling around my head no matter how much I swatted them away.  When my eyes finally opened the butterflies were gone, and a tiny sandpaper-like tongue was licking my nose.

"Ares!"

I threw my arms around the little kitten, cuddling him as I squinted into the daylight.  Ander's side of the bed was empty.  Judging by the coolness of the sheets, he was probably long gone.

"You hungry again?"

I crossed the room naked, remembering last night. Recalling the power and control with which Ander had handled my body, and the raw heat of our mutual explosion. God, I'd never come like that. Not in that way, and not that ridiculously hard, either. It left me shaken with anticipation of seeing him again. Of exploring so many other things more carnal things I simply didn't know.

*Meow!*

I grabbed my robe and slipped it on, then made my way into the kitchen. I spied a tiny puddle near the front door, and looked back at Ares accusingly.

"Litterbox..." I said, more to myself than him. I added it to my mental checklist. "That's on the top of today's list."

My heart swelled, looking down at the little orange tabby. He was *beyond* adorable. Soft and sweet and following me everywhere.

I still couldn't believe he was mine.

*You did good! Real good.*

Ander's words echoed in my mind, bringing back happy memories of last night. I had a *cat!* And maybe even a boyfriend, judging by what he'd told me last night. I still couldn't believe he and Senan had stopped taking on any more clients. All of it, apparently, because of me.

*Maybe you have three boyfriends, then.*

The idea made me shiver. I needed to know where things stood, and where they were going. Even if they weren't going anywhere at all, it would be good to know that too.

I deserved that much, at least. To know. It's all I wanted.

*But Kylie.*

That part I felt horrible about, and I didn't even know why. It warmed my heart to think about the guys all helping out with Senan's sister. It made me want to help as well. I didn't even know her, had never met her, but if there was anything — anything at all — I could possibly do...

I stopped abruptly, as an idea floated to mind. It expanded in my head, then exploded — as my ideas so often did — into something bigger and more complicated than I could handle at this very moment.

*Later.*

I pushed the concept away, then cleaned the mess and happily fed my new cat (not just a cat — a kitten!). Then I took a shower, got dressed, and fled downstairs to get busy. The day had already started on the right foot, but it got even better as I realized Ander must've swept and de-iced my car while waiting for his to warm up. I jumped right in, turned the corner, and headed to campus.

Two classes and a grocery trip later I was back at home, setting up things for Ares. He'd never replace Athena — not in my head or my heart — but they were both children of Zeus, and now children of mine as well.

Flipping my laptop open, I got a ton of stuff done while Ares explored the apartment. He napped near the heating vents, played with the curtains, and leapt up more than once to see what I was doing. Toward the end though, I'd reached my limit. My mind was constantly wandering back to the guys again, and to what Ander had told me about him and

Senan.    Most specifically, to that one earth-shattering admission that had rocked me to the core:

*A week ago is when we met you.*

It was well past nine o'clock when I finally broke down and called Senan.  I did it fast, without thinking.  Without giving that nagging little voice in my head the chance to stop me.

To be honest, I was a little shocked when he picked up.

"Hello, baby."

My breath caught in my throat.  Even his voice was an aphrodisiac.  And the smooth way he'd called me 'baby' already had me off guard.

"Hi," I said awkwardly.  "I— I didn't expect you to be home."

"I've been home all night," Senan answered.  "Actually I just woke up."

"You've been *sleeping?*"

"I'm taking over a night shift," he explained.  "I know the guys told you about the warehouse.  Someone else needed a favor."

"Oh."

"The money's nice too, of course," he said.  "But that goes without saying."

"Senan, what are we doing?" I asked abruptly.

With the words finally said, my heart beat so loudly I'd swear he could hear it.  But on the other side of the phone, Senan only answered smoothly.  "Uhh... talking?"

"No, not that. I mean like... what are *we* doing?"

"You and me?"

I paused to take a shuddering breath. "Yes," I said. "And Ander. And Brett."

"You want the technical term for it, or—"

"I just need to know where I stand."

There was a silent pause, followed by a cough.

"How'd it go with Ander last night?" he asked, completely ignoring the question.

His voice hadn't changed at all. It was like he hadn't heard me.

"Fantastic," I smiled. "I'm the proud mom of a new kitten now, in case you haven't heard."

"He told me all about it," Senan replied. "Very cute. And how'd it go with Brett, the night before? Did the two of you have fun?"

My stomach fluttered. I took the phone down to the bed with me so I could stretch out my tired body.

"Well you know," I teased, "a true lady doesn't kiss and tell."

"Is that right?" he chuckled.

"Sure is."

"Ander and Brett told me you had fun," he insinuated. "*Lots* of fun."

"Well Ander and Brett have big mouths, then."

"Maybe," Senan allowed. "Or maybe they're just

keeping things real. Clear. Unclouded."

"Then uncloud them for me," I countered, rolling over onto my stomach. "I'll ask the question again, one more time. Senan, what are we doing?"

The silence between us stretched for way too long on his end. I took it for discomfort.

"You wanted to learn," he said eventually. "You wanted to be taught the the ins and outs of sex. Your words, not mine."

I bit my lip. He wasn't wrong.

"And so you're learning," he said. "We're teaching you. Each of us in his own way."

My stomach rolled. "Is that all, though?"

Somewhere on the other end of the phone, Senan paused again. The pause was different this time.

"No," he admitted finally. "That's not all."

My hand gripping the phone relaxed. I set it down on the pillow before me, staring at it like it had a life of its own.

"What do *you* want, Chastity?" he asked.

Now it was my turn to be speechless. In the sanctity of my bedroom, you could hear a pin drop.

"Me?"

"Yeah."

Thrown back at me, my own question seemed to weigh ten thousand pounds. I struggled with it just as much as Senan.

"I... I don't know."

"Maybe we don't either," he said. "Not now, anyway." He paused again, then continued: "Or maybe in some ways we do."

I felt suddenly foolish, interrogating him for no reason. Shaking him down for answers I wasn't even willing to give myself. But that last part. That last sentence...

"Listen, what are you doing this weekend?"

The question came out of left field. It was the last thing I expected, but I was relieved he'd let me off the hook.

"No plans, why?"

"I talked to the guys, and we want you to come over Friday night," said Senan. "If you can, bring a bag too."

I could feel the heat inside me, rising again. Rousing the butterflies.

"An *overnight* bag?"

"Yes. With warm clothes. Outdoor clothes." He caught himself. "Oh, and bring your new friend too."

My gaze dropped to Ares, who was busy licking his paws. My heart was pounding now. Racing with excitement and speculation.

"Why?" I asked, my voice cracking. "What are you—"

"You'll see."

# Forty-Three

## CHASTITY

Friday couldn't come fast enough, at least not for me. But as with most things you look forward to, the wait seemed like forever and a day.

Eventually it came, and I was more than prepared. I got work out of the way early and spent the rest of the afternoon getting ready. Prettying myself up for whatever the guys had in mind, as well as packing for whatever mystery awaited me in the form of my overnight bag. I took some supplies for Ares as well, including the little red ball with the bell in it that he seemed to be carrying everywhere with him. If he wasn't so cute the constant ringing of the tiny bell might've driven me insane, but over the past few days I'd learned to tune it out.

When dusk fell I received a text from Senan, telling me they'd pick me up rather than have me drive there. I replied that was fine by me, and an hour later I was pulling my door closed and locking it tight.

"Let's go, punk."

Ares stared back at me from the cat-carrier, wondering what he'd done to deserve jail. I carried him down the steps and into the cold, along the walkway and straight to Senan's car, idling silently at the curb.

"Back seat okay?" Brett smiled.

He held the door for me as I ducked inside, placing the carrier on the floor. Then he jumped in beside me, pulled the door closed, and the car rolled off.

My eyes scanned the front seat, where Senan and Ander were smiling back at me. All three guys were dressed totally casual. Whatever they had planned, it sure wasn't fancy.

"So where are we going?" I asked finally, shimmying out of my coat. The interior of the car was warm and comfortable.

"About an hour and a half from here," said Senan.

I chuckled. "That narrows it down."

"Okay, ever been ice fishing?"

I blinked. "I—Ice fishing?"

"Yeah."

"No, never."

"Good," laughed Ander. He threw an elbow over the passenger seat and winked back at me. "Us either."

The car turned, then turned again, gliding onto the highway. It sped off into the darkness, leaving me at a complete loss.

"So there's this thing we do once a year," said Senan, "sometime after the holiday bullshit is over. The three of us pick something we've never done together before, and we go out and do it."

I nodded, beginning to understand. "So this year... ice fishing."

"Last year was snowmobiling," Brett confirmed. "The year before that, ice climbing."

Ander winced. "Ice climbing *sucked* by the way," he chimed in. "You should feel lucky you dodged that bullet."

"Oh I already feel lucky," I smiled charmingly, settling into my seat. "So, are we staying somewhere overnight, or—"

"We have a cabin," said Senan. "Two days, two nights. We come home Sunday evening, if that's alright by you."

Quickly I did the mental calculations to determine whether I had enough clothes, enough outdoor outfits to make it through an entire weekend getaway. I did of course, but I still double-checked my math.

"What's the cabin like?" I asked.

"Not all that sure," said Senan. "We've only seen a photo or two."

A thought suddenly occurred to me, and my eyes went wide. "It's not one of those little fishing huts, is it?" I cried in dismay. "The ones you slide out over the lake and cut your own hole in the ice?"

Nervously, Senan shrugged a shoulder. "Could be."

"Because if it is—"

They burst out laughing together, and I realized I was the butt end of their joke. I was relieved instead of angry, though.

241

"Look, ice fishing is probably not for everyone," said Senan. "So if it's really not your thing, just say the word and I'll turn around. No hard feelings."

"Does the place have heat? Beds? Blankets?"

"Yes, yes, and yes."

"Then I'm in," I said, smiling cheerily. "Make me warm and you'll make me happy."

The car rolled on, with the guys looking at each other pointedly. I had the brief, fleeting sensation of being a doe, surrounded by wolves.

"I've got another proposition for you," Senan offered.

"Oh yeah? And what's that?'

"We'll make you warm..." he said, looking back at me in the rear-view mirror.

"... and you make *us* happy," Brett finished for him.

# Forty-Four

## CHASTITY

The place was spacious and scenic — a single-room lodge built on the lake, made entirely with logs and stone. The back wall was a sprawling fireplace. Nearby, two sets of bunks were built into the walls, just opposite the island leading into the kitchen. The ceilings were vaulted. The windows, three-quarters of the way covered with snow.

Oh yeah, and the place was totally and utterly *freezing*.

"H—Holy s—shit..."

Ander flipped a switch, and the lights came on. They belonged to a single wrought iron chandelier, dropped from the log cabin's massive central beam. The rest of the place was in shadow.

"Turn on the heat?" Brett asked hopefully.

Senan laughed. He unzipped a duffel bag and tossed a lighter Brett's way. "Go ahead," he said, pointing toward the fireplace. "Let us know if you need any help."

243

Senan's extreme grin of satisfaction told me he wasn't bluffing. And by the look Brett gave Ander, I could tell the two of them weren't in on it either.

"Seriously?"

"Yeah. The fireplace *is* the heat."

I set Ares down and wrinkled my nose. "Don't tell me there's no hot water."

"Hot water heater runs off the system too," he said. "It should be plenty hot as long as we keep it stoked."

Thankfully an entire wall of the cabin was cubbied out and filled with firewood of all different sizes. Brett grabbed an armful and headed to the fireplace, while the rest of us unpacked the car.

*Ice fishing.*

I had to laugh. It was just my luck.

*With three guys.*

It wasn't exactly the getaway I'd hoped for, now was it? Then again, did it matter? The three of them had talked about it, according to Senan at least, and in the end they'd invited me along. They could've just as easily gone alone. If there was ever a 'guys only' trip, this would be it.

"We'll stock the fridge tomorrow," said Ander, dropping a large plastic bin on the kitchen table. "Until then, we have this."

He popped open the container, which was filled with snacks. I saw a few bottles mixed in. Vodka. Rum. Wine.

"You guys come prepared, huh?"

"The essentials," Ander chuckled. "Yeah."

"Speaking of essentials..."

I walked to the only other door in the entire cabin, crossing my fingers the whole time. It opened into a decent-sized bathroom. There was a toilet, thank God, and a shower. For any of them it would be a tight squeeze, but for me it was perfect.

Fifteen minutes later Brett had the fire going pretty well, and we'd put just about everything away. Ares was busy exploring his new surroundings. He looked at me a little worriedly at first, but the temperature in the cabin was rising minute by minute.

"So when does the ice fishing happen?" I asked casually, pulling the cork from an oversized bottle of wine. I looked back at the guys. "Or is that just code for something else..."

"Do we really need code for something else?" Senan asked.

I smiled coyly. "No."

"Good," he said, passing me his glass. "To answer your question though, the best time's at night. We've got a fish house rented out near the center of the lake. Should be good."

"Should also be freezing," added Brett, mock-shivering for effect.

"Yeah, well..." Senan's gaze shifted to me again. "We've got a few things here at the cabin that can warm us up."

The thrill I'd felt on the way here had morphed into an almost unbearable anticipation. I knew what the guys wanted. I knew what they needed. But while the innuendo was fun, I also desired to know the extent to which they'd talked about me. The full extent of their feelings for me.

And I especially wanted to know what Senan meant when he said '*maybe in some ways we do.*'

"So what's next?" I asked, walking through the cabin. One by one I handed them wine glasses before settling by the fire. The lingering eye-contact delivered from each of them left little doubt as to their intentions.

"Well," said Ander. "To tell the truth, we brought you here for more reasons than the obvious."

"Oh?" I asked innocently. I turned so that my back was to the fire. It felt immensely good, warming my ass.

"But first things first," he continued, holding out his glass. "We feed the hell out of this fire, and we finish that bottle of wine."

The others toasted together, raising their own glasses in salute.

"Then we need to *talk*."

# Forty-Five

## CHASTITY

The fire crackled noisily, roaring beyond its hearth. It filled the cabin with warmth and heat, to the point where we'd been stripping off clothes to keep from sweating.

"Dude, enough wood already," chuckled Ander.

Brett stopped mid-stride, holding two fresh logs. He paused, dropped one, and tossed the other one into the fire.

"Dick."

"I like it warm," he shrugged. "Besides, when we crash out later we'll want a good base of embers to last through the night."

From my cozy corner of the couch, I drained the remainder of my second glass of wine. The dregs at the bottom were a rich, dark purple. Or maybe that was just the lighting.

"So, big question," said Senan, breaking the silence. As he spoke, all eyes suddenly shifted to me. "What sort of feelings do you have for us?"

My head swam, but in a good way. In the way that said I was in the zone — pleasantly tipsy, feeling no pain.

"I think—"

"Better question," asked Ander, interrupting me. He steepled his fingers together from the opposite couch. "Which *one* of us do you have feelings for?"

It was a strange question, especially since I hadn't answered the first. I expected the others to glance back at him in annoyance, but their attention was still on me.

"All of you," I said simply. "I have feelings for every one of you."

Ander nodded, while Senan didn't move at all. Brett shifted in his seat, stretching his long, muscular arms overhead. He was practically shirtless in his thin, sleeveless Tee.

"We're not talking sexually," he said. "Those feelings are obvious. We're talking... beyond that." He struggled a moment, searching for the right wording. "What we mean is—"

"I think I'm in love with you."

The words tumbled out, one right after the other. They landed in the middle of the cabin like an alien spaceship, simply falling out of the sky.

"I do you know," I reiterated. "Love you, I mean. It's not even a question."

"Who?" Senan squinted.

"All of you."

The guys sat up a little in their seats, fidgeting and exchanging glances. I saw excitement in their expressions. Acknowledgment. Even relief.

"How can you love three people at once?" Brett challenged.

I shrugged. "Honestly, I don't know. I've never been in love with anyone before. I thought I had, but it was nothing like this."

"Then how do you—"

"I just *know*," I countered. "I can't stop thinking about you. The things we did, sure, but also the men you are. Senan, you're sweet and strong and so incredibly hard-working. And Ander, your self-sacrifice is equally amazing." I turned to Brett. "You — holy shit, you're a male version of *me*. Only way hotter and way more fun and confident than I could ever be."

A log snapped somewhere in the fire, sending a spark through the center of the cabin. It disappeared even before it hit the floor.

"There's so much I admire in all three of you," I smiled gently. "Plus you all rock in bed. From my perspective, anyway. It's not like I have anything to compare it to."

"Love," Senan said flatly. "That's a pretty big word."

"It sure is."

"You think you *love* us," he repeated.

"Yes."

He scratched at his beard, studying me intently. I felt like I was being quizzed. Or tested.

"I thought I'd been in love a couple of times," I went on. "But I was wrong. Whatever it was, it was nothing like this. Nothing like the emotions you bring out in me. The way you make my heart feel."

"So if you had the chance to date one of us, who would it be?"

"That's easy," I said. "It'd be all of you."

Senan let out a short laugh. Brett and Ander however, were staring back at me with the same strange look. Translated wordlessly, the expression said: *good answer.*

"So you wouldn't choose?"

"No," I said flatly. "It'd be all or nothing."

"Why?"

"For one, I met you all at the same time. I even fell into bed with you together." I stared into the flames and shrugged. "I could never parse out my feelings like that. Not after everything we've been through."

Ares chose that moment to leap into my lap. He circled clockwise three times — that was apparently his thing — before settling down into a tight little ball.

"I probably sound stupid, right?" I laughed nervously. "Like a lovesick little girl. After all, who in their right mind—"

"What would you say if we wanted you also?"

The words came from Ander. I turned to face him, absently stroking the kitten. "Wanted *what?*"

"Wanted you," Senan iterated. "All three of us. As a trio."

My mouth was suddenly dry. I looked down into my glass, wishing it were full again.

"I'd say you *had* me already," I joked, "as a trio. Or don't you remember?"

"What would you say to being our girlfriend?"

The fire crackled. The flames danced.

Deep in my chest, my heart was soaring.

"Are you serious?"

They nodded together, quietly, in unison. Their faces were mirthless.

"You want me to date all *three* of you?"

"You're dating all three of us now," Brett pointed out. "What would be different?"

I glanced down at the floor for answers. There weren't any.

"I– I guess not, no, but–"

"We talked about this," said Senan, "and we all decided we want the same thing. We want *you*, Chastity. We want to cement what we've been doing together, and make it concrete. Exclusive. Real."

"It's real already now," Ander jumped in. "I guess what he's saying is we call it something. We declare it. Say yes, and you'll be our girlfriend."

*Girlfriend...*

The word dropped with all the impact of a thunderclap in the back of my mind. At the same time, it made me shiver.

"The bad news for you is you'll have three asshole boyfriends," Brett joked. "Three individual dumbasses to make happy. Three different guys to take care of."

"Speak for yourself," Ander spat.

"But also," added Senan, ignoring the jabs. "Three guys to take care of *you*."

# Forty-Six

## SENAN

"So how would we do it?" she asked, her face all flushed from the fire. On the couch she looked feminine and beautiful, her smooth legs peeking out delectably from her sleep-shorts. Her lips were full, stained red from the wine. I wanted to taste them in the worst way.

"The same way we've been doing it, pretty much," I told her. "You'd be our girl. We'd do with you the same things we'd do with any girlfriend of ours. Only with four people involved, we'd also have the option of doing them together."

"And doing *me* together, too," she added carefully. "Am I right?"

She looked frightened, but only a little. The rest of her expression was excitement and exhilaration. Maybe arousal.

"You're right," said Ander. "Actually you're *very* right."

"So I'll be busy," Chastity grinned wryly.

"Three times as busy as any other girlfriend," I nodded. "Yes."

"Consider it one of the benefits of having to put up with three of us," Brett smiled. "I mean if you're going through all *that* trouble, there have to be some perks too, right?"

"Perks," she giggled. "Got it."

I squinted at her through the shadows. "What, you don't believe us?"

Chastity shrugged a sexy shoulder. "Sounds too good to be true."

"Why?"

"Because look at you," she said, sitting up. "The three of you should be statues, chiseled from marble. You should be in a museum somewhere, or being sketched by art students."

"Been there, done that," said Ander. "It's *way* too boring."

"Seriously though," she went on. "Any one of you could have any girl you wanted. Just because—"

"Delaina, *listen.*"

I saw her stiffen immediately, at the mention of her actual name. After a moment of silence she turned to look at me, her eyes shining in the firelight.

"Each of us has had girlfriends," I told her. "We've all had long-term relationships. Nothing's panned out for us. Not until now."

"He's right," Brett agreed, taking over. "Ninety percent of the women who are attracted to us for our looks end up being shallow, superficial, lame. Five percent are flighty and weird. Another four percent, just plain crazy."

"Oh yeah?" she asked. "And what about that last one percent?"

Brett smiled as she fell right into his trap. "Honey, that last one percent is *you*."

Chastity blushed — or rather Delaina — or whatever she wanted to go by. Truth be told, I didn't even care. I only needed to know she was on board.

"You really want to do this?" she asked hopefully.

"Do *you?*" asked Ander.

She searched her feelings for a moment, but a moment was all it took. "More than anything," she nodded.

Our smiles widened instantly. We couldn't hide the excitement as we got up and closed in, surrounding her on her couch. Ares didn't even stir as we took turns kissing her, our hands moving slowly and deliberately over her cheeks and face. Some of us even took two turns.

"This is crazy," she breathed, when we were done. "We're crazy."

"Uh huh," said Brett.

"I—I can't believe—"

I stopped her with another kiss, this one hungrier and more full of promise. It was the kiss you gave your girlfriend before you threw her over your shoulder and carried her into the bedroom.

Only we were already in our bedroom.

"You're *ours* now," I told her softly, "to do whatever we want with. And we're yours. Stop fighting it."

Our newly-appointed girlfriend smiled shyly. "O— Okay."

"And now, the first order of business in our new partnership... fishing."

I laughed as her expression went from one of heady expectation to sudden confusion. The three of us got up and began pulling our clothes on. Boots, snow-pants, gloves — everything.

"You're fishing *tonight?*"

"You are too, if you want. The fish house seats four."

"Gear's already out there," Brett confirmed. "Grab that key on the table, I think we're number sixty-one."

Chastity shook her head mechanically. "Not tonight," she laughed. "And not after *this* much wine. I'll go with you tomorrow though."

I smiled and nodded. "Good enough."

"As for him," she said, pointing at Ander. "I need him for something, just a little while longer."

I raised a semi-jealous eyebrow. "Something?"

Chastity rolled her eyes. "I promise to let him go after an hour or so. He can catch up with you then."

All at once Ander stopped dressing. He looked over at Brett and I, then laughed.

"What? I don't know anything about this, I swear."

"He doesn't," Chastity confirmed. "Trust me."

We finished putting our stuff on and left, pausing briefly at the door. "Sixty-one," I said to Ander. "Don't forget."

"I won't."

"Have a fun... *hour*," I said smarmily.

The last thing I saw was Ander kicking off his boots and stepping out of his snow-suit. But just before the door closed...

"Wait!"

I turned again, and she was in the doorway. Wet, pink lips. Gorgeous blue eyes, slightly glassy from the wine. For a moment I was seriously reconsidering fishing.

"How long have you known my actual name?" she asked.

I jerked my thumb over my shoulder at Brett.

"Since the first day of school," Brett said matter-of-factly. "Faculty registry. Simple search."

"Oh," she chuckled. "Yeah, I should've figured that."

"It was also all over your mail," I smirked. "That stack of bills, scattered across your kitchen table."

She tilted her head slightly to one side, pursing her lips together in consideration before continuing.

"Can I ask a favor?"

"Shoot."

"Can I still be Chastity for a little while?"

"I dunno," I shrugged. "Delaina is a beautiful name.

But if that's what you really want..."

"It's just that she's having a lot more fun than Delaina ever did."

The wind gusted, blowing her blonde hair back from her angel-like face. Taking her chin between my fingers, I leaned in and kissed her softly goodbye.

"For now she is," I winked as I closed the door.

# Forty-Seven

## CHASTITY

I closed the door slowly and turned around, still reeling from Senan's kiss. By the time I did, Ander was already inching his boxers down his tan, muscular thighs.

"Whoa!" I chuckled, holding up a hand. "Hang on."

He stopped, looking back at me quizzically. "What?" he asked. "I thought you wanted me for an hour?"

"Yes, but to show you something."

He blinked back at me with a wounded expression. Like a kid being told to stop opening a Christmas present.

"I just... wanted to..."

My sentence trailed off, with me still staring at his thighs. In a move that was most likely strategic, he had his shirt pulled up over his stomach. It showcased his beautiful eight-pack of quivering abs, still warm from the fire. And that sexy 'V' of his lower torso, the one that only a personal trainer might work on. The one that pointed dangerously lower...

259

"Alright," I sighed. "You're not going to be focused anyway, so we might as well take care of you first."

I sauntered over and dropped to my knees, taking his boxers down with me. Then, right in the middle of the kitchen, I took him straight down my throat and began blowing him.

"MMMmmm..." he groaned.

For the next three or four minutes I went down on him expertly, pulling out all the stops. Using every trick I had with my mouth and tongue, plus a few using both my hands. Ander moaned, sifting his fingers through my scalp, pulling my hair back into a ponytail so he could get a better view of what I was doing. It ended with one hand on his balls, squeezing gently while he exploded into my mouth. Draining him completely of every drop of his deliciously warm seed, until he was spent and satisfied, his legs practically buckling.

"What the *fuck,* Chastity," he gasped, his eyes fluttering as I finally let go of him. He eyed me suspiciously. "You've been holding out!"

"Yeah yeah," I chuckled. "When you're a virgin you do a lot of that. So you get to be good."

"Well you'll be doing it again," he insisted firmly. "You'll be doing it often."

"Fine," I agreed, leaping to my feet. "Now put yourself back together and come over here."

I pulled my laptop from my bag, laid it on the table, and opened it up. Ander looked surprised.

"I thought we said no work stuff?"

"Maybe you guys did," I shrugged. "I wasn't at that meeting."

He chuckled and pulled his chair over, as I pulled up a few screens. Over the next ten minutes I showed him the prototype for *Train Direct*. Not the workout part, with the unfinished peer-to-peer software. But the meal plan and calorie-logging software. The nutritionist lookup and motivational forum. But most of all:

"This part here," I said, "is a virtual calendar you can log into from anywhere. If I tweak it enough, and finish the last ten or fifteen percent of the programming, we can open it up to any and all gyms to do their scheduling."

He nodded slowly, taking it all in. He was more than interested, he was fascinated.

"So can people looking to train log in also?"

"When I finish it, yes," I said. "That's the idea. Your gym gives each member a login, and they can go schedule their own training sessions with any personal trainers available at that particular gym. The best part is it takes all the work out of the gym's hands. The trainers hook up directly with their clients to schedule sessions online. And if you're looking to train with someone specific, you just pull up the calendar to see his or her availability."

"This is fucking genius."

"I know."

"Tell me again why you didn't finish it?"

"Because the people I work with have short attention spans," I said morosely. "Most of them, anyway. They flit like dragonflies from project to project, never following through

261

with anything."

Ander turned to look at me. "So you're gonna do this yourself?"

"I think so. It's mostly done, to be honest."

"So what do you need me for?"

"I need you to go over the features with me. Tell me what else I need, and what I *don't* need." I poked him. "You're a personal trainer. You know this stuff." I paused to point at the screen. "I'm a coder. I know *this* stuff."

He nodded, smiling broadly, even letting out a short laugh. "This is amazing. Seriously. If you could get this out there—"

"Then you can help me sell it, gym by gym," I grinned back at him. "That's another thing I'd use you for. Sales."

"Use me, huh?"

I leaned in and kissed him on his stubbled cheek. "In more ways than one."

# Forty-Eight

## CHASTITY

I sent Ander away after a good forty-five minutes' worth of notes, with instructions to send me Brett right away. He geared up for the frozen lake and took off, my body still tingling from his goodbye kiss on the way back to my laptop.

A half-hour later, Brett showed up. He stomped the snow off his boots, pulled off his gloves, and headed over to warm himself by the fire.

"C'mere when you're ready," I said, barely looking up from my laptop. I was too busy typing, too busy jotting down the stream of ideas flowing through my mind.

"Nah uh," he said playfully. "Not until I get some of what Ander got."

I frowned playfully, then took off my glasses. "Seriously?" I chuckled. "Do you guys tell each other *everything?*"

"When it comes to our girlfriend?" he smiled, unzipping his snow-pants. "Yeah."

263

I let out my best mock-sigh as I made my way over to the fire. His body felt good, cool in my hands. Especially his backside, which I assumed was frozen from sitting in the fish house, staring at a hole in the ice.

"You catching anything out there?" I asked, working his boxers down.

"Does it matter?" Brett chuckled.

"No," I conceded. "Here. Get on the couch, it'll be more comfortable."

I pushed him to the cushions, then climbed between his cold, pink-hued thighs. At least he felt warm, gliding past my lips. It made me warmer still, sucking him with all the heat and enthusiasm I'd given Ander. Using my tongue, my hands, even my hair, to boost his arousal and add to the whole experience.

Not to mention make it all happen faster.

He lasted only slightly longer than his friend and roommate, gripping me tightly as he fired his load straight past my lips and down my throat. I took as much of it as I could, stopping to swallow only once before continuing to finish him off and drain him dry. It was strangely triumphant, feeling his body loosen up. Seeing him go from tense and borderline shivering to feeling warm and sated and totally relaxed.

"There now..." I said, wiping the corner of my mouth sluttily with the back of one hand. "Feeling better?"

"Much," he sighed.

"Brain clear? Mind focused? Ready to work?"

He nodded sleepily. "Two out of three, maybe."

"Good enough," I told him. "Now follow me into the kitchen. I'm gonna need your opinion on the best way to code something."

He did, and for the next hour or more I showed him the series of modules and function calls that made up *Train Direct's* interactive, web-based calendar. Brett was duly impressed by most things, and pointed out some flaws in others. He had some ideas for shortening things up, and consolidating inputs. Side by side, we also went over a rough outline of the tables in the database.

"I can help you with this when we get home," he said definitively, as we wrapped things up. "Ander thinks it's a fantastic idea, too."

My spirit soared. "He does?"

"Yeah. Not shitting, either. I'd tell you if he thought otherwise, but he seemed really ga-ga over it."

I beamed, both inside and out. I wanted to dance through the cabin. To spin outside and do snow angels, then rush back to the fire again. I was so amped up I was practically vibrating. That's how good it felt to be working on this project again.

"Wanna come fishing for a little bit?" Brett offered. "It's not *that* cold. Plus there's a space heater in there, and I'm pretty sure you could wrangle the seat next to it."

"Thanks," I said, "but I really want to keep working on this." I held up a hand. "Through tonight at least," I added, "while you guys are fishing."

Brett nodded in understanding, even as he gathered his gear. "I know how it is. You've got code-brain."

265

"Big time," I said. "But tomorrow?" I placed a finger into one corner of my mouth and threw him my sexiest look. "Tomorrow I'm all yours."

"All *ours* you mean," he winked.

"Yes," I said, as my heart skipped a beat. "That too."

My lover zipped up his jacket and laughed. "Alright. Get back to work and keep that fire fed. I'll tell the guys."

"Thanks baby," I said, throwing my arms around his neck and kissing him.

*Baby...*

I hadn't used the word in forever. Not like this. Not in any meaningful sense.

But God, it felt so *good*.

"Oh," Brett added, pausing at the door. He jerked a thumb outside and gave me a roguish grin. "Did you need me to send Senan back here for an hour?"

I sank back into the chair, stretching my arms overhead. I felt flush. Warm. Happier than I'd been in forever.

"Not unless he wants to," I winked back.

# Forty-Nine

## CHASTITY

I worked for the next several hours on my little project, twisting the source code away from its original 'live workout' purposes and into something more schedule-orientated. There was tons to be done. People I needed to call and talk to.

But that would all have to come after the weekend.

As it was, the guys didn't return until well into the wee hours of the morning. They were cold and frozen, which was good news for me because it meant helping strip their gorgeous bodies down to practically nothing so they could stand by the fire.

"You're in *my* bed tonight," Senan ordered, pointing to me and then one of the bunks. "The others already had their fun."

Not long afterward we were beneath the blankets, kissing like soulmates, rolling around in the shadows of the bottom-most bunk. I warmed him with the heat of my naked body, climbing onto his huge chest and laying my thighs atop his. Senan absorbed my warmth for a while before rolling me over, at which point my legs spread automatically in anticipation of the thrashing that was yet to come.

Instead, he made love to me slowly, leisurely, grinding himself into my dripping folds while basking in the heat boiling up from my core. I was a lot hornier than I'd realized. Going down on the others had me all worked up, but in focusing on my laptop I hadn't realized the extent to which I really, *really* needed to get drilled deep.

*And you're their* girlfriend *now.*

I turned as Senan entered me from behind, spooning and screwing me at the same time. On the opposite wall, Brett and Ander slumbered away. For the first time, it didn't feel the slightest bit weird doing this in front of them — even if they hadn't been sleeping.

We passed out shortly after bringing each other off, Senan's big arms draped over me protectively while the fire crackled away. The last thing I remember was staring into the embers. Thinking about how much my life would change once we got home, now that I was officially the shared girlfriend of three overeager, oversexed men.

Then I passed out and slept like the dead.

I woke to the smell of breakfast, which included not just sausage and eggs but also pancakes too. Apparently someone had gone to the store. The fire was still going — resurrected by whoever it was who'd gotten up first — and the cabin was still warm and toasty.

"Mmmmm..." I smiled, dragging the blanket from Senan's bed with me and draping it over my shoulders. "That smells *good.*"

We ate just before lunchtime — that's how long we'd slept. After that we took a walk along the lake, followed by a ride into town, followed by the standard cute little shopping trip that came with just about every weekend getaway. The guys humored me patiently while I picked out mementos and tchotchkes, then stopped at a local grocer to stock our fridge. We didn't buy heavy, though. We were only staying one more day.

*They're right you know,* the little voice in my head admitted. *You're doing the same things you'd do with any boyfriend.*

In that respect it was just like dating one guy, only times three. There was three times the laughter, three times the corny jokes. Three times the hand-holding, and even three different people to carry everything I didn't feel like carrying. That part I especially liked.

In the end we returned to the cabin, where the guys made dinner. They'd caught a single lake trout between them, and we split it four ways. They also blamed me for 'distracting them' before pan-frying a porterhouse and splitting that up as well.

"You'll catch more tonight," I giggled, vowing not to pull them away this time. "I promise."

Senan screwed the cap from a beer and pointed an accusatory finger my way. "We'd better."

We drank a little, talked a lot. Went over a bunch of different stories from our pasts, and spoke a bit about our future. As the night wore on though, it became more and more obvious the guys were stalling. Like they weren't in a rush to go anywhere, anytime soon.

"So are you ice-fishing tonight or what?" I asked finally, bringing the latest round in from the kitchen. Brett was still face-down on the couch, with Ares sound asleep on his back. Ander was busy feeding the fire. "Not that you need to be sober to do it," I chuckled, "but pretty soon nobody's going to be able to even bait a hook."

Nobody answered. Everyone — including the kitten — remained pleasantly motionless.

"If you don't want to go fishing, I vote you take me out for ice cream," I announced. "It's hot in here, and I could really go for some."

Senan met me halfway, taking the beers from my hand. He set them down on a side table and slid both hands over my ass.

"I can only think of one way you're not going to distract us tonight."

He kissed me so hard I actually whimpered, his hands clawing my ass with such possessiveness it left absolutely no question as to who owned it. I was suddenly breathless. Instantly wet.

*Ohhh... wow.*

Then his hands slid down my pants and my whole body melted into him.

"Still wanna go out for ice cream?" he asked teasingly. "Come to think of it, I think Brett has some in the freezer."

"I do," Brett chimed in. He rose to slide in behind me. "Of course, we could forget about fishing, forget about going out..."

270

His mouth nuzzled my neck, tracing a wet line along my shoulder that left me shivering all over.

"... and we could stay in and ravage you instead."

*Ravage me.* The words were hotter than hell. They invoked images that were so strong, so filthy, I wanted them more than anything.

"Hmmm..." I teased, moaning into Senan's mouth. "What flavor you got in the freezer?"

Another hand clapped itself over my ass so abruptly I jumped and gasped.

"Strawberry blonde," said Ander, closing in tightly from the other side.

# Fifty

## CHASTITY

"Alright... who's next?"

Ander withdrew from me, his naked body sweating profusely, his spent manhood still long and thick even after his roaring orgasm. It glistened in the firelight, with his juices and mine. Down between my legs though...

Down between my legs I was *full.*

Brett spun me his way, lifting one leg over his shoulder to take his place between my thighs. He pushed the bulbous head through my tender folds, which were already warm and wet and welcoming...

"Look at her, she's a mess."

I grabbed his ass tightly, pulling him into me. Reveling in how good it felt to have him spear me deep, taking the place Ander had just withdrawn from.

"God," he gasped, his eyes unfocusing a little as the heat and pleasure of being inside me washed over his brain.

"She's like a million degrees, too."

One stroke became two, then four, then six. In no time he was pumping away, driving his big dick deep into my body. Screwing me as I lay back and whimpered, my wet lips and open mouth waiting for whoever came next.

It had been like this all night: ever since they'd abandoned their plans to go fishing and gathered every one of the pillows and blankets in the center of the floor. They took turns feeding the fire, and the heat felt absolutely orgasmic against my naked skin. They also took turns feeding me, one by one. Kneeling beside my head, sometimes two at a time. Driving their warm, swollen manhoods into my wet, willing mouth.

"This is insane," Brett grunted, rolling his hips on the downstroke. "It's never felt this good," he breathed, "this so fucking *amazing...*"

I was on my back, my head lolled to the side, as I had been for the past half hour. I sucked them greedily, at all different angles. Gripping them. Guiding them...

And through it all, the non-stop fucking. The feeling of being constantly penetrated, of spreading my legs. The friction of a hard shaft gliding in and out, burying itself achingly deep inside me. Hands on my breasts. Cupping. Grabbing. Thumbing my nipples, or rolling them between fingers.

*Oh my God...*

The guys, switching off. Each taking their own glorious turn between my thighs. And I was *so* wet. Dripping wet, saturated, the blanket beneath me soaked with my own arousal.

And now, also with the significant deposit Ander had just given me... and soon enough, the ones I'd drain from Brett and Senan, as well.

"*Mmmpph...*" I moaned uncontrollably. "*Fuck...*"

I was sweating. Gasping. Whimpering softly. Nuzzling against the hands caressing my face, guiding me from one big dick to the next. I was screwing back against Brett. Sucking Senan deep into my throat, when suddenly

*SLAP!*

Brett's hand came down on my ass, hard enough to sting like crazy. I pulled Senan away, just long enough to look down. The pain was pleasure. The sting was exquisite, especially against the heat of the fire.

And then I saw it: the handprint on my ass. Four fingers and a thumb, outlined in angry red. And in the middle, still white, where the pads of those fingers would be.

"Do that again."

Brett raised a mischievous eyebrow, then raised his arm. He lowered it again, whipping his hand forward at the last second. Slapping the perfect curve of my humping, squirming ass, this time with an even louder SLAP than the first.

*Oh hell fucking YES.*

His eyes found mine, and through the bounces I managed a nod. He spanked again, then again after that. Each time I winced. Each time it made me hotter and more turned on.

"You like that don't you?"

274

Senan was leaning down now, whispering in my ear. I was still stroking him, somewhere near my cheek. I nodded fervently.

"We're gonna have to remember that," he smiled, and kissed me so deeply it took my remaining breath away.

For the next several minutes I was spanked, fucked, kissed and fed. The two of them pulling my legs back so they could take turns on the other ass-cheek, leaving bright red handprints on top of the handprints already there.

*SLAP SLAP SLAP!*

It was just hard enough, just forceful enough. It gave me the belly-churning sense of a well-deserved punishment for being such a bad, bad girl, and somehow through the sting and the pain it turned me on more than I'd ever been turned on in my entire fucking *life*.

"Roll her over," I heard Ander say. "I want some too."

I was on my stomach in seconds, as someone jammed a pair of pillows beneath my abdomen. My ass was exposed now, raised up a little and facing the roaring fire. I could feel the skin going pleasantly numb, my womanhood swollen and sated and full. I gasped in anticipation, as the guys did nothing.

"What now?"

"We need a paddle."

"Or a spoon or something."

I shivered all over. They still hadn't touched me yet.

"Or we could just keep using our hands."

*SLAP!*

The strike was so flat, so dead on, I felt my entire ass jiggle. I folded my arms beneath my chin. Closed my eyes...

*SLAP! SLAP! SLAP!*

This time I cried out, letting them know it hurt. But also wriggling my ass, begging for more. Letting them know the hurt was okay.

"I have an idea..."

Somewhere behind me the side door opened, and there was a rush of cool, delicious air. The guys groaned in pleasure as it swept over us, like stepping into an air-conditioned room on a hot summer day.

"Whatever you're doing," I heard Senan say, "leave that door open a crack when you come back."

*SLAP! SLAP!*

Two hands. Two cheeks. One from each guy, almost simultaneously.

*Holy shit holy shit holy shi—*

*SLAP SLAP SLAP SLAP!*

The barrage was thrilling and beautiful, and it hurt less and less. My ass was on *fire!* It felt like the heat your skin would give off after getting the worst sunburn, yet without the underlying pain.

"Here..." I heard Brett say.

Suddenly, abruptly, something glided over my ass like white-hot fire. It smoothed its way over both cheeks, and then suddenly I was dripping some more.

Or rather, *something* was definitely dripping.

276

"That's crazy," I heard someone chuckle. "Look at her legs, quivering."

They were quivering, but it was the feel of the liquid heat on my two spanked cheeks that had my interest more than anything else. I felt more liquid between my legs. Like I was gushing. Exploding—

And that's when I realized they were sliding a snowball over my skin.

"*Ohhhh...*" I sighed contentedly. Now that I knew what it was, I could actually feel the cold. I could make out how soothing it felt against the heat of their strikes. "*Yes...*"

I glanced over my shoulder. The snowball was already melted by half. Senan produced another one, and he started doing the other side. The water dribbled down my cheeks and onto the blanket beneath me. It also pooled in the little valley created when I'd clamped my legs together.

"Enough play," I heard Senan grunt. "I need to *fuck* her now."

He said the word roughly, grunting it through clenched teeth. With my legs still pinned together he straddled me from behind. His thighs clamped mine shut. Using one hand, he guided himself forward and downward, parting me easily.

"You feel incredible," he growled as he penetrated me. A hand slid its way upward, resting just beneath my chin. It pulled me back enough to kiss him, as the warm, heated flesh of his abdomen pressed tightly — and rapturously — against the now-frozen skin of my blistering hot ass.

I grunted as he began riding me, screwing his entire

277

body into mine. I felt almost like an animal, being broken. I wanted him to keep going, to keep riding me forever.

"Yes..." I sighed. "You feel—"

But it was already too much for him. Too hot. Too ridiculously tight.

"FUUUUUUUUUUUCK!"

Senan erupted at the end of his last stroke, burying himself deep inside me, filling my womb. The hand under my chin tightened, his sexy breath tickling my neck as he convulsed and spasmed, over and over again, filling me with a whole night's worth of teasing and trading and pleasure.

*GOD...*

He went on for a long time, jamming his tattooed body tightly against me. I could feel him contracting, over and over. Enjoying every last spasm as he filled me up, every tiny twitch and pulse until the last of them had finally subsided.

Then my own orgasm rumbled through my body like thunder.

*Unnnnghhhhh....*

The pleasure came in waves, and those waves were amplified by the fire-and-ice sensations of having my backside so thoroughly and completely dominated. I bucked back against Senan, milking him from within. Screwing my hands into the blankets in front of me, while the pillows beneath my stomach kept my rear-end pinned tightly against his warm, quivering six-pack.

*Yessssss...*

I came so hard I felt my back crack, and that made me

laugh. Even the laughter felt good, as eventually our mutual pleasure subsided to the point where our bodies were finally ready to kiss each other goodbye.

"Wow..."

My latest lover rolled off me, and I felt Brett's eager hands taking their place on the swell of my hips.

*Three boyfriends, remember?*

Yes, I definitely had to remember that little fact.

*Sometimes at once.*

Holy shit.

"Your turn now?" I asked huskily, rolling my ass backward as I threw Brett a tired wink.

He laughed merrily, like a kid on Christmas.

"You know what they say?" he smiled. "Best for last, right?"

My eyes rolled back dreamily as he surged into me, his face plastered with the best of all possible grins.

# Fifty-One

## CHASTITY

Evan rubbed his eyes in the top left corner of my screen, yawning as he did so. He'd wanted to postpone the call. Push it off to next week or something, because he didn't have anything 'new to report on.'

But I did.

"Alright," Claudia said, returning to her own corner of the viewing screen. "I'm back! Sorry about that, had to run off to—"

"No worries," I jumped in. "We're all good now. Jaime popped on also while you were away, so we've got a full house."

Jaime smiled and waved to the rest of the group, pushing his mop of hair back over his forehead. Before he could say anything else, I kept the ball rolling. If I took too long to speak, the small talk would start and we'd be talking about a vast array of mundane bullshit for the next twenty minutes.

"So you guys ready for some news?"

"Oh yeah," Evan replied. "Your text sounded a little mysterious, but intriguing."

"Nothing intriguing or mysterious about it really," I said. "The fact is, I found a buyer for our project."

From their little windows on my laptop's screen, all three of them appeared taken aback. It was a little comical.

"An investor?" Claudia's eyebrows went up. "Really?"

"No, not an investor," I corrected her. "Someone who wants to outright purchase *Train Direct*. They want the source code, the url for the website, even the server we've been using." I paused for an intentional moment. "Or rather, the server we *haven't* been using."

"Everything?" asked Evan, surprised. "They want it all?"

"Yes."

"That's... that's good!" Evan nodded.

"Sure is."

"So we're *selling?*" gasped Claudia. She couldn't hide her excitement. "W—Who's the buyer?"

"Me."

If they were excited before, they were absolutely shocked now. The top two boxes on my screen, anyway.

"*You?*" asked Evan skeptically. "You really want to buy us out?"

"If the price is right, sure."

He shrugged. "Well you already know our price."

"I do," I said slowly. "But I was figuring I'd get something of an employee discount. Let's say 25-percent?"

Evan's eyes went wide. "Whoa. We haven't even listed it for sale yet."

"So?"

"So maybe it's worth more that we were asking?" he theorized.

"And maybe it's worth even less," I said, crossing my arms. "After all, it's a non-working product. One with *competing* products. And the source code is—"

"She's right," Jaime butted in. "We don't even know that we'd get a fraction of our asking price." He sighed. "We might even get nothing."

Up on top, Claudia suddenly looked worried. It was a little funny, how fast she'd gone from being overly excited to utterly crestfallen.

"Seventy-five percent of our asking price seems pretty generous, don't you think?" asked Jaime. "And after all. It's going to a friend, right?"

Casually I moved my hands down under my desk, where I crossed my fingers on both hands. Then I waited.

"I–I guess so," said Evan. "I mean it's a little unorthodox selling it to a colleague without even *trying* to market it yet..." His eyebrows knit together. "What are you planning on doing with it anyway?"

"Not a hundred percent sure yet," I admitted. "But I have some ideas. Hopefully they're good ones."

Evan nodded, as a smile slowly curled its way across his face. "With you, they usually are."

Our once team leader took a breath and lifted his hand. "All in favor of selling to Delaina at three-quarters our ask price?"

Claudia's arm went up instantly. So did Jaime's. I raised mine sheepishly as well, for the hell of it.

"Congratulations then," Evan grinned. "You're the proud owner of this unfinished mess."

I smiled as the others cheered, and then we began the small talk. For another few minutes everyone talked about life, their jobs, their projects, their family. They talked about everything from how the holidays had been to what the current weather looked like. Finally:

"Well, I'm gonna run," said Evan. "Draw up the paperwork and we'll get it all signed, okay?"

"Already on it," I said with a smile. "And hey, thanks."

"Thanks from us too," Claudia chimed in. She let out a sigh. "I'm gonna miss these little meetings. It was always nice catching up with each other."

We said our goodbyes, each of us promising to keep in touch. It felt a little sad, ending our last meeting. Closing the last chapter on a very ambitious project that had taken up so much of my time, even my life.

But it also felt good to be moving forward again.

Claudia's corner of my laptop went black, followed by Evan's. With the two of them gone, Jaime's corner grew larger until it took up the whole screen.

"Soo..." he said slyly. "That went pretty much as expected."

"Thanks to you," I smiled. "Good job on the backup."

My coding partner let out a short laugh. "I still think you're overpaying," he shook his head. "You could've asked for fifty."

"Twenty-five's just fine," I said. "Besides, you're gonna get paid out now."

"Yeah. I'm happy about that," he admitted.

"And I'm gonna have enough to hire you on," I smiled.

Jaime's head tilted to one side. If he hadn't already suspected my intentions he knew now. His smile twisted into something inquisitive.

"Hire me on?" he asked. "For what?"

"To develop the mobile app side for the software we're gonna be working on," I told him smartly.

# Fifty-Two

## CHASTITY

For the most part, the next few weeks were a total blur. A balancing act between three different jobs and three separate boyfriends. In other words, a roller coaster of working hard and playing even harder, while trying to find enough hours in the day.

Professionally I focused on my classes, which meant getting into the groove for the new semester. I had faculty meetings. Assignment reviews. Meetings in the computer lab, where the more complicated work was done on mainframes that simulated many aspects of the business world, where students wouldn't just be programming with cutting edge tools and languages, but often updating code that had unfortunately been written in the 60's, 70's, 80's and beyond.

Personally, I had my hands full with the guys, and they made sure to take care of me. Since the consummation of our threeway relationship at the frozen lake, they'd been taking me out in ones and twos and sometimes threes... as well as taking me *home* like that, too.

I invited them over to my apartment one by one, sometimes two at a time if it were feasible. But over at their place, things got even crazier. As their girlfriend I was fair game to all three of them; open season, pretty much whenever they wanted me. That part was especially hot, because it made me feel wanted — and loved — like never before. No matter who was there, or when they'd arrived home, the guys were always happy to see me walk through their door.

For example I would fall asleep naked in Senan's bed, only to be awoken by Ander. Subsequently dragged into *his* bed and made love to, only to be roused awake by Brett. I got very little sleep, and so much sex it left my toes permanently curled. I was tired most of the time, exhausted sometimes beyond belief.

But I never once complained.

In fact, the more that I had them? The more it seemed I both wanted and needed them. The more the guys took turns screwing me silly, the more eager I was to see them, to kiss them, to jump their hard, muscular bodies and straddle them to the core, screwing them every bit as hard and as deeply as they did me.

Physically I craved them. Emotionally I was invested. We got along like best friends, in ways I sadly hadn't with any of my ex-boyfriends. Yet at any given moment one or more of us would get that lustful look in their eye, and a minute later we'd be screwing like rabbits. Sometimes wherever the hell we happened to be.

I'd been nailed all over the house, in every room, every corridor. I'd taken Senan on the pool table, which was *way* harder than it looks by the way. Ander had me in the freezing cold, our jackets still on, bent over the balcony of the front porch while waiting for a pizza to be delivered. And Brett and I had finally screwed at school — a dangerous but exhilarating romp in the stacks of the Baker Library. We'd all but gotten caught by a pair of undergraduates passing through, but I'd gotten my skirt down in time to make it look at least *probable* we were only searching for part of a lost earring.

Through it all however, every spare minute I wasn't with them I was working hard on the new iteration of *Train Direct*.

As with most projects still in the honeymoon phase, my newly-imagined version of the software was coming along swimmingly. I had the web-based interface working nicely, and the calorie counter hooked up to a constantly-updated database of the latest foods and menu items. Brett was prepping the server side of things, and making sure our hardware could handle a much larger user base. Ander was creating sales materials that would help him demo the finished product when he brought it from gym to gym, and Jaime was well ahead of me on the app design. That was his specialty, and often I hung his progress waiting on me to finish a few things on my end.

I knew two good marketing gurus, and a third who was a whiz with optimization. I also had an uncashed favor I could call in, when I was ready. If done correctly it would help garner some serious and instant exposure for us, as long as the product was polished to perfection.

By the end of the third week, Heather's wedding crashed into my schedule like a meteor I hadn't been checking the sky for. I ended up taking Senan, and we danced all night together in the same dazzling red dress he'd helped me pick out not long after he'd taken my virginity. Half my friends were

Corrupting Chastity - Krista Wolf

spellbound by how unbelievably hot he was, and the others were so uncontrollably jealous they pretended not to notice. We ended the evening buzzed and exhilarated, stumbling up to our hotel room sometime around midnight. Once there, he stripped me down to the matching bra and panty set I'd picked up just for the occasion.

I was on my knees in no time, going down on him hungrily when we were interrupted by a low knock at the door.

"Hang on a sec," he said, pulling himself from my greedy mouth. "Hold that thought."

His smile should've told me everything. I shouldn't really have been all that shocked and surprised as he opened the door... and Ander came striding right through.

"Well well well," laughed Senan, glancing back at me. "Guess whose night just got a whole lot better?"

My stomach rolled. My smile widened.

"Ummm... mine?"

My head swam with all new possibilities. Possibilities that included me having the hottest wedding night in the entire hotel — even better than the bride and groom.

Ander took one look at me on my knees — my ass all but swallowing my red satin G-string — and started unbuckling his belt.

"You didn't think I was gonna miss after-wedding sex," he chuckled, "did you?"

# Fifty-Three

## CHASTITY

*I want to meet her, Senan. Please.*

I only asked once. He didn't hesitate to deliver. It was a short drive to his mother's house – his birth place, the place he grew up in. The neighborhood was beautiful. Small. Quiet. The houses had been built a long time ago, and were dwarfed by the properties they sat on.

"Mom, this is Delaina."

His mother was a tall, thin woman who looked much older than I knew she was. Her smile was frail. Like it could break at any moment. So was her handshake, which was like closing my hand around a sculpture made of glass.

*Delaina.*

It was the first time he'd said it, really. The name sounded so strange and foreign coming out of his mouth, and yet it was surprisingly satisfying at the same time.

Senan stepped forward, leaving his mother to go back

to watching some old game show on television. She didn't even seem to notice when he reached out for me and I took his hand.

"Come. Her room's down here."

Down the hallway we went, past dozens of photos in old wooden frames. Some were of Senan and Kylie as children, smiling, laughing, playing in the sun. Sledding in the winter. Building a snow fort with those plastic block molds that made perfectly smooth snow-bricks...

The photos got older as we continued along. I saw Senan as a teenager. As a young man. I saw Kylie standing in front of a car that apparently belonged to her, grinning happily and holding up a set of keys.

*She's beautiful...*

The door at the end of the hall was open. Senan pushed through, and there she was: the girl from the photos. She sat upright near the window, in a high-backed chair. A blanket was draped over her lap. A glass of water with a straw sat nearby, a little more than half full.

"Hi sis."

Senan knelt before his sister, smiling as he took her hand. Nothing happened immediately. She didn't move an inch.

"My... friend is here," he went on. "Her name's Delaina. She wanted to meet you."

I stepped into Kylie's line of vision, but she still didn't move. I did my best to smile though. To show happiness, even though I was choking back tears.

"Hello Kylie."

Her breathing changed, or maybe it was just my imagination. Senan squeezed her hand, and I thought I detected the tiniest shift in her pretty hazel eyes.

"You have your brother's eyes," I said softly, looking closer. "They're all streaked with browns and blues. So beautiful."

If Kylie heard me she didn't show it. She sat utterly motionless in her chair, like a statue, or a mummy. They were shitty analogies, and I immediately regretted them.

"You're letting mom watch those old game show tapes again, aren't you?" Senan joked. "I told you to step up and stop her. She's seen them so many times she already knows who wins."

He stroked her hand gently, pushing her sleeve back. In that moment I saw it: the dark outline of a tattoo on her forearm.

"That's... that's the same..."

"It is," Senan nodded. "It's the same angel wing I have on my own forearm."

I swallowed hard, but couldn't get the lump out of my throat. My eyes were glassy. I had the sniffles.

"I got it after the accident," he said. "An exact replica of hers."

"That's cool."

"I wanted it to be more than cool," Senan admitted. "I had this romantic notion that if I got the same ink in the same place, and then I showed it to her, she'd have some kind of

291

reaction to it."

A tear rolled down my cheek. I swiped it away. "And... nothing?"

"No," Senan sighed. "Not that time."

"Not *that* time?" I raised an eyebrow, inviting him to continue.

"Well... she doesn't move on her own, you have to prod her. And she hasn't said a word since the accident. Not even during the rehab."

I looked back at Kylie, who was indeed breathtakingly beautiful. Her face was soft and feminine, but not entirely dissimilar to Senan's. Her hair was clean and thick and brushed perfectly straight.

"She speaks with her eyes, though," Senan explained. "Sometimes — just for a second or two, mind you — I'll get a glimmer of hope. I'll see a spark *behind* her eyes, sort of like a ghost or an after-image of the person she once was." His voice dropped lower. "If... that makes any sense."

"Of course it does," I choked. "It makes all the sense in the world."

Senan nodded, looking pleased with my answer. "That's why we keep paying for her treatments," he said. "They sure seem to do *something*. And if we get anything out of her. Anything even *close* to how she once was..."

"Then it's worth it," I finished for him. "It's priceless, actually."

I took Kylie's other hand, sniffed, then let out a short laugh. "Your brother getting your tattoo was pretty cool," I said. "However... you *really* should've stopped him from this —"

Abruptly I lifted Senan's shirt just past his navel.

"A biohazard symbol?" I laughed. "Around his *belly-button?*"

Senan rolled his eyes. In the end though, he couldn't help but laugh at himself.

"That was stupid just-turned-eighteen shit," he explained.

"That doesn't excuse it though," I needled him. "Does it Kylie?"

I turned to look, and Kylie still hadn't moved. Her gaze still hadn't shifted. Not as far as I could tell, anyway.

"Yeah, well, keep a sharp eye on him then," I told his sister. "Before he gets the Tasmanian Devil inked on his arm, or something equally cliché and ridiculous."

I rose, setting her hand back in her lap as Senan planted a kiss on his sister's cheek. As we left together I noticed a beautiful acoustic guitar with a butterfly strap, standing in the corner.

"That's hers, isn't it?" I asked as we re-entered the hallway.

"Yes," said Senan. "And thanks for that."

"For what?"

"For not using the past tense," he explained. "Most of the people who come here talk about my sister like she's already gone, or treat her like she's not there. They'd say 'that *was* hers' when pointing out the guitar." He shook his head.

293

"But not you."

"That's terrible," I said sadly.

We made our way back through the living room, saying our goodbyes. His mother smiled pleasantly and offered us iced tea, but Senan only hugged her and told her he had work, and we had to run.

"Next time for sure," I promised, adding my sweetest smile.

"Stop sucking up," Senan elbowed me as we descended the front steps.

"Hey, I'm not turning down some good iced tea."

"She makes terrible iced tea," he countered.

I was still laughing as we sank back into the car. When the doors closed however, my expression went serious.

"Senan I want to help."

"With what?" he asked casually.

"With Kylie."

# Fifty-Four

## CHASTITY

He put the key in the ignition as if I hadn't said anything at all. His face was stoic as he pulled away from the curb.

"I'm serious," I said. "I know all about the treatments, what they cost, and how the others are helping with them. And I want to help too."

My body shifted forward as his foot abruptly hit the brake. Turning the steering wheel, Senan pulled us straight onto the shoulder then turned to face me.

"You can't help, Delaina," he said. "It's a nice gesture and all, but—"

"*Gesture?*"

"You know what I mean."

"Look, I'm not asking," I said angrily. "I'm *telling* you."

There was a fire in his eyes now, an intensity that

295

almost mirrored mine. It wasn't anger though. It was something else.

*Shame?*

God, I hoped not! He had nothing to be ashamed of. He was doing the best he could, even working like crazy. Ander and Brett too. All three of them.

"You're launching soon, right?"

He was referring to *Train Direct.* I nodded.

"Then you're going to need all your money," he said. "Marketing is expensive. So is exposure. So are the ads you'll need to take out, in those first crucial weeks."

"But—"

"I don't know computer stuff like you and Brett do," he said, "but I know getting a new product off the ground takes resources. There's no way I'm short-changing your launch by accepting charity for—"

"It's not charity," I practically shouted. "It's because I *love* you!"

Senan stopped for a moment and lowered his eyes. His expression was pained.

"I love you too," he said. "I have for a while now. Maybe even since the very beginning."

"Then what's the problem?"

"The problem is I can't accept your help," he pleaded.

"But you can accept Brett and Ander's?"

He waved me off, a little more dismissively than I liked. "That's different."

"Why?"

"Because—"

"Because they're your friends? Because you've known them longer?" I spat. "So what? You wanted a team relationship, and that's what we have now. One that involves all *four* of us. Not just three."

Senan started the car again, and began driving away. I let him sit in silence for a while, giving him time to clear his head. He could've just been stewing, though. Making things worse.

"Look," I said softly, laying my hand over his. "Don't fight with me. Let's talk about this another time. It doesn't have to be now."

His inhale — and subsequent exhale — was just about all the response I was going to get.

*Great. Now he's mad at you.*

I couldn't imagine why. I was trying to do something helpful, something selfless. But the more I insisted on trying to help out, the more he pushed me away.

At first I thought he was too proud, but that didn't make any sense. He wanted to help his sister more than anything. I couldn't imagine him refusing assistance for something as stupid as pride.

*He's embarrassed.*

That didn't make sense either. Senan was fearless. Confident. I'd never seen him embarrassed about anything.

In the end, I decided it was exactly as he said: he wanted my launch to succeed. If *Train Direct* failed because I lacked resources — after having given some up — it would only leave him with another layer of blame. Plus, he was just stressed out. He was working enough for two people, and his shoulders were practically granite by the time he got home for me to massage them.

He dropped me off with a perfunctory kiss, and sped away to punch his timecard at the warehouse. Before he did he looked me straight in the eye and his expression softened.

"Thanks for today," he said. "It means a lot."

I nodded and waved, watching the street long after his car sped from view. I stood for a minute, letting the icy wind bite at my skin. I allowed it to wake me up. Invigorate me for the task ahead.

Then I dragged my ass upstairs, flipped open my laptop, and got right back to work again.

# Fifty-Five

## BRETT

I'd had many birthdays, and gone many places. I'd spent time with friends, with family. I'd partied until I was sick, then rallied and partied some more.

But nothing beat *this* birthday, all stretched out and relaxing on the couch with her.

*It's funny how things can change when you're not even looking.*

I chuckled inwardly at my own dumb adage. Was it an adage? I didn't even know. I wasn't even sure it was entirely mine.

*Either that, or you're just getting old.*

Now *that* made me laugh out loud. In an all-too-uncomfortable truth sort of way.

"You having fun, baby?"

Chastity reached up with a slender arm and traced a soft hand across my face. My stubble bit back at her fingertips.

I hadn't even shaved today.

Hey, it was my birthday. My rules.

"The most fun ever."

She was lying on top of me, my arms locked around her, the both of us watching television. It was take-out night, but not for another hour or so. I slid my hands over her tummy and squeezed, eliciting a giggle.

"You've got a lot more birthday *fun* coming, you know," she said slyly, laying her hands over mine. Surreptitiously she pushed them south, down the smooth expanse of skin just beneath her navel. My fingers felt the warmth there. The heat rising up from just below the all-too loose waistband of her favorite pink sweatpants.

Just then Ander stormed in, on his way to the kitchen. He'd been in his bedroom most of the day, working on materials for our shared project.

"Nerd alert!" he laughed, looking down on us. "You guys taking a break?"

"A much-needed one, yeah," I shot back.

He looked down as if considering joining us, then back at the television. "What are you watching?"

"Star Trek II," said Chastity. "The Wrath of Khan."

Ander laughed bitterly and shook his head. "Geeks."

"Yup," we answered in unison.

We erupted in laughter, Chastity wriggling her cute little ass even deeper into my lap as Ander frowned. He seemed torn.

"As far as Star Trek goes," I told him, "this is the Holy Grail of all the movies. Even people who don't usually watch —"

My sentence was interrupted by the loud opening and closing of the front door. Senan stomped in, looking animated and maybe even excited.

"Move in with us."

His request — which was really more of a statement — was directed at Chastity. She sat up immediately, driving my semi-boner even deeper between her cheeks.

"I'm serious," Senan said, without even waiting for an answer. "If you really want to help Kylie, if you're seriously looking to—"

"YES."

Our girlfriend's smile was bright and clear, and her expression left no doubt as to her sincerity. She'd talked to Senan through a text-message or two, but she hadn't seen him in two days. He'd been working so much, Ander and I had barely seen him ourselves.

"You will?" he asked. "For real?"

"Of course I will," Chastity grinned. She stood up and hugged him before turning around. "If that's okay with *you* guys, of course..."

"Are you kidding?" I smiled. "Hell yeah it's okay."

Ander nodded also. "We've got the room for sure," he said. "And having you around here all the time would be—"

She threw her arms around him and hugged him too. He squeezed her so hard she even yelped.

301

"You'll let me help with Kylie, right?" she asked Senan.

"The money you save on rent?" he sighed. "Sure. But not a single penny more." He cleared his throat. "But that's not why I asked. We want you here because you *belong* here. Because you belong to *us.*"

"And we to you," I winked from the couch.

"Besides," said Ander, "you're usually here anyway. Or we're there. It's about time you start pitching in on the laundry, the dishes, taking out the garbage..."

"Oh you shut up!" Chastity laughed. "I've been doing all those things anyway. Plus some of your laundry, to boot."

She had, and we'd been pretty happy about it. No one had asked her. She'd just started pitching in.

"Ares comes too, of course," said Ander with a chuckle. "If he'll have us."

I pictured the little orange tabby and smiled. Already he was significantly bigger than when we'd first met him.

"He might be a little territorial at first," said Chastity, "but he'll get used to it."

"Territorial?" Senan frowned. "What does that mean?"

"He'll piss all over your stuff," laughed Ander.

"*What?*"

"No he won't," Chastity said quickly. She threw Ander a pretend dirty look. "He might *shred* a few things... but other than that—"

She winked back at us when Senan wasn't looking, and we knew she was kidding. It was funny as hell, leaving him completely in the dark.

"So when is this gonna happen?" asked Ander.

"As soon as you big strong men can move me in," Chastity said sweetly. "My lease is month-to-month. I'd give my landlord a little notice, but he's been looking to sell the place for a while now. He was holding off while I was there just to be nice. It's a win-win."

I stood up, and we surrounded her like we so often did. This time we had reason to celebrate, even more so than normal.

"Hang on a sec," she said, slipping deftly away.

She disappeared into the kitchen, and we followed not far behind her. My stomach was rumbling. I was apparently hungry in more ways than one.

"Brett-san!" Chastity called suddenly, in her best Mr. Miyagi voice. She bowed low, and produced an ice-cream cake from the freezer. "Here is number one birthday present!"

I laughed and wiped the haze of condensation from the cake's plastic viewport. Beneath the red gel script wishing me a happy birthday, it looked delicious.

Ander and Senan however, were staring blankly at each other.

"You forgot his birthday, didn't you?" Chastity wrinkled her nose at them.

"No," Ander said instantly and defensively. Then a little more sheepishly: "Err... *maybe.*"

"We really don't do birthdays around here," Senan admitted. "I mean, we do, when we remember." He shot me an accusatory glance. "Or when someone *reminds* us."

"You're such guys," Chastity huffed. "You know that?"

"Yeah," we pretty much all agreed, nodding.

"You're lucky you're all so damned good-looking."

Senan reached for her, but she twisted away. She rubbed her stomach and looked at me.

"We're going out to dinner instead of ordering take-out," our girlfriend declared. She pointed to Senan and Ander. "And you two are paying."

My friends smiled wryly. "Fine."

"It's the least you can do to make it up to him," she insisted smartly. "And from now on, we're celebrating birthdays. None of this 'we don't do that' crap."

"Shit," Senan grinned. "She hasn't even moved in yet and she's already making rules."

"Damned straight," Ander countered. He threw Chastity an approving nod. "And I'm liking it."

"Good. Now everyone get dressed," she said, "and meet back here in ten. And you..."

She kissed me full on the lips before spinning from the room. It left me reeling with the taste of her soft, beautiful mouth.

"You get to pick the restaurant."

# Fifty-Six

## CHASTITY

"Are you ready?"

I poked my head into the living room, which had been dimmed to a soft, welcoming light. The pillows we usually arranged when I stayed over were already there, spread perfectly between the couches. Sheets and blankets too.

"After all the time you took in there?" Senan smirked. "Yeah, we're ready. Bring it on."

We'd had a fun dinner, followed by yummy ice-cream cake. Brett had blown out his candles and made his wish. And now here I was, hoping I'd be making at least some of it come true.

"And now, for your number two birthday present," I called in my Miyagi voice, then stepped into view. Sauntering sexily, I strutted halfway across the room, turned around, then bent over to lean on my mallet.

All three of the guys' mouths dropped open.

305

"Holy fucking shit."

"So you like my Harley Quinn cosplay?" I asked, my voice going low and sultry. Or rather, as sultry as I could while chewing two fresh pieces of Double Bubble.

The outfit was outrageous, as of course it was meant to be. A red and black checkered corset pushed my tits high and left my midriff bare, while the matching boy shorts were so tight they left absolutely *nothing* to the imagination. I wore black garters over white stockings that climbed high on my hip, one of them in an alternating black-and-white diamond harlequin pattern that looked cool as hell.

"Jesus, yes," swore Ander.

My sleeves were more of the red and black pattern, ending in white puffy wristlets. I also wore white face-paint with jet black eyeshadow and bright red lipstick. My blonde hair was teased all the way up, and sprayed with temporary pink highlights. Sitting on top was a floppy red jester's hat — jingling bells and all.

Oh yeah, and I had an oversized foam mallet painted brown with gold banded accents. The weapon itself weighed practically nothing, but it measured three-quarters of the length of my body.

"Who wants to hit this?" I asked, wriggling my ass in their direction.

"Me!" they said in stereo.

I turned to face them, blowing them a bright red kiss before spinning the mallet in a slow, easy circle. "And who wants to *get* hit?"

Senan laughed, while Ander grinned. Brett however,

looked like a kid lost in a candy store.

"YOU..." I pointed the mallet at him. Pausing, I blew a giant bubble and then popped it with my tongue. "Get your birthday ass over here."

He came dutifully and I shoved him playfully to his knees. Even like that he was tall enough to be staring straight at my breasts.

"Happy birthday to you." With a wicked laugh I pulled him deep into my cleavage, rubbing myself all over his stubbled face. Brett responded by nuzzling in even further.

"So let me get this straight," I teased, in my best character voice. "The three of you *really* think you can handle me?"

I threw my hips to one side, accenting the musculature of my legs. It made my ass look even tighter in my two-toned boy shorts, as I casually hooked a finger in the corner of my painted mouth.

"We're pretty sure, yeah," said Senan.

Ander shrugged and stepped forward. "Or we can die trying."

I reached out and bonked him with my mallet. He grinned and rubbed his head.

"I should probably let the three of you take turns," I teased, blowing another bubble, "so this whole thing lasts longer. So you don't all shoot too quickly, spoiling the whole thing."

"You let us worry about that," said Senan.

"Oh I'm not worried," I purred, pushing Brett's head

even lower. He was kissing my stomach now. Trailing his way downward, to where I was already sopping wet. "As long as I get to come *first...*"

I felt his hands on my thighs, sliding over my stockings. The rest of my outfit would survive, but by the end of the evening they'd probably be ripped to shreds. That was okay, I knew exactly where to buy more.

Reaching out, I crooked a finger at Senan. "Come."

Ander looked wounded. I laughed at him.

"Relax. You take your shirt off."

In less than a second Ander was scrambling to pull his shirt over his head. In the meantime I let the weapon drop from my fingers and pulled Senan in.

"There's no reason the birthday boy should be doing all the work."

I pushed my gum into his unsuspecting hand and kissed him wantonly, wickedly, grabbing hard at the back of his head. His sweet tongue traced every inch of my mouth as he kissed me back, amplifying the taste of the bubble gum. Down below, Brett was eagerly devouring me *through* my boy shorts — something that was unexpectedly hotter than hell.

*Fuck...*

My entrance throbbed against Brett's churning mouth as he pulled me in by the asscheeks. I was getting seriously into the role play, and so were they. With that in mind, I shoved Senan backward.

"I have *eyes* to look at," I said, using two fingers to point at them, "but these are better."

I reversed the fingers to point downward at my breasts, and Senan took the hint. Pulling my corset down just enough, he closed his hot, bearded mouth over one aching nipple.

*God...*

The sensation of being ravaged while still being in control was all new to me. I'd role-played like this dozens of times, but never sexually.

"You!"

Until now Ander was only watching. Now his eyes shifted upward to meet mine as I pointed out my other breast.

"I've got two of these, you know," I quipped. "And the other one's not gonna suck itself."

He was on me in a flash, and suddenly I had my hands full. Two smoldering hot mouths, working me from the front. Licking. Nibbling. Nuzzling...

*Ohhhhhhhhh...*

And then Brett, doing what he was best at down below. My boy shorts were saturated. He was sucking the juice from me there, and spitting it hotly back into the fabric as he ran his tongue *all* over the surface in slow, delicious circles...

I was throbbing. Panting. Clawing the backs of two gorgeous heads, as all three of my lovers took my body at once.

"Let's take this party to the floor," I gasped, trying my best to keep up the authority in my voice. It was a difficult task, though. Especially when every other part of my body wanted so badly to surrender.

# Fifty-Seven

## CHASTITY

They gave me exactly what I wanted, only a little differently than I anticipated. And that's because they devoured me one by one, without even using their hands.

They made me come just as I asked, only they did it three times in slow succession. I climaxed hard against the exquisite pressure of Brett's face, and my legs weren't even done shaking yet before Senan was inching my very drenched boy shorts down my quivering thighs.

I lay back, running my hands through his hair as he brought me back to the brink. His beard tickled as always, and I focused on the scratchy yet arousing pleasure it brought me as my hands curled into fists and I came for the second time.

During it all the others kept kissing me... deep, heartfelt kisses that made my very soul ache. They kissed my neck, my shoulders, my breasts too, but nothing could distract me from the heat down below. Senan brought me off with his plunging tongue, then switched with Ander, who was especially careful not to make me too sensitive, too fast.

*"MMMmmmmmm...."*

I moaned loudly, forgetting all about my character. Allowing the boys to enjoy my body, my outfit, my every dirty little asset. Ander took twice as long to bring me back to that edge between pleasure and ecstasy, and the others helped me over by *finally*, at long last, feeding me their warm, throbbing manhoods.

*Ohhhh yes.*

I devoured them greedily, lolling my head left and right. Feeling the hands of one pushing the back of my head while I swallowed the other, and then switching again and again.

"What are friends for?" I heard one of them chuckle. And that's when it hit me — my third great climax of the night. It wracked my body as I writhed between them on the floor. I was sweating through my outfit, my jester's hat gone, my stockings torn by groping fingers. But I was happy. Oh so gloriously fucking *happy*.

"Alright," I heard Ander grunt as he lifted my still-booted feet over his shoulders. "Our turn."

But halfway through guiding himself against my entrance I placed a boot against his chest and stopped him.

"Nah uh," I admonished, wagging a finger. "Not yet."

His face was a mixture of confusion and outrage. "What?" he snarled. "Why not?"

"Because he gets to go first," I said, pointing to Brett. I smiled up at my blond lover and winked at him. "It's his birthday, after all."

311

Ander paused, considering something invisible. Then, having made his decision: "Bah," he spat, dropping my legs on either side of his body. "I'm never first."

His disappointment was palpable. I decided to console him.

"Hey..." I said, crooking a finger. "Come here."

He leaned over me, leaving us face to face. His body hovered a few inches over mine.

"Always the bridesmaid, never the bride huh?"

The personal trainer seemed confused by my analogy. Instead I took his hand.

"Look, I know you lost deflowering me to a coin toss," I said sympathetically. "And now Brett's taking first crack too. But here, what if I told you..."

Pulling gently, I guided his hand between my legs. His fingers played a bit, getting coated in warmth and honey, before I dragged them even further down.

Then I covered his middle finger with mine... and pressed it firmly against my tight little asshole.

"Now *this*..." I said, teasing him by kissing along the outer edge of his ear. "This could be yours first if you wanted it."

I saw his whole expression change. He looked suddenly alive and animated.

"Really?" he asked.

I nodded my head. "In time baby," I said softly. "In time. In fact, maybe it would be better to wait a while. Stretch out the, uh... anticipation."

His shoulders slumped, but his eyes still held promise. "When exactly?"

I shrugged demurely. "Maybe for the honeymoon?"

"Don't tease."

"Who's teasing?"

"We'd definitely marry you," he whispered, just loud enough for me to hear. "All three of us. Together."

"I know you would."

"We'd find someone to perform the ceremony," said Ander. "Or shit, maybe we'd just perform it ourselves. Or even—"

I kissed him hard, wrapping my legs around him for a moment. I could feel the pulsations of his throbbing member, jutting against my belly. More than ever, I wanted it *in* me.

"I *know* you would," I repeated, my eyes deeply serious. "And that's what I love about you."

I pushed again, this time more firmly. For a second, the first part of his middle digit penetrated my nether-region, eliciting a gasp of excitement on my end... and a distinct gleam in the eye, on Ander's.

"You'll get first crack at *this*," I whispered huskily. "I promise."

"It would only be fair," he murmured, "considering I lost the coin toss last time."

"Don't fret. It'll be worth it, from what I understand."

"From what you understand?"

"Well I'm not a guy obviously," I said, "but from what

313

I hear..."

I kissed him harder, excited by the prospect. It was a private moment. A secret covenant, between the two of us.

"And you've never—"

"Nope," I smiled wantonly. "Never. Totally uncharted territory."

"I like that," Ander smiled. "I like that a lot."

I winked back at him as he climbed reluctantly from between my legs, passing me ankle-by-ankle over to the birthday boy. As Brett surged forward, plunging his way inside me, I grabbed Ander's head and put my lips right up against his exposed ear.

"I thought you might."

# Fifty-Eight

## CHASTITY

They plundered me like pirates. Divided me like spoils. I was the golden treasure to be shared between them, to be reveled in, to be cherished and made theirs.

And I wanted nothing more than to *always* be theirs.

Brett took me savagely in my Harley Quinn cosplay, screwing me with all the innocent desperation that came with fulfilling some comic book fantasy. To tell the truth, I could totally relate. I could imagine one or more of them dressing up like Conan the Barbarian. Carrying me off and ravaging me in ways only a barbarian horde could.

*Mmmmmmm...*

Senan pushed down on my shoulders, screwing me even harder into his friend. I turned my head and began blowing him, enjoying the distinct pleasure that came with their pleasure. The not-so-subtle feel of being used and dominated; of surrendering my body wholly and completely to the goal of getting them off. Of making them explode into me, onto me, all over me...

"Somebody take her before I lose it."

Brett was panting like a dog in heat as he passed me to Ander, who took his place so effortlessly we never broke rhythm. I was still blowing Senan wildly. Looking up past his dark tattoos and into his piercing eyes, the connection between us telling the story of just how hard I wanted him to fuck me next.

They flipped me over. Dogged me bent over the cushions of the couch, my face buried in a throw-pillow, crying tears of happiness. I screamed as they plowed me deeper and harder, their fingers digging into the supple flesh of my exposed ass. I was being fucked so hard I couldn't even think straight. My mind so flooded with pleasure, I felt my body going numb.

*Holy shit...*

Again they switched up, and each change brought fresh new energy to the array of sex acts being performed on my writhing, sweating body. I was spitroasted between Ander and Brett. Made to ride Senan, bouncing happily off his deeply-embedded thickness while the others stood over me, taking turns using my mouth. Everything between us was feverish and frenzied. Dirty and filthy and oh so fucking *hot.*

I came thunderously, grinding hard against a beautifully-muscled torso while screaming into another one. I was too delirious to know who was who. Too drunk on my own lust to even care. Someone pulled my hair and I came *again:* two distinct and separate orgasms ripping through my body. They left me shuddering and in tears. Shaking from the adrenaline and euphoria, until someone else reached out to pull me in their direction next.

Two hands lifted me into a chair, planting me onto another steel-like rod that throbbed and pulsed inside me. Eventually I opened my eyes. Brett had me in his arms, rocking me gently forward and back as my body recovered.

"You okay?"

I shook my head no, but smiled 'yes' at the same time. "I'll *be* okay," I sighed happily. "Eventually. I hope."

He slowed down, moving his hands more lovingly over my nakedness. The angle of the chair bent our bodies together nicely, bringing us face to face.

"I love my birthday present by the way," he smiled, dragging me in for a slow kiss. When he pulled back my makeup was smeared all over his cheeks. "Best Harley Quinn ever."

"That's probably because this Harley Quinn *fucked* you," I grinned back. "So you're more than a little biased."

"Maybe."

"Well happy birthday baby," I purred, grinding myself even deeper into his lap. I kissed him again. "Now... give me a present?"

Brett nodded distantly, and I knew the look. He was focusing on my bouncing, twisting body, and on the sensation of being inside me. He'd been holding back. Trying not to come.

Now all he had to do was stop holding back and let go.

"Inside me," I whispered into his ear, hugging him

greedily. "*All* of it."

He came in a series of breathless grunts, driving his balls tight against my churning ass. I could feel him filling me deep. The distinct twitching of his iron-like manhood, flooding me with heat and wetness as he chewed my shoulder.

"That's it baby," I cooed, clutching him against my breasts. "Just like that."

The others had given us this moment, but they didn't go much longer. Because the second he was done I was being torn from Brett's lap. Carried away and laid back down in the blankets, where the others wasted no time in filling the void between my legs.

"Birthday party's over," Ander grunted, nibbling roughly on my ear. "*Our* turn now."

He entered me excitedly, with all the pent-up passion and frustration of having had to watch for so long. I was so hot down there I was molten. I knew from the look in his eye he couldn't last long.

"What's wrong?" I teased, the moment he slowed down. "I thought you were you going to take your turn?"

I kicked my legs up playfully, wrapping them tightly around his flanks. Then I squeezed, driving him in. Taking him deeper than he wanted to go, while reaching up with my hands to run my palms over his nipples.

"You wanna come, don't you?"

Ander grit his teeth and closed his eyes. He kept fucking, though.

"C'mon, tell me," I teased. "Show me..."

I bucked some more, pushing him over the threshold. His hands shot down to my thighs, grasping them tightly as he unloaded the entire contents of his swollen, heavy balls... straight up into my already-soaked womb.

"Awww..." I laughed, holding him through his orgasm. "Did you want to go *more?*"

I touched his face and he reeled back, still mad at himself more than me. Eventually though, he relented. His expression went soft at first, before cracking into a grin.

"I'll go more later," he said evenly. The words were definitely more than a statement — they were a promise. "You just keep it hot for me."

I winked at him before delivering a very wet parting kiss. "Baby it's *always* gonna be hot for you."

He left me in a daze, open-legged and leaking. I was swollen. Dripping wet. My body stretched out and invitingly open, waiting for the last of my three lovers to slake his thirst.

"Look at you..."

Senan smirked as he lifted my legs high in both hands. Carefully he rested my ankles on his shoulders, sliding his way home between my thighs.

"This is how it's going to be now," he murmured, running himself through my dripping slit. "Every day — all day."

He pushed all the way up inside me. I let out such a long, low groan I barely recognized myself. It sounded like another person on a distant planet.

"Every night, too," he sighed, fighting his own arousal.

319

He began screwing me, doing push-ups in and out of my body. He was reveling in the heat and wetness. Relinquishing any last control he might've had, and trading it for pure, uninterrupted pleasure.

"You're going... you're going to..."

His eyes fluttered, and I merely smiled and nodded. I pulled him in tightly, clawing him against my chest.

*YES...*

Then he came, spasming over and over. Grunting unmercifully. Squeezing his ass tight as he pumped me full of his hot, sizzling seed.

And my world was finally complete.

When it was over we lay there in a tangle, chests heaving, the smell of sex hanging over us like a thick, cloying blanket.

*This is it,* I thought to myself. *This is your life now.*

I laughed, and my laughter caused the guys to all look my way. They propped themselves up on their elbows and stared at me.

"What?"

"Nothing," I said. "Nothing at all."

"You're scared, aren't you?" joked Ander.

"A little bit yeah," I admitted. "But it's a good scared. The kind of scared you feel the night before something you *know* is going to be amazing, but you just... well..."

"You really want it to go well," Senan offered.

"Yeah. Exactly."

"So you've got the moving in with three guys jitters," Brett joked.

"Not just three guys," I replied. "Three *lovers*." I laughed again. "Huge difference."

"A lot less sleep involved, I can tell you that," Ander winked.

My stomach tightened. I thought about life, about work, about the upcoming launch. But those things were insignificant in the wake of what I'd accomplished here. Not just finding love at the end of a very long road, but finding it three times over... and not shying away from it.

"You sure you can handle us?" asked Senan, raising an eyebrow.

"Me?"

Brett smirked. "Well we don't see any other half-naked Harley Quinns lying around."

"Maybe I should show you what I can handle," I grunted, rolling onto my stomach. I smiled back at the boys wantonly, scissoring my legs.

"And maybe we should spank you again," Ander countered.

Glancing left and right, I reached out and seized my mallet. Standing it on end, it towered over us menacingly.

"You can sure as hell try," I winked playfully.

# Epilogue

## DELAINA

"It's... just woods."

Brett laughed beside me, nodding his head. At least he agreed. But off to my left, Senan came stomping back into the tiny clearing.

"You've gotta close your eyes and look at the big picture," he said. "The picture that happens *after* we clear most of this out."

He raised both muscular arms and made a circular motion, like a wizard casting a spell. Nothing happened. The trees were still there, thick and tall.

"So I have to close my eyes to see it?"

"Yes."

"Okay..."

I closed my eyes, playing along. I expected at any moment that one or more of them would kiss me, or stick a finger past my lips, or do something equally spontaneous or funny. I knew them long enough now to know what usually came next.

*Two whole years...*

Well, almost.  Close enough to know their little tricks and idiosyncrasies.

"Look, the land was cheap because we have to clear it," said Ander, stomping out of the woods from the other direction.  "That's something we can do together.  To save money."

"Week by week," Senan nodded, "we'll get the property ready.  Five acres is huge.  We only need to clear one to start working on the house.  The rest we can clean up as we go."

The house.  Rather, our *dream* house.  The one we meticulously sat down and planned out.  The one we were ready to build, but only in the right place, on the right lot.

"Picture the backyard here," said Senan.  "And we'll build a huge deck back here, and a patio here."

"And a firepit," said Brett.  "Gotta have one of those."

"And the swimming pool," I added.  "One with a waterfall."  I smiled as Senan and Ander both rolled their eyes.  "That was the agreement, so don't forget that part."

"Yeah, yeah," Senan chuckled.  He reached out again and gestured.  "A kidney-shaped in-ground pool, right about here."

"With a waterfall," I pressed.

Ander laughed.  "What are you, a mermaid?  Why do you need a—"

"With a waterfall," Senan affirmed.  "We promise."

"And a hot tub," said Brett.  "We can attach it to the pool if you want.  Or..."

I let him go on, wandering away as the guys began talking animatedly between themselves. Senan was right, the property was definitely a bargain. A huge, secluded lot at the end of a cul-de-sac, all ready for someone to come clear it and build a beautiful house among the trees.

*No, not a house. A home.*

It was a long time coming for us. Two whole years as a quadruple. Two glorious years of sharing my love with the three most incredible men in the world, and them sharing their lives with me. As far as relationships went, it should've been the craziest thing in the world. Totally forbidden. Completely taboo. It should've been wrought with jealousy and infighting and problems that would stem from having four strong personalities butting heads together, both in business and in our personal life.

Only it was nothing like that at all. And that's because it *worked.*

The one thing nobody takes into consideration about a situation like this is the camaraderie that exists between friends. They focus solely on the sexual aspects: on the pitfalls and problems of there being one woman 'splitting her time' with three men. They miss the concept of friendship, of brotherhood. Of each guy having his two best friends constantly around, laughing and traveling and spending quality time together, without having to split that time between romance and friendship.

As Ander once put it, they had the best of both worlds. Romance and friendship existed simultaneously. Any guy who needed time to himself could take it, knowing I was well taken care of by the others. As for me, I had all the attention I could ever hope for. But during the few times I needed some space of my own, the guys were gracious enough to step back, enjoy time with each other, and let me breathe.

Not that I needed time to myself very often. I was having way too much fun with *them*.

"Nine-foot ceilings in the basement?" I heard Ander ask.

"Hell yeah," said Senan. He raised his arm and patted the top of his six-foot-whatever head. "Besides, our kids are going to be *tall*."

*Kids...*

*Holy shit.*

Every time we even talked about it my stomach exploded with butterflies. They all wanted children — each of them — and if it were up to them, two each. I'd laughed and shoved them away and told them there was no way I'd be bringing six kids into the world. Not while maintaining my life, our lifestyle, and my sanity.

That said, I definitely wasn't opposed to *four*.

"Who gets to sire the fourth one?" Brett had asked. "After you've had one with each of us?"

"Sire?" Ander had spat. "Did you just say *sire?*"

"We draw straws," Senan had answered smartly. Then, after throwing a wink my way, "Or maybe we just flip a few coins."

I walked deeper into the woods that would one day be our side yard. A place where we'd play games. Have fun. Lay around in the grass maybe, and stare up at the sky. And yeah, sure — a place where we'd raise our sons and daughters. Eventually.

I looked down at my engagement ring, the large, trillion-cut diamond gleaming brilliantly in the late morning sun. Children were on the horizon for sure, but marriage was first. A ceremony, somewhere out of the country. Somewhere distant and exotic and beautiful. Something private between the four of us, that would further cement the bonds we already knew were unbreakable.

I didn't need a church, although my parents certainly wouldn't agree. I didn't need some piece of paper telling us that we were legally bound together. All I needed was Senan, and his bright bearded smile. Ander's sweetness and impossibly strong arms. Brett's boundless intelligence, as well as his soft, loving heart.

No. I had everything I needed. I had a life, a relationship, a business too. *Train Direct* had survived a shaky few post-launch months before finally going viral on a national morning talk show. From there it exploded, the app being downloaded over ten million times by now, and the website garnering so much traffic Jaime had three people working under him.

The success of our little venture set Brett's after-college career in motion. It also opened the door for Senan and Ander, who together spawned a corresponding yet separate YouTube channel that provided workouts and uber-nutritional cook-offs between them in a sort of sibling rivalry that was rapidly approaching three million followers. A large portion of our house would be dedicated to designing their own gym space, where they'd continue filming exercise vids, cooking shows, and once in a while, some very goofy competitions between them that sometimes involved me and Brett as well.

I'd even allowed Claudia and Evan to buy back in on the *Train Direct* portion of the business, so I could take back some of my own time. They took ten-percent ownerships while Jaime had twenty-five, leaving me with a majority stake in what was rapidly becoming one juggernaut of a company — all thanks to hard work and dedication.

And oh yeah, and not giving up.

"Hey little red riding hood!" I heard Ander shout. "You wanna come out of the woods?"

The voice called me back from the trees, and I turned and went. I couldn't help smiling, thinking — as I so often did these days — about how ridiculously happy I was.

"How do I know none of you are the big bad wolf?" I asked, breaking back into the clearing.

"Maybe we are?" Brett offered. "Maybe we'll huff and we'll puff and we'll—"

"Blow my little house down?" I squeaked innocently.

"Something like that," smirked Senan. "And you know that's *Three Little Pigs*, right?" He cleared his throat. "Of course, it's easy to get your wolves confused..."

I returned his smirk with one of my own, thinking about the weekend the three of them had proposed. Senan was my *first*... and I was about to marry my first. That was romantic. Hell, I was about to marry my second and third, too, and that was even more romantic as far as I was concerned.

"You okay?" he chuckled, as I kept on staring.

"Fine," I smiled, sliding my arms around him. "More

than fine."

His expression softened, and he looked like Kylie again. More and more I saw it: that brother-sister resemblance. Since we'd been keeping up with her treatments, Kylie had actually been showing signs of improvement. She looked at us now, and not just blankly. She actually *saw* us...

My heart swelled just thinking about it. Once, a month ago, she actually turned her head all the way in our direction as we walked into the room. Senan's mother had screamed — literally shrieked and fallen to her daughter's knees, tears of joy streaming down her face.

That one scream had been worth everything in the world.

"Ready for lunch?" Ander asked, rubbing his stomach.

"You mean brunch?" Brett countered. "Because I want eggs."

"Whatever, man."

He elbowed his friend, who elbowed him back. As the two of them got into it, Senan smiled at me over the both of them. He made the gesture of knocking their heads together, Three Stooges-style.

"When do we start clearing?" I asked him.

"As soon as the machines get here."

"And you guys can drive them?"

He laughed. "Umm... we can operate them," he said a little defensively.

"Don't worry," Ander winked. "We'll get better with practice."

I rolled my eyes and the guys laughed. "Just make sure you don't take down each other."

"Roger that," Brett saluted.

"Because I need all three of you," I said. "In one piece."

Ander shook his head playfully. "I dunno," he sighed. "Sounds greedy."

"Yeah," Senan went along. "Three guys. For one girl?" He shrugged dramatically. "I'd think you could afford to lose one and still be happy."

I sauntered into the middle of them, pulling them close. One by one I kissed them, slowly, sensuously, with meaning... and love.

"I'm not losing *anyone*," I declared. I took their hands and placed them on my stomach. "If anything, we're multiplying."

Senan grinned. Ander and Brett's eyes went wide.

"A—Are you saying you're—"

"NO!" I broke out laughing. Then more gently, "No, not at all. But I will be, eventually. Not long after the honeymoon, hopefully, when I hand the three of you my birth control pills..."

"And we throw them right in the ocean," Ander said with a nod.

I smiled, remembering our agreement. "That's right. But for now..."

My hands slid over their chests, and slowly down their stomachs. I let my fingers slide past their belts. Linger

329

teasingly over their jeans — as well as the lumps in the front of those jeans — before throwing my head back with a wistful sigh.

"For now it'll be plenty of fun to just *practice*."

 **BONUS EPILOGUE**

Wanna read the ULTRA-HEA, tear-jerking,

sugary-sweet, flash-forward

BONUS EPILOGUE?

Of course you do!


<u>TAP RIGHT HERE TO SIGN UP!</u>

and have it INSTANTLY delivered to your inbox.

# Need *more* Reverse Harem?

Thanks for checking out *Corrupting Chastity.* Here's hoping you totally LOVED it!

And for even *more* sweltering reverse harem heat? Check out: *Theirs to Keep - A Reverse Harem Romance.* Below you'll find a preview of the sexy, sizzling cover, plus the first several chapters so you can see for yourself:

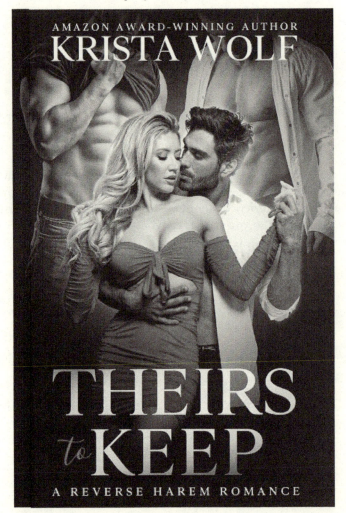

AMAZON AWARD-WINNING AUTHOR
KRISTA WOLF

THEIRS
*to* KEEP

A REVERSE HAREM ROMANCE

# Chapter One

## KARISSA

"We've got the plasterers here tomorrow," I said, "and the plumbers in the morning. The electric should be all roughed out on the east wing already, but contact Marius just to make sure. We can't be ripping the walls open once they're stuccoed."

"No," my foreman smiled in agreement. "Wouldn't be good."

"Also, the HVAC guys need to get this shit all cleaned up before they leave today." I pointed with my pencil, to where several jagged piles of sheet metal trimmings littered one side of the courtyard. "I saw two of them sneak off for the day already. The rest aren't leaving until it's all in the dumpster, though."

"HVAC. Dumpster." Oscar scratched at the side of his head. "Right."

"You writing all this down?"

As usual, Oscar wasn't writing anything down. That pissed me off, especially since I'd gotten him a new clipboard last week. I'd even threatened to duct tape it to his arm, but my foreman had only laughed.

"Speaking of dumpsters, I need that one emptied," I said, pointing again. "Should've happened yesterday, really. Got it?"

"Yeah."

"'Yeah' doesn't cut it," I said, noticing he was already looking down again. "Oscar. Hey. Look at me."

The foreman's gaze finally swung my way. He stopped scratching at the back of his head.

"Tell me you got it."

"I *got* it."

I nodded one time, firmly, never taking my eyes from his. "Okay, then," I said warily. "Good."

Oscar wandered off while I surveyed the rest of the massive worksite. The fifty-five room manor was more like a palace, almost even a castle. At one time it had a name, a history, a purpose. But right now, the only thing that mattered was getting it back into shape.

I made my way along the cobbled courtyard, dodging two groups of roofers and a man running a loader stacked with large clay shingles. A crane was operating on the north side of the property, delivering the stacks up to the roof some fifty feet high.

"Well hello there, boss..."

The voice was deep and beautiful, and immediately

335

changed my mood. Stepping through the next alcove I came face to face with Camden, his arms folded, leaning against a smooth stone wall.

"Boss, eh?" I chuckled. "The three of you are paying *me*, remember?"

He was wearing his sleeveless shirt again — one of the black ones that hugged his beautifully-sculpted chest. With his arms folded, his biceps and triceps looked absolutely enormous. Like he could crush boulders just by hugging them, or—

"Karissa...?"

I snapped back from whatever daydream I was about to step into. Camden's gorgeously-stubbled mouth was curled up on one side, his crystal blue eyes piercing me like two shimmering jewels. I felt myself growing warmer, even in the shadows of the alcove.

"Everything alright?"

I pulled out my clipboard and consulted it, temporarily setting my pencil in my mouth. "Peachy," I mumbled around the writing implement. "Today at least."

Camden glanced at my list without seeing it and chuckled. His laugh was velvety and masculine. "Good."

"How about you guys?"

I could see the dirt of the day upon him. Camden's deeply-tanned arms were covered with light brown hair, and that hair was covered in sawdust. He smelled like all good things: sweat and steel and freshly-cut wood. My gaze wandered down to the worn leather tool-belt, slung low around his waist.

"Can't complain," he replied. "Got off to a slow start waiting for an inspector to show up, but we still did a shit-ton of framing today."

"A metric or an imperial shit-ton?"

His smile widened. "Whichever."

"It matters, you know."

"Uh huh."

Our eyes had found each other's, and now neither one of us was willing to look away. It was like this often. The flirting happened between our look, our movements, our body language. One day, soon I hoped, it would go even further than that.

"So... you got a guess for me today?" I asked, the pencil still clenched between my teeth.

"Not yet, but Bryce does."

"And?"

Camden shifted from one foot to the other. "It's a good one."

"Okay."

"I'm hoping he's wrong of course," he added hastily.

"Obviously," I said slyly. "Because then he'd win."

Camden took a half-step closer. The movement brought our bodies to within a foot of each other. "And *I* want to win," he said. His voice dropped even lower. "Badly."

I took the pencil and casually tucked it behind my ear. "Then make sure you guess correctly."

"Wanna give me a hint?"

I inhaled, letting his deliciously manly scent wash over me. Basking in the warmth I could feel radiating off of his hard, muscular body.

*Hell yeah,* I thought to myself. *Of course I want to give you a hint...*

"No hints."

Camden's mouth went tight. "Too bad." He leaned back against the wall again with an almost imperceptible sigh. "Bryce thinks you were a wedding planner."

Silence. Dead silence. In the sanctity of our shaded alcove, I didn't even move.

"Holy shit, he's not *right* is he?"

I let my handsome employer stew for a moment, saying absolutely nothing as my own grin widened. I could feel his panic growing. His internal alarm.

"No," I said finally. "I was never a wedding planner."

Camden exhaled, long and slow through clenched teeth. His shoulders slumped in relief.

"Was he at least *close* though?" he squinted.

I smiled sweetly. "No hints. Remember?"

"Yeah yeah..."

I tucked my clipboard back beneath one arm and stared up into those gorgeous blue eyes. It would be so easy to make a move right now. So simple, to just close the distance between us and plant my lips on his.

But he was my *boss.* One of three of them, anyway.

And not that it would've stopped me if *he'd* made the move, but for me to make the choice myself... well...

It would be like snubbing the other two.

*Not to mention, opening a huge can of worms.*

I sighed internally. The can of worms I could deal with. In fact, I was actually looking forward to it. It had been *way* too fucking long since I'd had any sort of... release.

Besides, I rationalized, the guys had flirted with me off and on for weeks now. Or at least, two of them had. Roderick on the other hand...

"The deal still stands though, right?"

Camden stared down at me, his expression hopeful yet mischievous. His full, beautiful mouth looked so kissable right now I could barely stand it.

It would be so easy. So simple.

"Yes," I said, choking my way past the lump in my throat. "Of course it still stands. I'm not exactly a woman who goes back on her word."

It was a deal I'd made on an almost nonsensical whim, after they'd spent half a day rattling off various guesses. But now I only gave one guess per week, for each of them. One chance for my three employers to figure out who I was.

Or rather, who I'd been before *this.*

"First one of you to guess what I used to do before I came here..." I said slowly, reaching out to run a teasing finger along the outer edge of my Camden's arm.

His eyes flashed. My lips curled into an even bigger smile.

"Gets to take me bed with him."

# Two

## KARISSA

Not only did the key stick in the lock again, but this time the door itself refused to open. I shouldered it, trying to channel Ripley from *Aliens*, and promptly bounced back into the darkness of my front porch.

The frogs and crickets laughed in chorus from the surrounding woods.

I got up again, this time determined to use mind rather than muscle. The old wood was swollen, the paint flaking. Hell, it was humid enough out here that everything was swollen, including me.

*Why in the world did you even take this place?*

Because it was cheap, that's why. I'd driven out to Rhode Island for a fresh start, a new beginning. A beautiful apartment in Newport, maybe even one with a balcony and an Atlantic breeze.

But Newport was *way* too expensive. Ditto for Middletown, Bristol, and even Ocean Grove. The further north I bounced, the more affordable things got. I ended up north of Swansea, renting an old vacation bungalow on some forgotten lake.

But the realtors were treacherous, and the photos I'd seen had put lipstick on a pig. The place turned out to be a dump, the lake a swamp. Even worse, it was in the middle of absolutely nowhere. I convinced myself that I'd move in temporarily and search for something better, just as I'd convinced myself I would enjoy the solitude.

That was almost a year ago, and neither of those things had panned out. Living out here was lame at best, and downright spooky at its worst. If it weren't for the reno job keeping me at work twelve hours a day, I'd probably have already packed it in. The pay was solid, the work rewarding. Even better, turned out I was *good* at it. Real good.

*Hey, who would've thought?*

Right now I had bigger problems though. I was dirty, exhausted, and in need of a shower. If I didn't get inside soon I'd be likely devoured by mosquitoes swarming in off 'the lake.'

"Fuck you, door."

Approaching the knob again, I examined the old lock. My key wasn't fitting because something was broken off inside it. Something shiny and jagged, like the end of a paperclip.

*SHIT.*

A chill shot down my spine as I glanced nervously around. Someone had broken in, or at least tried to. Again.

*This is bullshit this is bullshit this is bullshi—*

342

I kicked out in frustration, and to my surprise the door swung open. It slammed into the opposite wall with a dull bang, sending a blizzard of paint-chips floating down like snow.

"Hello?"

Even the sound of my own voice seemed scary. In my own home.

"Anyone still here?"

I flipped the switch, and the overhead fluorescents flickered on. One of the bulbs refused to catch though. It sat there fluttering darkly, maybe ten-percent illuminated. The lack of any real light made my kitchen seem even more dreary and depressing than normal.

"You're probably pretty disappointed," I called out, still talking to my phantom intruder, "and I can't blame you. Nothing much to steal here, I'm afraid. Unless you want that stack of bills over on my—"

I whirled into the living room, flipping that switch too. The lights came on. Everything seemed okay.

"If you're in my bedroom that's even more disappointing," I continued, creeping along. "Not much going on in there, either. Unfortunately..."

Halfway through the kitchen I grabbed it: the sawed-off baseball bat I'd found in the crawlspace. It wasn't much, but it was definitely better than nothing. The tape-wrapped handle felt heavy and reassuring in my hand.

"If you want out by now, I can't say I blame you. I'll just step aside, and you've got a clear shot to the front door..."

I pushed on the bedroom door, then hugged the wall. Nothing happened. The world was silent, except for the constant buzz of insects.

"Alright," I said, overly loudly. "If you're still here, and you're still looking for trouble I'm—"

Mid-sentence I whirled, spinning into the room. Looking quickly in every direction at once, I held the baton that used to be a baseball bat out before me.

Nothing.

Carefully I checked my little bathroom, even drawing back the mildewed shower curtain where every serial killer in the world ever hid. Still nothing. The place was empty.

"Whew."

My shoulders slumped in relief... and then I noticed it. It should've been obvious when I first came in, but I'd been preoccupied with other things. But now that I *did* see it? My heart sank.

"Awww..."

My bed was nothing but a box spring. My entire mattress was gone.

"MotherFUCKER."

Dropping the baton I made my way into the kitchen, wondering if I would call the police. The irony of the situation made me laugh bitterly, as I opened the fridge to at least salvage the night with a few beers.

Only my beers were gone too.

I threw my head to the flaking ceiling and laughed.

"Perfect."

I'd only had a six-pack, but at least it was *my* six-pack. And now it was someone else's. Someone presumably enjoying it from the comfort of my own mattress, snuggled up beneath thirty-dollars' worth of Walmart bedding.

*What else did they take?*

I glanced into the tiny living area to see my television was still there. Only it was cracked now, the frame broken. Someone had apparently destroyed it while trying to pull it off the wall.

"It's a removable mount, jackass," I sighed to no one in particular. "You pull the string behind it and lift. It's not rocket science. It's not like—"

*CLINK.*

A noise from over my shoulder caused me to whirl in panic. I spun around, gripping my weapon. Ready to defend the very last of my worldly possessions — the coffee maker maybe, if it was still there — while willing myself to feel anymore more than apathy and defeat.

Instead I saw the broken window, shattered inward. A 'lakeside' breeze had blown my threadbare curtains against the jagged glass, causing another shard to drop.

"Straw?" I laughed, and my laughter seemed almost maniacal. Rather than echo through the empty room, the swollen walls seemed to absorb the sound. "Meet camel's back."

Fishing my keys from my pocket, I left without even turning off the lights.

# Three

## BRYCE

"So uh... remember when you guys offered me the option of staying on the worksite?"

Karissa stretched her long arms, arching her slender back. As always she looked absolutely stunning; her bright, beautiful face framed by acres of shining blonde hair.

But it was her last sentence that sent a shiver of excitement bolting through me.

"Wait, what?"

"When you first hired me," she reiterated, "all those months ago. You guys asked if I wanted to stay here. You said it would be a lot more convenient than driving back and forth, and it turns out you were right."

Camden and I exchanged hopeful looks across the large, unfinished kitchen. Even Roderick, leaning against one of the framed-out countertops, raised an eyebrow.

"If the offer still stands, I'd like to—"

"Hell yeah it stands," I jumped in. "You're welcome to any of the rooms that you like. The finished ones anyway."

I saw her pretty mouth break into a half-smile, as her gaze swung toward Camden. He set down his coffee and nodded.

"It would be great to have you here," he said. "Another pair of eyes on the place."

"That's it, huh?" she chuckled. "Another pair of... eyes?"

I shrugged. "Well that, plus we can use the company. Since we moved back into the west wing, things have been kind of quiet."

"And lonely," Camden added.

"And lame," I tagged on with a wink.

"Yeah, well it would just be temporary," Karissa went on. "You know, until I found a new place."

"What's wrong with your *old* place?" asked Roderick.

He was still off to the side, still leaning at an angle as he looked back at us over the rim of his coffee mug. His eyes weren't soft, or welcoming, and they certainly weren't filled with excitement. Suddenly I got the impression he might blow the whole thing for us.

"Are you retracting your offer?" Karissa asked boldly.

"I never made an offer to begin with," said Roderick. "That was Beavis and Butthead, here."

He blew across the surface of his coffee and took

another sip. The expression on his face was so smug I wanted to smack him.

"Alright," Karissa shrugged. "No biggie. If you have a problem with me staying here, I can always—"

"I never said that either."

"Said what?"

"That I have a problem with it."

Karissa's mouth had gone tight during their exchange. Now however, she let it curl back into a sly smile. "Oh. I see."

"See what?" asked Roderick.

"You're the one who likes to play games."

He raised both eyebrows this time. "*Games?*"

"Yeah," she continued. "The sarcasm game. Or maybe fun with semantics." Kicking up both of her long, beautiful legs, she crossed her boots on the opposite chair.

"How exactly am I playing games?"

"Well either you want me to stay here or you don't," Karissa went on. "The others have already decided, but not you. You like to walk the middle road. If things work out, you never really opposed them. But if shit happens to go sideways, you get to play the 'I told you so' game. Either way, you win."

"Maybe I just like to win," Roderick shrugged.

"I'll bet," she said, eyeing him over. "Still, when it boils down to it? The 'I told you so' game is your favorite game of all."

My mouth was already open in disbelief. I didn't know whether to laugh out loud or cheer her on. It occurred to me I should probably do both.

"Am I right?" Karissa asked. "You can say it. We're all friends here, so it's not like you're gonna hurt my feelings or—"

"Lawyer."

Roderick's answer was more of a question, really. It came with the squint of his two brown eyes.

"That your guess for the week?" Karissa asked, amused.

"It is."

"Well then nope," she shook her head. "I'm not a lawyer. Never was."

*Whew*, I thought happily.

"My mother always did say I should be one though," she added. "'Testardo', she called me. That's thick-headed in Italian."

"You sure it doesn't mean pain in the ass?" smirked Roderick.

"It could," Karissa allowed. "Wouldn't surprise me one bit."

She got up abruptly and crossed the room, moving like she owned the place. She grabbed the coffee pot and swished it around a bit, then frowned and put it down.

"Make another pot," I told her. "I'll have some too."

The little sideways smile she shot me would've been worth downing ten pots of coffee, and all the visits to the bathroom that would follow. Karissa raised her empty mug my way.

"A man after my own heart."

The room we were in would be the main galley — a sprawling, cavernous kitchen located at the very heart of the one-and-a-half century old palatial mansion. There were three other kitchenettes on the premises, including one in each wing and another in the guest house. But this, when finished, would be the beating heart of Southhold Manor.

It still didn't seem real that we were actually *doing* it.

Karissa took my mug back to the coffee maker. She glanced back at me, this time with a mischievous sparkle behind her gorgeous blue eyes.

"Sugar? Cream?"

"Plenty of both, please."

God, she was so fucking *beautiful!* And yet as our employee, totally untouchable as well.

*Sorta.*

No, forget sorta. Definitely untouchable.

It was pure dumb luck the way we'd found her: sitting there drinking alone, at the ass end of some ramshackle bar. We'd never gone to the place before, or returned since. But all the way in the corner, sipping on a gin and tonic, we somehow unearthed the best house assistant, supervisor, and ultimately, GC we'd ever had.

And hell, the three of us ran a *construction* company.

"So something happened with your place, eh?" Roderick guessed.

Karissa nodded. "It got broken into."

"*Again?*" I swore.

350

"Yeah," she chuckled. "Right? They took my mattress for fuck's sake! Who the hell *does* something like that?"

We only stared at her, standing at the opposite counter as a beam of sun filtered through one of the high windows. It lit up her back, turning her long blonde hair into shimmering stands of spun gold.

"The joke's on them though," Karissa chuckled, "because it was the worst mattress in the world, too. I think it was like ninety-five percent springs."

She formed a makeshift funnel from a paper towel, then poured coffee grinds into it in lieu of a real filter. She did it like a professional. Like she'd been doing it all her life.

*Waitress,* I reminded myself to guess next time. *Maybe in an Italian restaurant.*

"You sure you're okay with this?" Camden asked. "This place might seem big, but only the west wing is livable. And even that side's only half-finished."

Karissa laughed. "Have you ever seen *my* place?"

"No, but all three of us are sharing one bathroom," I said. "Living room, too."

"Got room for one more?"

"Of course."

"Then what's the big deal?"

Roderick folded his arms across his chest and leaned back in his chair a bit. As the kitchen filled with the steamy scent of freshly-dripped coffee, he seemed amused.

"Living with three grunting, burping, snoring guys might cramp your privacy, no?"

"Are you rescinding your offer?" she asked for the second time.

"Not at all," Roderick said smoothly. "I'm only pointing out we made that offer before we moved back in here, when you would've had the place to yourself. But now we're here too."

"And we walk around in our underwear a lot," smirked Camden. "Just so you know."

Karissa chuckled. "Cool."

"It might even be a house requirement, actually," I said, before Roderick kicked my chair. "Er... I mean—"

"Look, I need a place to stay," she said, leaning her elbows back on the counter. "If this works, let me know. If not..."

"Oh it works," I said quickly. "Everything else is us joking around. Like Camden said, it would be great to have you."

Camden nodded. Roderick too.

"Good," Karissa smiled warmly. "Consider me a roomie, then."

The coffee maker misfired, sending a brown rivulet down the side of the glass. The droplet hit the warming plate and turned to steam, sending a hissing sound through the kitchen.

"You need any help moving your stuff over?" asked Roderick.

Karissa broke into a cathartic laugh, one that was long and loud.

"Considering I can fit everything I'm taking with me under one arm?" she grinned. "Thanks for the offer, but that would be a 'no'."

# Four

## KARISSA

I took the third room on the left, counting back from the end of the hall. It was a huge room. They all were. But this one had a tremendous four-poster bed, as well as its very own fireplace. It was somehow large *and* cozy, and welcoming too.

A hundred years ago, someone had painted the walls and ceiling a lovely powder blue. Between all the fading and peeling, it resembled a serene sky filled with fluffy white clouds. I lay across my new mattress *and* bedding, that the guys had insisted on purchasing for me, and stared up into some fresco I couldn't quite make out. I saw angels, or cherubs maybe. A pair of trumpets, aimed at the sky. The tip of a spear...

*This is incredible.*

The manor was impressive enough while I was working on it, but I'd always been busy. Now that I was living here, I had time to really soak it in. I walked the halls slowly,

354

touching everything, realizing just how much work and effort went in to every tiny detail. Everything was carpeted, or paneled, or gold-gilded to perfection. Anything made of wood wasn't merely molded or manufactured, it had been ornately carved by dozens of pairs of talented hands.

I'd checked all the rooms of course, before making my decision. All of them except one.

Because the room directly across from mine had been locked.

"You can have any room you like," said Roderick, noticing I was struggling with the knob, "but that one stays locked." He paused for a moment, perhaps realizing he was coming off kind of dickish. "You wouldn't want that room anyway," he added. "Trust me."

Trust. It was something I wasn't ready to give, even to my three jovial bosses. Well, two anyway. Roderick wasn't exactly jovial, but I meant to figure him out when I got the chance.

Either way, I trusted this place a lot more than the last. I was safe and secure here. Surrounded not only by a century and a half of rich, silent history, but by three strapping construction workers walking around in shorts and T-shirts. I'd been here three nights already, and still hadn't seen any one of the guys in their underwear. But not for lack of trying.

*Easy, killer.*

It was funny, how their presence in the house was made known even when they weren't here. The guys owned a contracting company with a remote office in Fall River and two satellite sites. Most times they left before I even woke up, and came back long after the last of the crews here had left. It

355

was the main reason they needed someone here with eyes. Someone to keep things rolling on the one construction project they weren't directly involved in: their own.

But in the house, they'd taken their own three rooms back from history. They'd painted the walls in modern colors, and put up all new LED lighting fixtures that looked outright silly against the Victorian-era decor. They'd turned a spacious parlor into a comfortable living room. And one of them had hung a monster, high-definition television on the wall... right over the mantle of a fireplace engraved with a keystone dated 1867.

It was both funny *and* tragic.

Still, nothing compared to their more flagrant affront at the end of the west wing. There, they'd turned a sprawling, beautiful library — complete with thousands of books built into richly carved shelves — into their own combined version of a home gym.

There were whole racks of iron plates. Standing arrays of dumbbells, in every size, weight and shape. One of the walls had been refinished and completely mirrored, with three adjustable benches spaced equidistantly in front of it. Behind that were two treadmills and two stationary bikes. An elliptical glider for low-impact workouts, and a standing Smith machine that could be used for a variety of exercises — anything from bench pressing to squats.

I knew all this because I'd once been a gym rat. In another place, in another life, I'd spent six mornings a week in a place like this, honing and toning my body. The sweat had felt good, even if the cardio hadn't. Yet it kept me in shape. The adrenaline became an addiction, and it kept me coming

356

back.

If the guys worked out in the morning, I didn't know. But they certainly worked out at night, each of them taking turns at cooking meals while the others did their thing. Bryce and Camden had invited me to work out with them, but I was still getting settled. It wouldn't be long however, before I took them up on it. Especially since I'd gotten a glimpse at how beautifully pumped they were afterwards, their muscles all swollen and glistening on their way to the shower.

God, I needed to get laid.

"The ghosts of this place are going to haunt you," I'd told Bryce earlier, leaning against the doorway as he finished his last set.

"Oh yeah?" The big blond teddy bear had dropped his towel over one massive shoulder and smiled. "And why's that?"

"Because you shoved all the books aside to make way for your weights," I smirked back at him. "You blocked the fireplace and took out the chairs. You covered the oak floors with rubber mats."

"So?"

"So a ghost comes in here to read up on a little Stephen King?" I chided. "He's assed out. He's stuck watching you animals primp and preen and flex, in front of that mirror."

I pointed, and Bryce laughed. He blew hard at a lock of errant hair, sending it flopping back over his forehead.

"Ghosts enjoy Stephen King, huh?"

I nodded like I was an expert in the field. "They fucking *love* the guy."

"Pretty sure they didn't have Stephen King back in the nineteenth century."

I wrinkled my nose. "They're *ghosts*, Bryce. They transcend time. They move through walls and shit."

"You sure seem to know a lot about them," he admitted.

I got lost for a moment, looking him over. Letting my eyes wander that shredded sea of perfect abdominals, that not even his workout shirt could contain. Bryce was always doing sit-ups, constantly doing crunches. Wherever we were, whatever we were doing, it wasn't out of the ordinary for him to drop into a ball and tear off a hundred of them, just to keep them polished.

And wow, was it ever working for him.

"Maybe you'll take me on a midnight tour of this place," I found myself saying. "Point out some of the history. Scare up a few spirits."

His already-friendly smile twisted into something a little bit more. "You mean like ghost-hunting?"

Holy shit, had I really said it? It was too late now.

"Yeah. Something like that."

His light brown eyes found mine, and my heart started pounding. Did I just ask the boss on a ghost-date? Or was it nothing more than—

"Sure. I'd love to."

He took two steps forward, and I realized I was

partially blocking the doorway. Rather than move, I stayed exactly where I was.

"Tonight?" I squeaked.

Bryce took another step, twisting himself sideways through the archway. Our bodies ended up a foot apart, and I could feel the heat coming off him. His scent was all work and exercise. Musky and strong, yet somehow sweet.

"Any night you want," he half-smiled.

His eyes dropped for a split-second, sizing me up. They crawled down and up my body in all the time it took to blink, before once again locking on mine.

"You know where I sleep," he breathed huskily. "Right?"

I tried to speak, but I could barely swallow. Eventually the word dropped out. "Sure."

I was so close I swore I could feel his heart beating in his powerful chest. Low. Slow. Steady.

"Wait until midnight one night..." Bryce winked, before turning away. "Then come get me."

# Five

## KARISSA

Three hours later I was tired but awake. Physically exhausted, but still mentally charged up from my encounter with Bryce, which I kept running again and again through my head.

*Is this really such a good idea?*

The voice of reason in the back of my mind was nagging and annoying, but it was also right. I was about to go off with one of my three hot employers, to parts of the manor that would be silent and secluded. Alone. At midnight.

Holy shit.

Of course, I could just as soon crash until morning. Sleep on the whole idea, and not have to worry about what might or might not happen. Seeing things in the light of day might bring some much-needed clarification to this important decision. It might talk me off the ledge. Keep me from making a potential mistake.

*Or you could stop being a coward and just see what happens.*

And that was it, really. The devil on my other shoulder giving me full permission. Telling me to run off and fulfill my own base urges, and as always, worry about the repercussions later on.

*What do you* want *though?*

The answer to that question took all of two seconds. I wanted *him.* Or to be brutally honest, even Camden, or Roderick too. All three of my employers were well beyond gorgeous, and any sane, red-blooded girl with an above-average libido would be thrilled to bed any one of them. Yet for some strange reason there wasn't a girlfriend in sight.

This intrigued me, when I'd first been hired. I'd even explored the possibility that one of the guys might be dating another. But no, the more interaction I had with them, the more I realized they were most certainly straight. I'd caught all three of them giving me the once over, usually when they thought I wasn't looking. I'd even heard Bryce and Camden in a heated discussion about whether my naked ass would be tight enough to bounce a quarter, dropped at arm's length.

It was an experiment I wouldn't mind taking them up on.

But no, the guys had always been professional. Always courteous. They'd showered me with nothing but praise over the job I was doing, and had given me free license to take the renovation and run with it. Their credit card never once reached its limit, and they never provided me with a budget. Still, I was frugal in how I spent their money. I did my best to squeeze every ounce of labor from our current resources, which meant keeping on top of numerous crews, all of which were looking for shortcuts.

*Which is why it's probably best not to bite the hand that feeds you.*

I definitely wanted to bite *something*. That was for sure.

Pushing the voice of reason aside, I nuked a bag of microwave popcorn and headed into the living room. The couch had been beckoning all day, and I meant to answer the call. Maybe I'd fall asleep, and I'd miss my rendezvous. Or maybe I'd find something interesting enough to keep me up, and I'd be knocking gently on Bryce's door at the stroke of midnight.

Either way, I was going to let my body decide.

I walked the carpeted hall, through something the guys referred to as 'the sitting room' and into the makeshift living area. Camden was already there, one foot up on the leather ottoman. He was munching on a bag of Sun Chips; Garden Salsa, the flavor I liked.

"Movie night?" he smiled, as I walked in with my bowl.

"Sure. What's on?"

He flipped me the remote, stretching back to interlace his fingers behind his head. It brought out his beautiful biceps. They looked like two giant potatoes, perched atop his tanned, well-muscled arms.

"Do you *really* want to put me in charge of the remote?" I laughed, as I sank down beside him.

"Why? You're not gonna put on *The Notebook* are

you?"

"Nah."

His grin widened. "Kate Hudson? Matthew McConaughey?"

I ignored him, flipping through channel after channel. The guys had an impressive array of add-ons, I had to give them that. Finally I settled on an obscure movie I loved, then pushed the remote out of reach.

"*Prince of Darkness?*" Camden blinked twice.

"Ever see it?"

He shook his head.

"Get ready to be scared."

Horror had always sort of been my thing. Not so much the jump-scare bullshit they were putting out today, but more of the slow burn, suspenseful type movies that really immersed you in the story.

"You can hold my hand if you need to," I joked, popping a handful of popcorn into my mouth.

"Here..."

Shifting closer, Camden pulled a blanket down from behind the couch. He threw it over the both of us, until it covered us from the waist down.

"Don't get any ideas," he winked, as the movie started up. "This is just so you don't get popcorn all over me."

I chuckled, then pointed to a mess of crumbs all over his chest already. "You sharing those Sun Chips with your shirt?"

Camden blushed, but only a little. "Maybe."

I scooted closer and plopped my bowl down between us. "Well share some with me, and I'll let you dig into my popcorn," I told him.

When his smile turned up at the edges, I added:

"*Just* my popcorn."

## THEIRS TO KEEP
## IS NOW ON AMAZON!

Grab it now — It's free to read
on Kindle Unlimited!

# About the Author

Krista Wolf is a lover of action, fantasy and all good horror movies... as well as a hopeless romantic with an insatiably steamy side.

She writes suspenseful, mystery-infused stories filled with blistering hot twists and turns. Tales in which headstrong, impetuous heroines are the irresistible force thrown against the immovable object of ripped, powerful heroes.

If you like intelligent and witty romance served up with a sizzling edge? You've just found your new favorite author.

Click here to see all titles on

Krista's Author Page

Sign up to Krista's VIP Email list to get instant notification of all new releases:  http://eepurl.com/dkWHab